# ROOTSTOCK

LACHAPPELLE/WHITTIER VINEYARDS - BOOK 2

KELLY KAY

Published by Decorated Cast Publishing LLC
Edited by: Erin Young, EY Literary Management
Copy Edit: Holly Jennings, Freelance Editing Services
Cover Design: Tim Hogan www.timhogancreative.com
Copyright @2020 by Kelly Kay/Kelly Kreglow
www.kellykayromance.com
All rights reserved

❀ Created with Vellum

## ALSO BY KELLY KAY

Five Families Vineyard Series

**LaChappelle/Whittier Vineyard Trilogy**

Crushing, Rootstock & Uncorked

**Stafýlia Cellars Duet**

Over A Barrel & Under The Bus

**Gelbert Family Winery**

Meritage: An Unexpected Blend

---

CHI TOWN BOOKS

**A Lyrical Romance Duet**

Shock Mount & Crossfade

**Present Tense:** A steamy romance 20 years in the making. Coming late 2021

---

STANDALONES

Side Piece

---

www.kellykayromance.com

# ABOUT ROOTSTOCK

Rootstock is the second book in the LaChappelle/Whittier Vineyard trilogy. **Crushing** is the first book and is available on Amazon and through Kindle Unlimited.

You're welcome to read this one right away but if you haven't read Crushing, you might get a touch lost.

Please enjoy.

End of Crushing

**Elle**

I gave up control, and this is what happens. Not only did I let him see my vulnerabilities, but he rejected them. I need to get a hold of myself. I need to wrap up this project and get the hell out of the Whittiers' life and work. I'll get someone to handle the day to day. I need to leave.

**Josh**

The pain and guilt I feel are crushing me. She's safe. I can't believe I have to do this to her. I read her texts and I can't breathe. All I want is to be buried inside of her or have my arms wrapped around her. It's killing me. I won't let anything happen to her or my family. If I lose her, there won't be a day that passes that I don't make Salvatore Pietro pay. There won't be a moment that I don't make him suffer at my hands. Both physically and financially. I will find a way get out of this and back to her. I have to get back to her. You want to play dirty, you fucking Capo, let's dance.

I can't lose her. I won't. She's mine.

# Family Trees for the 5 Families

## LaChappelle/Whittier Vineyard

Will Whittier • • • • • • • • Sarah LaChappelle Whittier

Josh Lucien LaChappelle Whittier

## Schroeder Estate Winery & Vineyards

Adrian Schroeder • • • • • • • • • Bellamy Schroeder (d.)

Baxter Schroeder    Tommi Schroeder    Ingrid Schroeder

## Stafýlia Winery & Ranch

Costas Aganos • • • • • • • • Goldie Aganos

Tabitha Aganos

## Langerford Cellars

James Langerford • • • • • • • • Theresa Langerford

Sam Langerford    Jims Langerford

## Gelbert Family Winery

Tina Gelbert ⟩————⟨ Arthur Gelbert • • • • • • • Jana Gelbert

Poppy Gelbert

David Gelbert    Becca Gelbert

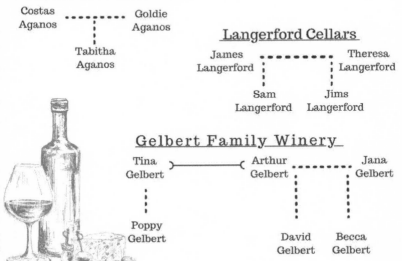

## DEDICATION

This one is for all the women, waiters, friends, strangers, men, bartenders and employers who have endured me scribbling on slips of paper, conference materials, festival programs, spreadsheets, notebooks, receipts, binders, PTA handouts, folders, purchase orders, my left hand, backs of envelopes and menus when I should have been working or paying attention.

Thank you.

# DEFINITION

ROOTSTOCK: /'ro͞ot,stäk,'ro͝ot,stäk/
*Noun*: rootstock; plural noun: rootstocks

Rootstock is a wine word used in regard to viticulture and the growing of wine grapes. This means that they are not planted on their own roots; rather, the vine is grafted onto the root of a different vine species to create a hybrid or a stronger union.

# 1

## JOSHUA

Her last text was three weeks ago. It shreds me. I should have known that my Hellcat wouldn't forgive so easily, not that I'm able to apologize or even explain. It came a week after I left. I desperately want to respond to her. Keeping this phone active is the only thing I have defied Sal on since I've been back in Santa Barbara. He ordered me to get a new number. I did. I gave it to my parents. But I couldn't give it to Elle. I keep this phone just in case I can finally call her or if she needs me. I had no choice but to leave her and stay silent. Salvatore Pietro, the mafia kingpin of LA, threatened her and my family. I had to return to my Santa Barbara office instantly to invest his fucking dirty money and make it clean.

I have to keep her safe, but I can't tell her that. He threatened me if I had any contact with her. I had to leave to keep them all safe. I have to face what I've done. But I thought she'd at least get back to being cordial. Four fucking weeks of agony without hearing her voice. Four fucking weeks knowing she thinks I betrayed and abandoned her.

*ELLE: I'm not mad anymore, just sad at the never was. I know you won't respond, but I need to write this. We are done. With all of it. Respect me enough to leave me alone if you ever crawl out of your self-serving hole. We are nothing. Not friends or anything I thought we were moving towards. Nothing. I know you talk to your parents, so Josh is in there somewhere. You should call Sam. He misses you. Don't leave him too. I was a fool to believe you wouldn't leave me. I'm wiser. Colder, more closed off, more realistic, but wiser.*

Fuck me. Every part of me tugs in pain at her words. I'm dying inside, but I have to do something to salvage myself. I have to move out of this pain. Sal Pietro fucked everything up. I fucked everything up by ever trusting Sal. I should have told her. It's too late now, she's gone. And I would never ever be able to live with myself if anything happened to her. Whether it's at Sal's hand or the mysterious threat he keeps in the dark shadows of his business. My job is to turn the money legit as soon as it hits his account. He wants all of it turned now. His timeline to legitimize the cash has gone into overdrive. The original plan of five to ten years seems to have moved to five to ten months. Somedays it feels like five weeks. I'm exhausted. And there is not out, not right now.

I never should have worked for Sal this long. But I never had anything to lose that I cared about until her.

The two of us made a shit ton of money together in the past. Sal and I would talk about scotch, women, or the Cubs but not any real details about his life or money. I take the clean cash, from formerly illegitimate businesses and put it into real investments. I thought I was nobly helping this mob boss become legit. I never felt threatened or worried until I decided to spend more time back with my parents in Sonoma, rather than at my venture capital firm in Santa Barbara.

Elle changed everything in my life. How I felt about the home I'd turned my back on, my parents who'd I cut out of my life and love. I can't say we were in love, but I certainly find it hard to be away from her. Maybe it was love, I'm not so sure I know what that feels like. But we were definitely on a collision course with that emotion. I've never really felt that way before. Elle changed every fucking thing.

And I messed it up by forgetting Aesop's fable of the scorpion and the frog who meet on a riverbank. The scorpion asks for a ride across the water. The frog asks, "How do I know you won't sting me?" The scorpion replies, "Because if I do, I will die too." The frog is satisfied. But then midstream, the scorpion stings the frog. The frog feels the onset of paralysis and starts to sink, knowing they both will drown, but has just enough time to gasp "Why?" Replies the scorpion: "tis my nature..."

Sal and I have worked together for nine years. A chance meeting, we felt a kinship in our histories and forged a partnership of sorts. I invest his clean money as he divests himself of the dirty lifestyle he was forced into by his family. He loves his family and wants to create a safe and clean world for his sisters, nieces, and nephews.

He had a ten-year plan to be entirely out of the rackets. But threatening my family and me was the first I ever saw of the other half of this man. The dark, violent connected man haunted by his past. But fuck him and fuck me for being in this position. I don't care what the hell he's got going on, I need out.

I've been with Salvatore often in the last month, and our dynamic is forever changed. He took her from me, and I'll never fucking let him forget that. He forced me into a being Joshua again, instead of carefree Vineyard Josh. I don't see how she'll ever come back to me.

My only hope is that I can find a way through this. If I can secure my friends and family's safety, then maybe I can convince her to be with me. I'll bury this asshole the first chance I get. I need to be back on an even playing field with him. I need information to orchestrate a power shift.

I reached out to Elle's former employee, the hacker. She sent me a burner phone in an overnight package with a note that said to only use it if I wanted to talk about Sal. It's all a bit melodramatic cloak-and-dagger, but I played along. I called the only programmed number in the phone. She was blunt and odd but said she'd help me for a price. She is one of the most curious people I've ever encountered.

Melissa warned me.

*"You made her cry. I told you. Don't fuck her over."*

*"Didn't she fire you?"*

*"Yeah, but she also believed in me. No one believes in a fuck-up except a pure soul. She's the shit."*

*"I'm aware. Mel, for her safety, this can never get to her. What I tell you and what I'm asking you to do. Know that this is one of the hardest things I've ever done. For her safety, she has to hate me."*

*"No problem there, dude. She despises your ass."*

*"Good. Now, I need you to help me get back to her."*

*"Shoot, cowboy. Is this about the money and the gang war in LA?"*

*"What?!"*

*"Shit, man, you don't even know how fucking deep you are."*

She told me she was doing this for Elle, and I told her the same thing. She's looking for anything we can use as leverage. Anything that will unravel me from this mess.

Sal did indeed have quite a lot of money to unload quickly. I've found legitimate deals all over the world. I want to figure out where this cash came from. I've taped every conversation we've had and uploaded every email to an encrypted server as Melissa told me to do.

IT'S BEEN close to six weeks since I made love to Elle when Mel uncovers proof of Sal's ties to the Latin Kings. I call a buddy from Stanford who works for the FBI. He's helping me decipher his web of connections. I am aware that it's his oldest nephew who is causing the rift. He discovered that Sal was taking the business legitimate, and he wants control before the illegal holdings are gone. He's ruthless, and I heed any and all Sal warnings and directives because of it.

I didn't tell my FBI friend, Mark, about Melissa. I need something that sets me free of threats. And I don't care who gets me out first. I won't do anything with the information I get on Sal unless he threatens my family or my Hellcat again. Elle is off-fucking-limits. Even if she never speaks to me again. Off-limits.

I hope no one's picked up on the fact that the new vineyard maintenance man and new tasting room host are ridiculously out of place. They're security I hired to watch over them. There's a night crew that sleeps in shifts on property and should anyone leave property they always have a tail with them.

This won't be forever. My parents have pleaded with me to come home. I keep making excuses not to visit so I can keep the mob at bay. I can never be with Elle if she's in danger. And she's made it clear that another chance is an impossible feat. There's definitely no way to get her back from this far away. She's gone. Nursing my heartbreak like only a man can do, I've started to slip back into Joshua patterns. I messed around with other women to prove that she's not what I thought. It's hollow but still feels good. Elle's the first thing I think of in the morning and the last thing at night, regardless of whose bed I'm in.

I've opened up communication with Sam. Sal said it was

okay in limited doses. I've caught a world of shit from my best friend for ditching Elle. Sam's pissed off at me for leaving him too. I can't fucking tell him why. So I lie. Sam and Sammy are all lovey-dovey now. I'm sure he thought we'd be on some malt shop double-dating track. So fucking wrong. I love Sam and would kill for him, but his heart is too soft for business. He stays tucked away at Langerford, pretending it's a life. He hides at his family's winery in the lab and making wine or working the vines.

I have someone at Langerford Winery as well. Just in case the threat extends to them. Sam's a brilliant musician and is playing the Vintage Festival, not that I can go. I hate that I still know Sonoma's event calendar as well as anything from my childhood. I also don't know if I get to go back there anymore.

I have a short fucking leash. I flew to LA on another deal and then got my ass handed to me because I didn't tell him I was in town. I have to fucking get something on Sal. Mel has to get her hustle on. I'm paying a freaking fortune for her dark web skills, let's see if she's worth it.

---

EIGHT WEEKS and half weeks back in Santa Barbara and I'm feeling more familiar with my life. Sonoma and Elle are fading every day. The memory of our connection will always haunt me, but I can at least get to a place mentally that rationalizes that this is for the best. It's been fucking agonizing. My forward motion doesn't mean I don't ache for her, but I have to live with the mess my life has created. They all deserve to live a life without my consequences. I screwed all of us, but I want to be the only one to pay the repercussions.

I've cut my hair back to a respectable length and purchased a whole slew of new products to hold my formerly floppy hair in place. There's something about the crispness of a custom shirt and perfectly tailored pants that make me feel the part.

My partners have been generous hustling new business, and I'm here to close all of their deals and make money for all of us. I was at a dinner every night in July and slaying it. I went to LA for a week, and it was the most fruitful trip I've ever had. Sal letting me do other business these days only makes bigger deals for him to be a part of. He understands this now.

This week I'll put to bed a deal to finance a new small chain of California hotels for close to a hundred million, Sal making up a third of that investment. He's pleased. My firm gets a sizable chunk of that hotel deal. Putting it in the category of my biggest one-day payday. I feel like the master of my universe again. The only problem is she keeps creeping into my fucking thoughts. Even while fucking. It's still painful to think of her. I wonder constantly if she's with someone. If someone is kissing the lips that belong to me.

I've been out with several women since I left Sonoma and her goddamned scent lingers in my memory. I had to move tables at brunch last week because of fucking orange blossoms blooming around the patio.

When I first got home, I thought I was going mad. I kept conjuring Elle's scent in my bedroom. Then I realized the fucking smell was coming from my closet, perfuming my clothes. I discovered that stupid pair of flowered tropical shorts in the front zipper part of my suitcase with her thong in the pocket. Lilacs, orange blossoms, and sex dripping off everything, and my dick would get immediately hard upon entering my closet. I took it out of there and threw away the duffle. I dry cleaned everything so that my closet and home are now Elle free.

But I'm actively torturing myself at work. In my desk

drawer, there's an open bubble mailer with a familiar address on it. Her coral lace panties and the black leather cheekies from our first night together sit inside of it. Initially, my thought was that I should return them. La Perla's expensive, and I should have my assistant slap some postage and mail it. Then I thought about replacing the bra I believe I ruined, but it seemed too much like a boyfriend move. I can't bring myself to seal the fucking envelope.

Every time I open the drawer, her scent surrounds me. It's begrudgingly comforting. I like the way my pants become a little too tight for a moment when I smell her. My dick reacts to it, and I can't stop it. It's the carnal part of her. I can't seem to get rid of her thong or those leather peekaboo cheekies.

John, my assistant, thinks she was just a good lay that I can't quit chasing. But more often than not, I think about the nights on the roof talking about her family and mine. Or our phone calls about nothing and everything. I want to hold her hand and stay there all night. I keep using that memory to calm me down, not the memory of her bucking underneath me. Although that is a damn good one that I use as well, mostly in the shower.

I need to get her out of my head. I call out to John.

"Can you set up a reservation at The Lark and see if Claudia Maier will join me?"

"Yes, sir! Right away, sir. Good. Anon!"

I love that whack job of an assistant. I used to like a good "yes, sir." Claudia seems like she'd give a good, "yes, sir." That's exactly what I need, someone who will listen to me and understand when I give a directive it should be followed, not played with. And someone who isn't so concerned with changing shit around. Someone a little less Noelle Parker is exactly what I need to get over her.

I have to figure out a way to close that chapter. It's not

like I can chase after her. I can't follow her around until she listens to me. And I can't get out from under fucking Sal. Time to move on. The best way to get over someone is to get someone else under me.

I want easier. I don't need to work that hard for any woman. I don't need to mess with love. Just sex and companionship. Fuck it. I wish to be respected for who I am instead of having to prove it. Claudia is dark and exotic like my ex-fiancé Serena was, but she seems to not have a stick up her ass. She has a feminine giggle and a body like a supermodel. Long and lithe. A tiny little ass instead of the luscious curves of Elle. She's going to be my antidote. She's my anti-Elle.

I'm terrified every day that I'll give in, that my resolve will weaken, and I'll run to Elle. That I'll tell her everything and beg for to take me back. The reality of her life being in jeopardy if I do keeps me rooted. It's that truth that is propelling me to move forward. Maybe the pull won't be as strong if I have someone, I care about in my bed here in Santa Barbara, a safe distance from Noelle Parker.

I met Claudia at a cocktail thing last week, and we've been to dinner twice. There was a little rubbing, licking, and kissing. Now it's time to see if she'll be able to handle my needs. See if she fits into my world seamlessly. I want no compromises and no ripples. Despite how it will hurt like hell. I have to stop the bleeding. I need to stop pretending I deserve or will get the life I wanted. Time to deal with reality instead of fantasy.

Claudia's dark eyes and light, lilting laugh are the only things that have even remotely gotten past the constant loop of Noelle Parker's face, smell, body, and moan.

---

CLAUDIA'S A GOOD LISTENER, even when I'm merely

talking about traffic. After a quick and adequate blow job in my car, post-dinner at Lark the other week, I decided to keep seeing her. We're on our fifth date. I had dinner catered at my house. I can hear the ocean crashing through my open patio doors. I invested well and took the right risks to have this life.

My glass and steel castle that overlooks the ocean defies all feminine touches. I have precisely one decorative pillow on the couch, but it's made of leather. Everything has its place, and I decided where that place was going to be.

The vintage Porsche Spyder and my four-bedroom home on the ocean are things my parents have never seen. I drive the Jeep up in Sonoma, but it's time to sell it. My parents can visit me from now on. I'm done with my dusty and directed upbringing. But I am ready to have my parents back in my life. Sam and the others have been giving me shit about missing Wednesday nights with them. I have been drinking hardcore with my bros here in Santa Barbara. I can't keep living a half existence. I have to invest somewhere, and Sal's ruined Sonoma for me. I'm not sure I could ever be there again.

CLAUDIA'S DONE everything I demanded of her. She bent herself backward without a whiff of defiance. There were positions I didn't even know a woman could twist herself into. I fucked her raw. We're lying here sweaty, our clothes in a pile on the floor. She drifts off quickly, after a single orgasm that culminated with a quick high-pitched squeak. She called it decadent to come, explaining that she never allows that kind of pleasure. It's not really her thing, but she enjoys giving pleasure. She's fucking nuts. If I were a woman and able to come over and over, I'd never leave the house. It was somewhat athletic but different. I'll need to tell her how to put her head back to take all of me in her throat without gagging next time.

Elle already knew how to do that when she took my cock in her mouth. Now suddenly I'm intensely jealous of how Asher knows that about her as well. I have to let it go. My mind drifts back to Tommi Schroeder's Instagram post from tonight of everyone at Starling bar. Elle's sitting with my friends and too close to the new chef from Cafe LaHaye. He's tan and Mediterranean-looking and has his arm around Elle in the picture. Tommi hashtagged it #wednightcrew.

I texted Sam about him, but he was vague. I also raged at my friends for letting Elle invade Wednesday night. My friends and I have a long-standing tradition of getting together on Wednesday nights that dates back to our Cub Scout meetings in first grade. My friends told me to fuck off because she's there, and I'm not. Fuck Sal.

I keep imagining the brooding eyes of that black-haired cooking weasel and wonder if Elle's seen his cock. Elle's ruby swollen lips around my cock and the gold dancing in her green eyes are the images that pop into my head. I need to shake all of this off and focus on where I am now. I have to push on and hope that she understands that this was the only way to keep them safe. I know her too well. She already had abandonment issues, and I expertly reinforced them.

Sal will pay for taking her from me forever. Without contact, she's an idea at this point. I can't even imagine being with her any longer. I have no context. Maybe I'm actually moving on from what might have been.

In my present moment, not my past, my $12,450 Sferra Giza bedding is inviting me to sleep after a satisfying sex session. Her long dark hair twisting around her back is empirically sexy against the stark white sheets. I know I could do anything I wanted to Claudia right now and she'd consent. I could wake her up and tell her to go get me a glass of water, pour it into her snatch, and let me drink it, and she'd do it without question. Elle would ask me why and then tell me to fuck off and get my own damn water. I roll away from Claudia when I hear her softly snore. I can't sleep. I can't stop my fucking head from comparing them.

## 2

## JOSHUA

LEAVING CLAUDIA TO SLEEP IN MY BED, I HEAD OUT TO THE deck by myself, restless and haunted.

I'm staring at the dark ocean and sipping my dad's latest invention, a red blend, from random varietals that aren't super popular. He plants small blocks of not very popular wines or hard to grow varietals; Carignane, Barbera, Tempranillo, Cardinal, Pinot Blanc, Albarino, Grignolino, Roussanne, Mourvedre or Cinsault. He loves an oddball. And indeed, loves to honor my mother's heritage to include so many Rhone varietals. None of these are made as a stand-alone varietal wine for LaChappelle/Whittier. Dad does it for his own amusement. He does a white and red blend every year.

The mini blocks are all over the property. He hand-harvests them and then he and Alena, the winemaker, make crazy limited production blends. They always name them with a phrase or sentence. This one is called *Go home, Bacchus. You're drunk.*

They're always fantastic wines. It started as their secret creative outlet within my grandfather's strict regime of rules and restrictions. My dad blends and my mom hand-paints the labels. They don't sell the bottles, so they don't need government approval. They give them as gifts to the staff or area friends and colleagues. Once a year they throw a wine dinner themed around their micro collection. I didn't even know they still did it.

I never told my grandfather, who would have been furious. I took enough beatings from him just for the shit I did. Nothing too terrible, a cuff on the head or ear from time to time. He was fond of saying, "Nothing happens on my land or in my walls that I don't know about and control." He said it enough that I embraced it a little too much. I think that's why Noelle threw me so hard. The caught off-guard girl. She was not part of any plan and certainly not ever really under my control. Well, maybe a little.

I hadn't thought about their DL wines for years. When I left, my dad handed me a case to take with me. I thought it was my favorite Malbec, but it's actually a curated case of their blends from the last couple of years. My mom hand-painted the bottles with my name on them and little notes about life and enjoying the moment. She used to do the same thing in my lunch box. I took a lot of shit for her hippie Zen notes, but now, it's comforting.

I'm half a bottle in, staring at the dark ocean hours before dawnbreak. The sound of the ocean and the air are where I find comfort in the middle of the night. Then I hear light footsteps. She places her long spindly fingers on my shoulders, and the tanned skin is stunning against my shoulder. I push the thought of Elle from my mind again and embrace what's in front of me.

"Sorry to disturb you."

I pull her down onto my lap. She's wearing an old t-shirt of mine that should be sexy. It just bugs me a little at the presumption.

"You could never disturb me." I mean it. She's too meek to disturb me, and it's precisely what I think I need. I don't have to work at this. I don't have to justify my behavior. She's unchallenging, and I welcome it. I kiss her lightly.

"Your phone is blowing up. And woke me. I have a shoot tomorrow, so I need to sleep."

There are six messages and I've missed four calls. The messages all say the same thing. It's three-thirty in the morning, my heart drops, and my body goes numb.

*DAD: Call me now. It's an emergency.*

# 3

## ELLE

THE KITCHEN IS FULL OF COFFEE, AND STICKY BUN SMELLS. I slept in after working on a proposal for a new idea for *Brides* magazine into the wee hours. I've been staying at Will and Sarah's house in California for almost five months now. They've sort of adopted me, and since my parents are long gone, I welcomed the paternal and maternal attention. I depend on them in a pretty unhealthy way. But it seems reciprocal, so I stayed. The only problem is that they're actually Josh's parents.

I probably should have rented out my New York apartment. My business partner, Evan, who is basically running the New York office of my marketing firm, Parker and Company, has his parents stay there when they visit. At first he thought I was having a breakdown by staying out here. Now he realizes that it's just a break. I'm glad someone's there in my place every once in a while. I've been paying my HOA and maintenance fee. I own the place outright, but I'm not sure what my next move is quite yet.

After he left me for Santa Barbara, I went home to New York. I sat in my apartment and at work. A shell of a person.

I ate all my former favorite foods and drank all the cocktails, not wine, with people who filled some time. I cried and walked the streets. And aside from my breaking heart, I desperately missed California. I missed Sarah and Will. I missed the Wednesday night crew.

When Will called and asked me to come back after a couple of weeks, I jumped at the chance. He made up a lame excuse and I let him. That was a month ago. I worked out a schedule with Evan to let me return to Sonoma just at the beginning of harvest.

But now, my time here is done. I'm not sure where my home will turn out to be, I don't think it's New York, but it's not here in Josh's childhood home. My heart is still so broken over something that almost was that I can barely take it.

I've done a good job at raising the LaChappelle/Whittier winery profile. I found buyers, with Asher's help, that will honor what they do here. They may be moving out of their house soon, but I'll miss living this vineyard as well.

Sarah and Will are walking away from a one-hundred-forty-seven-year-old business and their jackass son, Josh, wants no part of it. Since the jackass tucked himself into Santa Barbara, I've discovered a whole life here with his friends and without him. The kids of the five families have become my friends. The only hold out is Sam Langerford. Sam and Josh are brothers from different mothers, and I wouldn't want to get in the middle of that. I'm careful not to ask about him. We keep that elephant in the room tucked away.

His girlfriend and my friend, Sammy, does let gossip slip from time to time. It's too painful to deal with, so I simply shove it down and compartmentalize it. Move forward. Josh left me. Sarah and Will are selling then traveling far away from here. My brief security blanket will leave me again. Sarah's sick, and selfishly I can't watch her deteriorate. Everyone leaves me. It's my reality, and it's time to face it.

It's time to get the hell out before anything more can hurt me. I'm alone. I know how to do alone. I'm good at being alone. I've had lots of practice. But it was nice to pretend I had a village for a moment.

It's nearly 10:30 a.m. as I make my way towards the kitchen. I was up late on the roof with the stars. I'm dressed for my day and evening in what seems so foreign. I even dug up my favorite YSL lipstick *Rose Libertin*. Today is a deep pink lip kind of day. I used to wear clothes like this every day, but I've gotten quite used to jeans and a t-shirt or maybe a beat-up hoodie. But I'll leave soon enough, and it's time to remember the girl I built from nothing.

My Fendi mesh tobacco kitten heels are my new favorite thing. I bought them last week in San Francisco, in another impromptu shopping spree to put him out of my mind. The man is costing me a fortune as I try to expunge him from my thoughts. My heart hurts because I let him in. I can't bear it most days, so I shop. You'd think after eleven weeks and six days I could fucking get it together. Almost three months and my sadness and anger still bubble up too often. I'm still pissed at him but really pissed at myself for letting down my walls. I'm an idiot, and it will never happen again. He never came after me. He never called or wrote. My texts went unanswered and the message of being discarded came through loud and clear. I'm nothing to him. He never came here to explain anything. I have to be done.

My shoes look out of place on the rustic wooden plank floor. I have to run down to Silicon Valley for the day and glad-hand some Google execs who are thinking of expanding their partnership with Parker and Co. I adjust my favorite ribbed green Armani pencil skirt that highlights my ass. It's a dumb ploy, but I need this business. My striped crepe blouse clings a bit too much as it softly drapes over my chest. I feel like I'm in a costume. I join a concerned-looking Sarah at the island with my cup of coffee. She blurts out their problem.

"Sarah, really? When?" The vineyard managers are gone, left in the middle of the night just on the verge of harvest. The weather has been cooler, so the harvest got delayed a couple of weeks. Here we are just into September and not a grape has been picked. They've told me that now harvest must happen in a flurry. The vines won't be rushed. But when they're ready, the picking needs to be as fast as possible.

I ask, "What happened to José and Manny?"

"José woke Will at two this morning to tell him. Their mother took ill back in Guatemala. We certainly weren't going to keep them here. Now we're in a hard place. The normal field crew left as well. We lost fourteen more workers as of this morning."

"Why?"

"I don't know. The men said that they only work for José and that they got a better offer. They didn't even let us counter. They've been with us for years. We're flummoxed and fucked."

I react to her language. I've never heard Sarah talk like this. I feel bad, and I don't know how to help. "Tell me what to do. I can push back my return date if that helps."

I was heading back to New York the day after tomorrow. Evan and I need to be in the same room. You can only do so much work by email and text. It was our plan, and I'd made peace with it.

I also need distance between everything that reminds me of Josh and myself. I was getting away from all of this and back to who I'm supposed to be. I tried this on for a moment. I had fantasies of being the girl with dirt under her finger-nails again, like growing up on our family farm in Kansas.

But I belong to my concrete jungle. I have to belong some-where. With the sale happening just after harvest, it's time to get back to my clamoring clients. The finalizing of the offer is coming in any day, and it's a large sum of money. And Josh left me the day after he claimed me. I have no ties here.

The deal now encompasses the other four family wineries. It's a hell of a distribution idea to highlight Sonoma family-run businesses. The wineries are made up of basically Sarah and Will's closest friends, the Wednesday night crew's families. The Schroeder, Gelbert, Aganos, and Langerford families. It's an excellent way to get closure for Will and Sarah, to share the success with their support system.

The other wineries keep producing their wine and working their land, and the Vino Groupies will take on distribution and marketing.

I've been vamping here holding out for Josh. Three months and I finally start to see the light. There's no grand gesture coming. I told him we were done, and he listened. There's been no contact. Not that I gave him any encourage-ment. Time to become Noelle Parker again. Not Elle, the nickname given to me by Will, one I only use here in Sonoma.

Although Evan is terrific at what he does, I do understand that I'm the reason the clients ultimately signed contracts. I haven't been there for them. I got swept up in LaChap-pelle/Whittier. And that asshole.

I felt a part of things here that were bigger and more important than me. It was nice to climb away from my ego for a moment and see what to value in life. Josh ruined a lot of it, not Sarah and Will. With his absence, it reminded me that I have another life to reclaim.

It still stabs at my heart like cut glass when I think of Josh. I've only let myself cry over him when Sarah and Will couldn't see. He's left everything in his whole life. Why would I be any different?

And the sex. Sigh. We were really good at that. I hope I find someone to make me come like that again. Doubtful, though. I wish it had just been hot sex. It mattered to him where I was in the world. He checked in and called. Someone needed me for things other than work, and someone cared if I slept well. Being a partner with Josh was everything. But he destroyed me. I push it from my mind again, unwilling to go back to the depressing place I lived in just after the Members party back in June.

I'll put off my return as long as I'm useful to Sarah and Will. I owe them that, for all they've given me in return. I haven't felt a sense of place or family since I left Kansas. I've treasured every moment.

Sarah exclaims, "Elle! Thank you. Thank you. I knew we could depend on you. I know this isn't really your arena, but can you reach out to the other families and tell them what's happened? They might be able to help us. We'll pay off-hours or double shifts. We need help. Desperate for help."

"I'll call The Five. And I'll roll up my sleeves and pick too if that helps. But I do need a room at the El Dorado or MacArthur Place for Evan. I have a ton business to contend with, and I'm going to fly him here for the week."

"I look forward to meeting him. And let me call and see if we can get a room comp for him."

"No. I can pay for Evan's room."

"You'll do no such thing. If we can get it comped, then we'll take care of it. He's heading your marketing firm, and we're stealing their CEO and founder to pick grapes and preform farm work. It's the least we can do."

"I can also drive any farm vehicle you put in front of me. Don't forget that."

Sarah sips her coffee and smiles. "We need all hands on deck, farm girl."

"When's your next doctor's appointment?"

"Tomorrow. But I called for more meds today. I can't take the twitching at night. I don't sleep." Her Parkinson's seems to be amping up again. It goes in spurts, but I hate that she can't sleep.

"I'll run and pick up the prescriptions after I cancel my meetings for today."

"Don't cancel them." Sarah insists.

"I can reschedule. Evan can take the meetings next Monday. Did you take all the supplements yesterday?"

Sarah nods her head at me. "Stop fussing. You know you're leaving eventually, and I'll be the one taking my pills all by myself like a big girl."

"I do but don't think I didn't figure out a system to make sure you do. Now let me get you some more caffeine. That should calm down the pinkie a bit."

"Saw that, did you?"

Her right pinkie has been shaking since I came downstairs. It's not a big thing, but it's a big enough thing. Her head is starting to roll a bit too. Most people think she's being funny. I wonder who they've shared this news with besides me. I stand up, squeeze her shoulder, and circle back around the island to face her. I lean over it to get closer to her.

"I'll get some of the more mundane admin stuff handled by some of my staff in New York. I'll tell Randy to handle the tasting room and club inquires. I'm going to promote Sammy to assistant manager to aid in all of that. Devote time to sleep and harvest. And I can pick up the paperwork if you're needed elsewhere. And handle the phones with Mrs. Dotson. I'm going to let them do it on their own. Can I give them that authority?"

"Of course. I trust your judgment. It's amazing how quickly you can take control of a situation."

"Thank you. I have lots of practice. You two concentrate your energy here. I'll devise a plan for the staff to help pick as well. And I'll call Sam for immediate help."

She hugs me, and it's nice to be helpful. She's looking over my shoulder towards the door absently and then back to me. "We appreciate all of this, and you. But there's one more thing I need from you."

"Anything. Name it. Seriously."

"Play nice."

My adrenaline surges as I sense what's behind me. My breath is just about gone as I ask the next question. I can feel him. My stomach rolls with fear and anticipation.

I grit my teeth as she smirks at me, "With what?"

"Not what, my dear. Who."

"Who?" I exhale loudly.

My skin pebbles and flushes already knowing the answer. His musky cedar scent fills my nostrils before I can turn around. Then the voice that makes me infuriated and exhilarated at the same time rasps and vibrates the girly parts of me from the kitchen backdoor. Goddammit, I hate my body and him.

"Me."

I whip my head around to the door. In a tailored charcoal grey suit that's cut to fit his muscular torso, duffle bag in hand, and a much shorter cropped haircut, he fills the doorway. His defined jaw brushed with a sexy five o'clock shadow and his indigo blue eyes taking in every inch of me. I only wish he wasn't hot as hell. I wish I still didn't feel a connection to him. One that defies explanation. My stomach twists in knots and then flips at the sight of him, but I turn away, so he doesn't notice that he stole my breath. Give it back, asshole.

"For you, Sarah, I'll try. But you do know I have to stay somewhere else."

"I already thought of that. Josh, you're staying in Lookout cottage on the ridge."

"The what? No. Mom. This is my house."

"Please stop whining," she says, and I grin at the little whiner. "Wait until you see what we've done. You'll have privacy to work. It's gorgeous and perfect. It's the way I always dreamed it could be. I want to share it with you. You'll love it. And you can pee outside. That's your favorite. The toilet will be installed in a couple of days."

My cheeks flush from attempting not to laugh that his mother just told him he can pee outside like he's a four-year-old. Will and the boys rebuilt it and insulated it with a contractor from town. All of the outbuildings have at least begun to be repaired, restored and insulated now. The Lookout was the second renovation. Josh has already seen the Longhouse, the large conference room/event space in the middle of the woods, complete with kitchen and storage facilities. Sarah and Will are throwing their annual wine dinner with their custom blends just after harvest to show off the new buildings.

I helped with the planning and execution. Sarah and I worked with my friend from the city on the interiors. It was insanely fun. Although the Lookout's toilet is on backorder, the shower is to die for.

"Great. As long as there are walls and running water, I'll be fine. I'll just dig a hole if I have to do more than take a piss."

Sarah and I laugh. His lips curl up at the corners. I forgot how cute that wolfish grin could be. He turns towards me and says his first words to my face since the morning after the Members party almost three lonely months ago.

"You know I wouldn't be here if it weren't an emergency. And I'd appreciate it if you don't ignore me, Cosmo."

I narrow my eyes at him as he uses that name. I've been seething angry with him, but I turn to him and pretend I'm fine. "I don't know what you're talking about, Suit. You have a wonderful day peeing outside. If you'll excuse me, I have a lot of work to do in block fourteen with the vines, you know the grapes. It's why we're all here."

"Little overdressed for harvesting, aren't you?"

"Not at all, Joshua. This is the perfect outfit for testing the Brix."

"It's just Brix not 'the Brix.'"

"Whatever—the sugar level in the damn grape." I snort at him.

Sarah kisses her son. She whispers something in his ear that I can't hear, and she walks out to get to work. He calls out after her.

"I will do what I can. But you should have told me." We're alone in the kitchen. The tension is too much.

I know he's answering her plea for him to play nice too. I scurry around the kitchen table to dump my coffee and attempt to leave. He steps back in the doorway and blocks my way. His chiseled and tan body makes me remember things I'd rather forget. My chest begins to flush. Dammit.

"We need to talk."

"No. We don't. It's fine. It's so fine. It could not be finer. I'm fine." I speak as quickly as possible so I can get the hell out of here.

"So, I take it, you're fine?" He grins at me.

"Yup. Totally. Fine. I mean, totally."

"Liar. Look, Elle, there are things I can't share with you. Things that would make you understand what I've done."

"I'm sure you've had three months to come up with something but no need. There's no use for that now. Those were things you should have shared before you left. You didn't. And now it's fine. But I do give you credit for showing up for your mom and dad even if you couldn't for me. Maybe a version of the real you is still in there." I try and hustle out the door.

He shakes his head and scrubs his jaw and exhales loudly. He speaks insistently, "You are an infuriating woman. Slow down for a second. You have *got* to understand…"

I cut him off. Stop fucking talking to me. I need to regain composure before I fall apart and say, "I don't need to understand or know anything. Please leave me alone. You have a life, a career, and apparently a new leggy girlfriend who gives good duck face." A tidbit Sammy shared with me that Sam dropped by accident. She's all over Instagram. Josh is the background of her pictures lately. I'm not sure if he knows that. He looks pissed off and that suits me fine. "I'm going back to New York. We had too much to drink. It was a massive mistake that won't be repeated. Stay out of my way, and I'll stay out of yours. Please excuse me, I have work to get to."

"We're not done, Noelle Parker."

I round on him and get as close to him as I dare. I need him to hear me. "We sure as shit are. There are no third chances at trust. We're way past that fool me once crap."

"In your text you said, and I quote, *I'm not mad anymore.*" He did read my text he just chose not to respond. Asshole.

"I lied. Now. I've gotta go. The rows of grapes are calling my name. And I have to check the sugars."

I grin at her lack of wine terminology. "I'm going to change my clothes, but you go right ahead and test Brix in that tight little skirt that matches the green in your eyes and highlights one of your best assets."

I turn around quickly and speak cuttingly. "You lost the right to say that to me. Now it's harassment."

"Just an observation from a fan of that skirt."

"Shut up."

And now I have to ruin my new Fendi kitten heels out of spite as I trek down towards the muddy Pinot Noir block where Will is testing the sugars to see if they're ready for harvest. But I won't give him the satisfaction of changing. I'll ruin ten pairs of Fendi shoes if it means putting him in his place. And I do hope my perfect ass is torturing him. Jackass. I hurry away from him, so he doesn't see the tears building in my eyes.

# 4

## JOSH

MY PHONE RINGS. I SEND IT TO VOICEMAIL. FUCK. I'VE HURT her so badly, and it's all fucking Salvatore's fault. Never-fucking-mind. I *wish* it were all his fault. It's mine. I'm the asshole who thought you could keep a pet snake and not get bit. I did not know she would be here. Last I saw she was back in New York. Evan tagged the social media hell out of her: #backinthesaddle, #backwhereshebelongs, and shit like that. Fuck. Fuck. And now she's here, I'm here, and there's a fucking crime boss calling. Shit, there he is again.

Mark is supposed to tell me today if the FBI has found anything, I can use that's not classified. I should know if I can pin him to a major heroin shipment in Long Beach that Melissa found. My phone rings again because I'm on the shortest fucking leash ever.

He speaks before I even answer. "Joshie. You're not in your office. You know I don't like that shit. This is not what I expect. I thought we were past this disappearing crap."

"Good morning, Sal. I had some pressing matters to take care of."

"The Guatemala sick mama really screwed with your

parents. I get that, but hire them some damn help and get the fuck down to LA today."

And now I realize that he's tapped my personal phone. Melissa was right. Duh. There's no way he could know that. Thank god I've been using the burner for my Stanford buddy too. They're also trying to get intel on the nephew as well. I'm hoping to offer the intel to Sal in exchange for the end of my indentured servitude. I only hope that today is the day I get out from under this asshole. Now that I'm here, I can't imagine going anywhere.

"Tell me that it's just my phone you listen to. That you're only invading my privacy and leaving my family and friends alone."

"Joshie. I will do whatever I have to do. You fucking get that right. I have no fucking choice, so you have no choice. I protect my family and business. I'm in a tight spot. So, you're in a tight spot. It's not how I wanted things, but here we are. You owe me for years of feeding your career. The bill is due now, Josh. That's the best I can explain it. Sarà quello che sarà."

"Seriously, 'it will be what it will be?' Fuck you, Sal."

"Watch your temper. I've got a mountain of shit going wrong. I'm goddamned sideways. I need to get this money out of my accounts *today*. You better be in my office today. Or maybe I start looking into investing with some companies that might have a great marketing company all lined up. Set me a personal meeting with their blonde founder and CEO. If you get my point."

"Sal, you're the least subtle person. Send me the amounts and accounts. I have an idea. But all this shit will just go into escrow today. I'll shove it somewhere. But I will only move it if you stay far the fuck away from her."

"Good. But you know I need the personal touch, so I'll see

your arrogant ass this evening in my office. There is much to discuss. No excuses."

I hang up my phone and fucking throw it across the kitchen island. I text Mark from my burner.

*JOSH: Threats from my best friend to appear in front of him in LA today. Needs a "mountain of money invested today." Tell me I don't launder.*

*MARK: You don't. He's kept all his accounts with you clean and pays taxes on it. The info you got us is incredible. Tell your source thank you and wouldn't mind knowing who it is. We can't find a trace of them anywhere.*

*JOSH: Source stays anonymous. I'll tell them they're still a ghost. They'll like that.*

*MARK: There's a shit-ton of gang activity going down in the next few weeks. He's connected to some of it, but we have discovered he is actually pulling out and handing over territories to others. He seems to be doing it slowly so as not to upset the balance. He's a thug by birth not by choice. It seems like once he's out, he'd help flip on the others. If he makes a score, he cleans the money, then gives it to you to invest instead of putting it back into the rackets, illicit things, or drugs. But someone is working against him from the inside. We're not sure who is backing the nephew. The kid didn't threaten the king without serious cash and muscle. Sal is scrambling to prevent an all-out fucking war. And keep his family safe. He sees yours as a liability. They could be leverage to twist the knife in his back. It's why he cut you off from them and obviously how he's controlling you.*

*JOSH: You think?*

*MARK: We know. We can get you enough info today to get out. He's supposed to be at the heroin deal this morning. We'll get photos. But I need you to turn Sal into an asset. Consider the favor to be the back rent you owe me for that dump we lived in our senior year.*

*JOSH: Deal. I'll do whatever I can. If you get what I need then*

*someone has to deliver it to him. Say it's from me. And send me a*
*copy. And tell him to fuck the hell off.*

*MARK: I'll be in touch.*

*JOSH: Thanks, man.*

*MARK: Of course. No one fucks with Sarah and Will.*

Pretty grateful I did keg stands with that guy. He worked the vineyard a couple of summers and stayed with us. Mom makes a butter cake he still dreams of, apparently.

I have a plan to move away from all of this, and getting out from under Salvatore Pietro is step one. I wish the son of a bitch didn't make me so much fucking money. I mean, we've made stupid money together.

Once, long ago, he promised me that the clean money and investments never got put back into the mix of the mob. He also said I'd never be connected to anything. We had mutual respect once. At least I know he's telling the truth about the money.

On to my next pressing issue. My dick is now semi-hard watching as Elle flips her stupid perfect golden hair in the sun while standing ankle-deep in the mud. Fuck me, she's hot doing just about anything.

It slashed at my heart when she called us a massive mistake. She's so fucking stubborn. I know she has baggage in this area. I wish she'd believed in me a little bit more. I know it appears that I don't care and that she was disposable. That's the part that hurts the most.

I thought I had made strides to move forward and forget about Elle. She knows about Claudia. But now, as I stand near her again, I realize Claudia was only ever a distraction. I need to prove to Elle that it wasn't a mistake. I was a fool to pretend that she wasn't ever the end of me. I miss the challenge of her and the feel of her. Fuck me. I'm done. She's everything. Now to get her to listen to me.

I whip out my now-cracked-screen phone and order her

a replacement pair of Fendi heels, remembering her size from when I bought her Louboutins as part of a different apology. She's currently ruining her Fendis to spite me. It's adorable, really. She cares enough to prove to me that I don't affect her. Maybe new shoes are the way back into her heart. The least I can do is drop some cash on the issue.

I step away from the door and watch her leave. I'll text Sam that I'm here. I gotta get some scoop. See if he'll tell me who was the target of that green skirt. I need to know if that chef touched her. Because the skirt wasn't for my mom or me. Who's the beneficiary of that ass-hugging skirt? Nothing happens in this town without Sam knowing. Plus, I have to grab some second shift guys from him, see if we can rotate workers. I leave the Porsche at the Farmhouse and climb into the farm's Jeep to head up to the Lookout cottage.

The entire ride I'm excited to weasel my way under her skin again. Just teasing and waiting for her to lose her composure so I can have a conversation with her. I nod to my planted security guy who's hauling wine from storage to the tasting room. I got a report that Elle was headed to Silicon Valley today, but now she's literally standing in the muck in eight-hundred-dollar shoes in order to be right and prove me wrong. She had to control the moment, so I let her.

I have to uninvite Claudia to visit. She incredibly understood that I had to leave at a moment's notice to jump in and be an ad hoc vineyard manager with my father. Claudia would have been the first girlfriend I brought home since high school. That seemed a solid plan before I stood in the kitchen and saw the light play off her skin. Or heard her sassy voice get angry at me again. Or inhaled her scent. All the things about her that I rationalized away and tried to bury come flooding to me, and I know Claudia has no place anywhere in my life.

I never brought the college girls here because I didn't want them to meet my grandfather or assume that I was going to be a farmhand for the rest of my life. I never wanted to share because I didn't see the good in this place. Lucien has colored so much of my life. I'm only starting to understand how deeply ingrained my grandfather is in me. So much of my life was built in opposition to him. I'm grateful for the way he taught me to find my balls to stand up to men like Sal. But I'm also starting to realize that I might have gotten my father's capacity to love as well. A part that I was taught by my grandfather was frivolous but turns out my father might just have more secrets to life than I initially thought.

My parents are everything to each other. I know they love me very much, but their love for each other is epic. My father also loves the people in his life profoundly, and they feel it every moment they're with him. He's incapable of hiding anything.

Even Elle feels his love for her. She basks in it. My parents are the perfect argument for destiny, soul mates, and all the cosmic shit you want to explain their connection. I never truly appreciated it until I couldn't walk away from fucking Noelle Parker. I want to know all of her. I want her to discover everything about me as well. If I could have even a sliver of what my parents have, then I'd be the happiest man with Elle.

---

HOLY SHIT, the cottage looks great. The stonework is slamming. It seems as if it's always been here. They continued the stone into the walk-in shower, and the bed is luxe. Grapevines and willow branches are knotted together to create a frame of a gray leather headboard. The bed itself is low with four-posters made of birch wood. It's masculine and feminine.

The lighting is soft and bright. Somehow, it's all inviting and homey but has clean lines and angles. The ceramic dishes and mugs are all my mom. Like the ones in the Longhouse, she probably made them at the Community Center in their pottery studio.

I stop in the living room and stare at a breathtaking landscape canvas. It's the vineyard at dawn where my mom does yoga. I'd recognize it anywhere. Elle got my mom to paint, and that's fucking amazing. Everything else is magazine chic, which means Elle did it as well. My mom's a little more 'craft show' than 'arts and craft mid-century modern.' At least Elle had the decency to only leave a small whiff of her scent in this cottage.

I'm shrugging my jacket off when my dad appears in the door. He rakes me into a bear hug. He's a good hugger.

"Son. My boy. Thank fucking god you're here. But the suit's not necessary. We already have one of our new vineyard workers in business attire. I told her it was casual Thursday, but she showed up in that get up anyway."

We laugh at Elle. "I just threw on what I was wearing last night to get up here as fast as possible. I didn't feel like flying. I left early and missed most of the traffic. In my Porsche Spyder." I wink at him.

His eyes widen. He never gets toys like that, but I'm sure he'd love to see it. I've hidden everything away from them for so long. I should have shared much more than my rich boy toys. But the least I can do is let my dad drive the car.

"I forget you're loaded. Damn, boy. Can I drive it?"

"We'll see."

My Dad scrubs his jaw with his hands and then takes a deep breath. His words tumble out of his mouth. "I'm headed up to the upper deck ridge to see how the Cab is coming. There were a few blocks way off their timing. The sugar is up and down this year. And a couple of stubborn blocks didn't hit veraison in time with the others. And when I tried to explain it to Elle, I mean she picks things up quickly but I don't have time to explain everything. Bless her heart but she kept calling veraison, "the color changing" or the "ripening". I need someone who just knows. A short hand. Fuck I'm glad you're here, son. Come with me, so we can plan out the harvest. I'm so fucking overwhelmed."

"Breathe Dad. I'm here and I know all the terms. But it is cute when she calls Brix, 'the sugars'."

My dad laughs and puts his hand on my shoulder and pulls me into another hug. He's stressed and I get it. My dad's a genius who knows the soil and the land. He reads people better than anyone. He's charming and jovial. He under-stands the chemistry of wine. He has a keen business sense, but as for an organized plan, it's not his thing.

Fortunately, between Elle and myself, a plan of action won't be a problem. I pull out a spreadsheet and a map of the blocks, something I whipped up early this morning after his call. I couldn't go back to sleep, so I planned. I hand it to him, and he lunges at me with another giant bear hug.

"We need to verify all that info, but I think that's the order to pick down to the blocks. And I can adjust based on Brix levels. But it's getting to be blazing, so we're going to need to spark the sprayers immediately."

"I didn't think of that. I just kept them on the normal shuffle schedule."

"I'm here now but you need to hire someone. I'm not staying. This is an emergency and a favor for you and Mom."

"I get that, Josh. We're grateful that not only are you here but that you came when we called. Love you, boy."

"Love you too, Dad. Now, I want nothing to do with the

sale. I won't pose for more pictures or be her winery poster boy. No more interviews. You can do that, but I'm done."

"Elle. You're done with Elle?"

I laugh. Visions of her ass in that skirt are driving me wild. "Just done with the sale, Dad. Elle's another matter altogether."

"Whatever you say. I don't know what happened between you two, but she left here just after you did very suddenly. She went back to New York. Your mother had to beg her to come back here like coaxing a freaked-out raccoon out of the garbage. But you should know she was leaving us forever the day after tomorrow. Her goodbye dinner was tomorrow night. Once again, your mother worked her magic, and she's staying to help us through harvest. You've got a limited window. Don't fuck it up."

"I didn't know any of that. There are things to be said, if she'll listen. I'm not that hopeful right now."

"That doesn't sound like the Josh I know. You can get anyone to do anything. Thought you were a conqueror?"

"That's her, not me."

"Interesting you think that, but I agree. Fix it, or you'll regret it. We see you, Josh. And we know a thing or two about the stray we picked up six months ago, we see her too. Meet me up on the ridge. Block eighty-nine." He winks at me and exits.

My dad's hug and visions of that skirt lead me to the ballsiest, most impulsive decision of my life. I'm not fucking going anywhere. He can come after us. I'm done being a pussy missing out on my life because some thug told me to. I'm not that guy.

I'm not going to LA or Santa Barbara until she talks to me. Really talks and really listens. And after that, if I still lose her, then I'll be able to move on. But not without a fucking fight. She wants a chase; I'll give her one. I'm done hiding from my future, so Sal's is protected.

I text Sal. I'll protect them while standing right next to them. Which maybe I should have done in the first place, but I'm new to caring about people. I'm a little dense sometimes. Now that I have amassed an army of security, Mel, and Mark, I'm ready to stay planted. Come at me, thug.

*JOSH: Not coming. I've done everything you have fucking asked. But not doing this command performance. Deal with it. I'm nobody's bitch. Send me your shit, and I'll make it all legit. But don't you fucking summon me, ever. And don't you dare come up here. I'll be down there soon enough. You're a big powerful thug, surely you can handle disappointment, fucker.*

*SAL: I don't have time for your shit. Fix the money. You're lucky I'm too fucking busy to find you. Be here tomorrow at 9:00 a.m. And you are my bitch for as long as I say, Joshie. Deal with it.*

My final word on who is whose bitch will be delivered tonight, thanks to Mark and Elle's hacker, Mel. It's time for me to go dark and let the Feds handle it.

I head towards the shower to rinse off. My dick could use a little work out as well. I soap up and am in awe of the water pressure. It's like a world-class hotel shower on the top of basically nowhere. She can do anything, and the thought of that alone gets me going.

I yank my cock for a second and see if it wants to come out and play. I close my eyes and think about last night, only because I had sex last night. And let's see if it was as good as I'm pretending. Let's see if my cock thinks it's the right decision to stay. I imagine Claudia riding my jock with her petite breasts bobbing above me, and I crank it harder. I picture her tight little ass and her shaved pussy. It's not working.

Then that damn woman's skirt comes to mind and the thought of throwing her over the hood of the Spyder and lifting it up over her ass. And now I have some stonework of my own. Hard as anything and I pump it. Takes very little time when I think of Elle's mouth on mine, and before I know it, I'm unloading all over the brand-new shower. I roar as I paint the door.

Elle. Only Elle.

# 5

## ELLE

IT'S WEDNESDAY. JOSH'S BEEN HERE NINE FREAKING DAYS, AND despite his best efforts to talk to me, I've steered clear. I wait for him to leave the kitchen in the morning before I come downstairs for breakfast. I always have an escape route when he's working in the same area. There's nothing to be said and as soon as this fucking harvest is over, I'm gone. I'm back to my life in New York. I need a Josh free existence in order to let my heart close up again. When we do see each other it's curt and snippy. It's so freaking stressful and exhausting hating someone so much. The staff and certainly Will and Sarah are probably sick of us bickering.

I spent a few nights in San Francisco having drinks with my interior decorator friend and his husband, to avoid him. Then Evan came to town three days ago, and it's been glorious. We spent the first night together at MacArthur Place hotel, up late gossiping and sipping. Poppy cooked him a feast at her restaurant yesterday, and he met a couple of my new friends. We shut the place down. Sammy and Sam were there, and thankfully, Josh was not. I think Evan hooked up.

He's a love 'em and leave 'em guy, so I'm glad he's getting a little while he's here.

Currently, I'm at the Cooperage chatting with Mrs. Dotson. Actually, she's telling me about how I don't clean coffee mugs correctly or put them 'handle in' into the cabinet. This is not the first time I've had this lecture. I smile and nod. Then there's a series of air horn sounds. I jump a foot in the air and almost out of my skin. Mrs. Dotson's pencil cup falls on my head after I knock it over. I duck under a desk and try to pull her down. Everyone else in the office is cheering, and Mrs. Dotson is full-on bent in half, laughing at me.

Sammy strides over squats down and yells, "Juice break!" Everyone files out of the office, and I'm dumbfounded. Sammy explains as my adrenaline begins to even out. "It's the first juice crushed, and we all sip it together. I'm so excited about it. It's Gewürztraminer!"

"No one told me this was a thing. Or that there would be air horns involved."

The entire office walks to the crush pad while laughing at me. We're handed stemmed wine glasses filled with muddy green liquid. I'm in my favorite red capri pants, and I hope I don't have to go into the fields again. I've already ruined a staggering amount of clothing tromping around the vines. Maybe I should purchase overalls or something.

I whisper to Sammy, "This is the juice? Why is it so cloudy?"

And then out of nowhere, he's at my ear, "It has yet to go through débourbage."

I turn my head and whisper loudly back, "I don't know what that means, and I asked Sammy."

They both laugh. Sammy explains. "It's a French process used for white wine to let everything, or as it's called, the musts, settle before it's fermented and racked. You want clear juice, and if you just let it settle, you'll get exactly what you want. Let the musts get out of the way. Then it doesn't need heavy filtration or fining. Clarity comes with time. The less messing with it, the better the outcome. That's the theory behind the process."

And the jackass is back at my ear. "It's why our Chardonnay is better than Langerford's."

I need to step away before the wetness building between my legs makes me do something stupid. That damn breath in my ear. His lips so close to me. I hate my body. It's betraying me. Thank god Will is standing up on top of a barrel now. Every single person who works at the winery is here and paying attention to him.

"Quiet, hooligans. My rough and tumble crew, it's time to pay attention. I know you wanted Sarah. It was a battle royale. I wrestled this speech away from her. Honestly, I pinned her so quickly it was pathetic."

Sarah raises her middle finger to her husband. I do adore them. He blows her a kiss and raises his glass just to her. She catches the kiss. They're inanely adorable.

"The first press is sacred. Always has been. This story has been passed down through Sarah's family, and I'm going to tell it again. Like I *DO* every damn year.

Emma LaChappelle was so excited by her first harvest. She was thrilled and stunned that she'd actually grown viable wine grapes. She went all over town pouring her first press juice to anyone she could find. She toasted them with this phrase, 'Je suis la terre et laisse-moi partager mon soleil avec toi.'"

Josh whispers it in perfect timing in French in my ear. How does a girl stay dry when a hot man—albeit a jackass—whispers French in her ear? Fucking Josh.

"I am the land and let me share my sun with you. She toasted over a hundred people that day, and the legend is that the first bottle of juice is for the people. For those who choose to share the sun with Sarah, Josh, and myself. There is no LaChappelle/Whittier without all of you. I am the land. But you are the sun. À votre santé!"

Everyone repeats the French toast and drinks. Alena gets up and says a bunch of lovely words, but I can't pay attention. He's now standing directly behind me and playing with my ponytail. He's whispering in French. It's killing me. I have no idea what he's saying. Goosebumps all over my neck are giving me away. My skin is tingling, and heat is pooling down below. He could be ordering me to scrub toilets, but it's so freaking sexy in French. His breath is soft and warm on the back of my neck. I let it go on way too long. I lean back and turn my head.

"What are you saying?"

"Do you really want to know?"

"No. Never mind."

His lips brush my neck, and my skin sears from the heat. "I was telling you why I left. I can translate for you, belle femme têtue."

"No. I'm good. I know that belle means beautiful so thank you."

"And têtue means stubborn."

"How do you say jackass?"

"Le crétin." I giggle. That makes sense. I lean back into him.

"Go away, le crétin."

He chuckles way too close to my ear.

I turn away from him and sip. It's bitter, musty, and rich. "If I said it tastes like the color green, would that be strange? Almost like a way too tart Granny Smith apple and bamboo."

Alena the winemaker beams as she joins us. Thankfully he's stopped touching me and speaking in French. Josh's attention is pulled to a group of people standing behind me.

Alena explains excitedly, "That's exactly what I was hoping it would taste like. Your palate is coming along."

"Can I ask how long that doobie doobie do thing takes? Isn't that something with dancing horses? And what do you do to make it happen?"

She laughs. "Débourbage. The horse thing is spelled differently. And it takes as long as it needs. You do nothing. That's the beauty of it. Let it find its own way. We'll monitor closely and take it from there. As soon as we can move this juice out of the tanks, the next set of varietals can come in."

"Thanks for the lesson."

"Josh knows all of this stuff cold. You should have asked him."

I know he can hear me. "Yeah. I try to not need Josh for anything, you never know when he'll be around." He leans his head towards me when he hears his name.

"Cold. Did not realize you two had gone cold." Alena smiles.

"We were never hot, just overheated."

# 6

## JOSH

NOT SURE WHY I DIDN'T THINK OF THIS BEFORE, DÉBOURBAGE. She needs her musts to settle. She needs time for all of her sentiment and crap to sink to the bottom of the tank, and then she'll be clear-headed. Clarity comes with time. Find her own way back to me. She'll see what I need her to see and hear what I need her to hear, but only when she's settled. I can't rush it.

As enchanting as she can be, I do need her to do work for me tonight. I don't have the patience or strength to be rejected or fight more. I have to work on some Sal shit as well as winery stuff. Then get a couple of other deals put into place for other clients. And as a bonus, I get to figure out what everyone at the Vineyard is doing tomorrow and the next day. Scheduling a full staff is a bitch. I need her to pick up some of this tonight.

I catch her on her way back up to the Cooperage. She picked up her pace when she caught sight of me following her. "You might not need anything from me, but I need you to file the crush reports. And can you see what that liquor board email is all about? I can't get to it. And we need to divide staff scheduling. I put a doc in the Google Drive that I need you to help with."

"I don't work for you."

"So I've heard. But you'll do it anyway." I'm tired. I tried to flirt. I can speak French. That alone should have gotten her to smile. I'm so stressed waiting for Sal's retaliation for the papers I delivered to his office last week. I need to hear from Mark that we're secure. It's been rather quiet from LA, and that's not a good thing.

I gave the security guys a heads up, and all four take turns watching the house and winery. I have no patience for her nasty attitude right now. Give it up already. She walks away, rolling her eyes.

I yell after her. My patience is done. "Don't walk away from me."

She stops and turns to me. "I'll do as I please, and it has nothing to do with you. I'm tired. I'm leaving. I have somewhere to be."

I notice she's wearing her favorite lipstick, Tom Ford *Fucking Fabulous*. I bought it for her to go with that Halston dress. The dress I still dream of seeing live and in person. I sent a MUA to her suite that night and told her to send me the bill for anything Elle wanted to keep. Who are those fuckable lips for? I do not like the idea that her red bodycon capri pants and matching lips are headed out to see someone else.

I will do what I can to keep her from meeting this mystery man I've just conjured up. "No. You'll finish the fucking job today. Mom said you were doing paperwork. This shit has to be done. As well as the scheduling. I'll do the grounds crew if you can take the desk jockeys."

"If it must be done, then you do it."

"I don't have time. I too have somewhere to be. And it's not in my job description. So take your sweet…"

She turns to me and puts her hand up like she can stop me from talking. "Don't you dare comment on my ass."

"I wasn't going to. I'm sorry, that was uncalled for and you don't deserve that level of disrespect. But I do need you to help me out." She's close enough to me that I could pull her to me, but she's been clear that's not happening today. Her scent is intoxicating and as much as I love looking at her, right now I'd settle for a cease fire. I miss sharing my day with her. I think about all the things in a day I want to tell her, and I try to remember them. I started writing them down in my phone about a month ago. Random things like a TV show I think she'd like or absurd things that happened to me that day. It started as a journal to try and work on my anger and frustration, but it's turned out to be one very long and probably boring letter to her. I hope I can show her someday.

Her voice softens and she nods at me. It's a step in the right direction. "I will get the crush reports done if you leave me alone. The liquor board thing can wait." She begins walking away. I say nothing. Then she turns back to me. "Scheduling is already done for tomorrow. Look at the doc before you fucking question me."

She's far away from me now, and I'm pissed off that she can make me so freaking aggro. She disappears into the Cooperage.

"Yes, I will," I yell to basically no one.

---

I'VE NEVER NEEDED a drink more. I drive the Porsche to Starlings to meet the boys. Thank fucking god for Wednesday night. Baxter Schroeder, Bax, is in town. His job as an environmental lobbyist has him frequently in DC or Sacramento. His sister Tommi is joining us tonight. And the only girl in the Five that's the same age as I am, Tabitha Aganos. I also believe Jims Langerford, Sam's little brother, and David Gelbert will be there as well. It's all of us pretty much, and I'm so fucking excited to just let loose a bit. Even though they're all still a little pissed off at me at the way I skipped town, I've known them too long for them not to forgive me. We're family.

Sam isn't sure if he can get away. We're all on high alert because of crush. But the entire crew hasn't been together in a while.

I'm a bit paranoid about Sal, so I leave my phone on the windowsill of the Sebastiani Theater's faux ticket booth that's out front. It's a gorgeous old theater and now they sell the actual tickets inside, but they've kept the historical ticket booth out front. It's manned by Trixie, a mannequin. I'm trusting her to keep trouble at bay. If Sal is tracking me, then he can think I went to the movies for the night. My parents are home sleeping already, they have to be up for harvest early.

The bar is bustling, there's country music blaring, so Bax must be here. It's the only place he lets his secret shame out of the box. He's also super health-conscious and fit but secretly eats McDonald's when he's in town. I spot Jims Langerford just inside the door. He's trapped an overdressed and stylish man in a dark corner.

The man is slight, with light brown hair and dark brown eyes. His lips are curled and looking at Jims as if he's Thanksgiving dinner. I've never seen this man before, but it appears they're on a date. Jims is a predator, so I hope this guy is prepared. He must be from out of town. Jims has already broken all the in-town hearts. He's often said, "No man unturned."

Jims gives me a huge hug but quickly returns his hand to

the man's shoulder. He's usually not this open so he must really like this guy.

"Hey, man." I slap his shoulder and turn to his companion.

"Josh! Allow me to introduce Evan Bixby."

We shake hands, and his smile is bright and earnest. "It's a pleasure to meet you. Hold up. Not Josh Whittier?"

"Yes." I look at him skeptically as he uses one of Elle's favorite phrases.

"Oh. Then never mind. Not a pleasure. Not a pleasure at all. Move along." And the slight man turns away from me as Jims laughs. I'm dumbfounded. What the fuck did I do to this guy?

"Where'd you get this one?" I whisper to Jims.

"Met him at Poppy's the other night. And you might want to ask your girl about him."

"My girl? Elle? She's not..." Jims gestures with his chin towards the bar, and my blood boils.

Standing with her back to me is fucking Elle. Not only has she usurped my friends, who I need tonight, but she's supposed to be working. She's toasting Sam and Sammy while Bax and Poppy Gelbert appear to be filling out the vineyard reports at a high-top table. Those are the ones I asked her to do. I figured it would take her a while since she'd never done it before.

Bax sips his Old Fashion, sees me, and raises his drink. I don't smile back. He nudges Elle. She turns around slowly and smiles, then turns back towards the bar and sips her drink. I am instantly standing behind her, and I wait. Finally, she moves back into me and then turns. Dammit, she smells good. The bartender hands me a beer.

"What?" she says as she pushes me back to arm's length.

"I told you to do those reports. Why are Bax and Poppy doing them?"

"I outsourced."

"Did you at least pay them?" Both Bax and Poppy raise their cocktails to indicate she bought them. And she gestures to them with a bit of a voila gesture. Sam belly laughs. Elle turns away from me to the bar to order another drink.

I address the group. "Who's Jims' boy toy that seems to hate me? He doesn't even know me."

Everyone looks at me quizzically, like I should know who he is. "Do we know him from somewhere?" My eyes dart to Sam.

Sam explains, "He's Elle's business partner and Creative Director. He's been in town for several days. And out to your winery, Mr. Observant."

"Then he does know all about me. Interesting." I pull Elle's shoulder to face me as she tries to walk away. "Also, why are you here on Wednesday night with *my* friends?" I raise my eyebrow.

She turns her head slightly as if talking to them. "I told you he'd get jealous and possessive." Then she reaches her hand out. David hands her twenty bucks, and she tucks it into her bra. And now all I can think about is her bra, which I now know is Rosé-colored.

Everyone stares at me with bated breath. "Fuck it. Let's get drunk, Cosmo. I might hate you less that way." I laugh. She's actually friends with my friends. Not just hanging out with them, but they know each other. My heart warms as we all tease each other.

"You can try," David yells. "But I don't think there's enough booze here."

She stares at me and goes up on her tiptoes to get more eye to eye. I wish I didn't find it so freaking cute.

"I think there might just be enough booze. And I hate you too." She says it in a flirty tone that's been missing from my life for a couple of months.

Then everyone repeats Sam's mantra in reference to Elle and I. It's like a Greek chorus shouting in unison. "Fine line."

For the first time since he started dispensing that bullshit phrase, I do hope it's true. I hope it's a fine line between love and hate.

Evan and Jims stroll over to say goodbye. Elle hugs Evan deeply. He holds her out at arm's length and then pretends to dust her off. Her eyes glass over, and I want to comfort her. Evan holds her again and then squeezes her hand. I've not seen any of her world. Just some business meetings or dinners she's held, but this man is a piece of her. And he doubts me. Just like she does. It tears at my heart that I can't explain to both of them what's going on. As soon as Mark tells me Sal is in hand, I can explain myself. But it seems that tonight no one cares why I left, only that I'm back.

She watches Evan walk out the door holding Jims' hand. It's endearing, watching her life and mine mesh together. I stay rooted where I am. Débourbage. Let her settle and find her way to clarity.

She finishes her drink and Bax hands over the reports. She kisses him on the cheek, and I watch every second of it with some kind of high school jealousy. She and Poppy hug, and then she blows a kiss to Gelbert. Times they have a changed since he called her a bitch at the Members party. She appears to be leaving, and I block her way.

"Hey." She puts her hand on my arm to keep me away from her.

She speaks softly, "Josh. I don't have it in me to fight right now. Please leave me alone."

"You don't have to go."

"I do. I have a lot of work to do. I need to look at some contracts for Evan. I need to not be near you right now. It's too hard to be this angry or sad all the time."

"Then don't be."

My stomach wrenches as she speaks honestly to me for the first time since Member night. It's slicing me from stem to stern as I see the pain in her eyes. She's not fighting with me, she's not spiteful, she's defeated, and it's the worst feeling in the world.

I want to do something to make her feel better. Anything at this moment. I tell her, "I'll go. You stay."

"No, I have to go. I just didn't want to miss Wednesday. You know…"

"Never miss a chance to drink on Wednesday because the weekend is too far away. We made that bullshit up when we were sneaking vodka into junior prom." She smiles weakly at me. "Are you sure you're okay?" I reach out to pull her into my arms, and she pushes me away. It's like a dagger to my soul. I mutter, "Sorry. I didn't mean to make you uncomfortable."

"It's ok. I'm just tired. Please, just…" I see her fighting to keep those tears in her eyes.

"What? Anything. Let me do something for you, just tell me. Ask me." I plead with her.

She answers in a broken voice that punches me in the stomach. "Can you please just stay away from me for a bit?" She takes a step back from me and won't look me in the eye. She's quiet and insistent but not herself.

"I can. You can stop running away. I'll steer clear of you for a while if that's what you need." I mean it. If that's what she needs. I don't care if she settles anymore. I just don't want to see my Hellcat defeated. I can't be the one responsible for her loss of spirit.

She says in a very matter-of-fact manner devoid of all emotion. "It's just I'm burning the candle at both ends and hating you takes up so much energy. I'm so tired of being mad or sad because of you. It's a reality I need to face, but I can't do it right now. I can't with you. It's too much." And yet another twist of a knife to my heart.

"I can do that, Cosmo." She puts her hands up, and I quickly correct myself. "I can do that, Elle. I will give you space." She turns and walks out, and the room is a little gloomier. I'm responsible for her mood a lot more than she's been letting on. But if it's space she needs to settle, I'll give it to her. Débourbage. Find your clarity without anyone filtering or fining you.

# 7

## JOSH

I KNOW HE WON'T DO ANYTHING TO ME, BUT I'M SWEATING. My palms, my forehead, and my nutsack. I don't sweat, but this is Sal. I thought I knew the man. I hope I still do. I've gone out on a limb for him, and I'm about to find out just how sturdy that branch is.

"Joshie. To what..." he stops dead in his sentence when he sees I'm not alone. Mark is with me.

My friend is wearing an ill-fitting brown suit and brand new shoes that scream law enforcement. He's usually a 'jeans and white button-down guy' and always has his FBI jacket on. He's also brushed his mousy unruly hair into what I know is his "date" look. Slicked back and then he pushes the front up just a little. He has earnest green eyes. They don't sparkle and dance like Elle's. They're deep and dark. This is a man who was born to be a protector. He's a man you want at your back and not at your front door.

"Who the fuck is this?"

"Sit down, Sally." He doesn't sit down but winces at my use of is mob nickname. He stays standing and I see him casually reach for his desk drawer. "And back away from that button. No one is coming in here. Do you understand me?"

"Look, who the fuck is giving the orders now?" Mark pulls his badge from under his collar and lets it hang down the front of his shirt. "Oh. So that's how it is."

"It's not what you think, Mr. Pietro."

"Well, if I'm going to get fucked up the ass, perhaps you call me Sal. Josh, did you at least bring lube?"

"My name is Special Agent Mark Rance, and you should be thanking Mr. Whittier. Let's all sit."

We both sit, and Sal continues to stand. Mark opens his briefcase, which I think is pleather. I'm buying him a real fucking case. I know he won't want it or care, but I'm getting him one. He pulls out several thick envelopes and folders. The papers I had delivered to Sal were simply pictures of him at the heroin deal. The note told him to leave me alone and that I would be in touch. He didn't know I was working with the FBI, simply that I'd gained some leverage.

Mark places the thick files on Sal's desk. I had to sign all kinds of paperwork for the FBI, stating that I was going to learn a fuck of a lot more than I should, but it protects me from being an accessory.

Sal sits slowly. "I'm listening. Tell me the tale of how Josh fucking ratted me out. Know this, he doesn't know shit."

I speak, "Sal, he's not here to take you in. He's here to work with you. He's a man I trust with my life, and despite our rocky past three months, I said the same of you."

"You fucking vouched for me to the Feds?"

Mark continues, "Yes, he did. Along with the evidence he's turned over, the specific amounts he's invested for you to turn your business legitimate, your ass is safe. He's your saving grace."

Sal shifts in his chair. He leans back, holding a pen so tightly I feel as if he's going to snap it. He could still shoot both of us, get rid of the bodies and only mystery Mel would be the wiser. And I don't have a lot of faith in a shadowy hacker who reads Elle's email for fun. Then he speaks. Sal's voice is a little shaky but vulnerable.

"I had no choice. I needed the cousins, my sisters, and the nieces and nephews out and safe. I've never felt the sense of honor or duty toward this work that was demanded of me. I was bred for this shit, and I've played along until I met Josh. That's when I started figuring out a plan to get my famiglia out. I don't want them to have to grow up in this world. Not if I can fucking help it."

"I get that, but you're aware who started this war, right?"

"Giancarlo. My fucking nephew. My sister's oldest. Piece of shit human. He likes the wrong side of this business. To him it has nothing to do with honor, tradition, power or money. It's all about a bloodthirst and domination."

Sal thumbs through the folders and winces as he sees the volume of crime folders and autopsies. "This is not the time to lie, I did some of this. I'm responsible. I may not pull the trigger anymore, but some of this I sanctioned. I had to. He pulls a picture and throws it across the desk."

I look down briefly at a man with a hole in his head. "Josh, he was in Santa Barbara a month ago. I don't know who else knows about you, but I always had a guy on you. You were my one weak spot. That's why I cut you off from your loved ones. To mitigate my weakness."

I nod to him and try to keep cool, but I'm freaking the fuck out inside. Someone was going to kill me. I come from farm people. This is not fucking real. I cross my leg, and it's shaking. Mark reaches out and places his hand on my arm.

"I got you. Sal. Giancarlo is on a rampage, and he's sloppy. He's uncoordinated where you're shrewd and calculating. I'm going to ask some things that are not in those folders. And

trust me, you won't believe how much we do know. I want
you to answer me."

"To what end? Lompoc? What's this little dance about?'

"I don't want you. You're not killing to kill. You're setting
things right. I don't love that you handed over the heroin
territory to Latin Kings, but I can see why you had to." His
eyes get wide. "You're careful, and it took someone extraor-
dinarily skilled to find out the bulk of this information. But
I'm a student, and an expert of this world and Giancarlo
makes no kind of sense. Why groom him?"

Sal laughs profoundly and stands. I'm still on edge,
hearing about the fact that I almost died. He pulls out cigars
and gestures to the two of us. Mark smiles and nods and I
shake my head no. He clips them and collects ashtrays. Mark
puffs and lights his as does Sal. The smoke is curling up
around our heads, and I'm staring in disbelief at the two of
them.

Each of them is precise and calculating in their reactions
to each other. They're sizing up the moment. I would be
brash and bold in this situation and charge forward, but
these men are slow playing each other. After another minute
or two, when the tension is thick, Sal finally speaks.

"I'm not grooming anyone. I'm actively looking for a legit
CEO. Giancarlo wasn't even going to get a role in the legitimate Raptor organization. He has a chip on his shoulder and
not a brain in his foolish head. Blames me for his father
getting shot, but his father was as dumb and arrogant as he
is. You know, don't you?"

Mark nods. I'm lost. "Have you ever heard the name
Phillip Koch or Les White?"

Sal contemplates, and I'm on the edge of my seat. I don't
know who that is either. "What does he want with me?"

"He figured out you were going legitimate, and he wants
your power in L.A. Your people, their loyalty, your territory,

and holdings. The man brokers in power and has a lot of it. We think he's based in California, but we can't seem to find him or get anything concrete on him. Rumblings of his misdeeds have been kicking around the Bureau for a decade. We suspect he wants your territory, and he wants to own the cash going forward. Giancarlo is his pawn. He staked him and convinced him to threaten you."

"Let's give him a shit ton of money and send him on his fucking way. Clearly, I'm out of the protection business with the Feds sitting in my office." Mark laughs and puffs on his cigar.

I stand and head to his wet bar and pour two fingers of scotch for myself and the others. I shoot mine and pour a second one before I deliver the drinks. Both nod in approval. It's odd to see them together, and they are remarkably similar people. Their devotion to what's right and wrong is what makes them two sides of the same coin.

"The man usually works in the shadows and comes from unprecedented money. We don't know a lot about him except that he likes to play god. You're a powerful man Sal, and that's his favorite commodity. He wants your throne, not your gold."

"And I'm destroying the throne piece by piece."

Mark nods, "Exactly. From what we can understand about this man, he's known internationally. We don't know if there's any terrorism connection, but we do know that he likes to play a political game, not one of blood. So when he discovered what you were doing, he must have panicked. The thought is that he's been targeting you for years, and he would eventually bring you into his organization and absorb your influence."

"Shit."

"But this rash mistake on his part, using Giancarlo and starting a gang war, that's not his M.O. It's left him exposed.

It's the first real lead we have on this ghost. We want this guy bad, and if you cooperate, everything goes away."

"Turn states?"

I lean forward. "There's more Sal. There's so much more, and it's the part you won't like."

"Let me know that the money that's already invested stays where it is, and my sisters get to keep it."

Mark puts another set of paperwork on his desk, and Sal sits back.

"What's that?"

"Witness Protection once we take Giancarlo down, and we get a step closer to the man. It will take time. I know you want out now but for the greater good we need you to stay put a little longer. We need to end this war, bring in Giancarlo, and make it seem as if you've changed directions. We need you to draw the ghost out. We have a plan and want to work with you. I'll be in your office and at your side every step of the way."

"Like my own fucking federal fairy godmother." We all laugh, but Sal's face is strained. He gets up and walks around his office.

"If I go under, it won't be where even you can find me. My family goes now before we start stirring the pot." I nod at him. Sal is his own man.

"I've always had an exit strategy if anything got too hot or too close. Ironically, I thought it would be you RICO assholes that would make me go under. And in a way it is. Fine. How do we fucking do this?"

\* \* \*

We talk for another hour or so about Mark's immediate plans. He's going to go undercover from here on out, and I'll walk out of the office with the briefcase full of evidence. There's a safe box in Santa Barbara that I was instructed to put it in. Only Mark knows the combination, and it's the only set of hard evidence all in one place. They still don't know Melissa's name, but they asked me if she could do some digging around about this other guy, and they'd pay her a lot of money. She said no. She said she was busy this season, but maybe at a later date. Whoever this woman is, she has bigger balls than all of us. I stand up to leave, and Mark hugs me. "When all this is done, I'm going to need some butter cake. And a big fat hug from Sarah. Look in on my sister, please." I grin at him. "And tell Sam I said to shut the fuck up."

"I will. I'll make sure your sister and the kids need nothing. I promise. Thank you for everything. Take care of yourself."

"It's what I do." My friend steps back, and I nod at him.

Sal stands and looks at me in the eye. "I'll make sure he stays alive. I'll see you in a while. As much shit as I have on my door right now, you know that you just dumped more. We'll see what the fuck is what Josh. I still can't believe I underestimated your punk ass. This was not the way this was supposed to go down."

I nod to him. "It had to. The moment you touched your fucking helicopter down at Emma Farm, you involved a whole lot of innocent people and you pushed me too far. Leave me the fuck alone. Leave everyone I know alone."

"We're not done, Josh."

"Oh, yes, we fucking are. This portion of our relationship is now fucking over. We'll see what the future looks like from your fucking shackles."

He's at is full height with his voice seething. I hold his gaze even though my heart is beating extremely fast. But I will not back down from this piece of shit. "My hands may be tied right now but make no mistakes, I'm still in fucking charge. I say when we're done. If I have to appear to still be

me, then that means I still have cash that has to go somewhere." He grins at me.

I look at Mark before I punch his smug face. He nods at
me and indicates that I should go. Fucking Sal Pietro. Hopefully, I never see that fucker again.

## 8

---

## ELLE

DAY ONE JOSH-FREE WAS HEALING. I SLEPT TWELVE HOURS that night and woke up in the same position that I fell asleep. I was ready for my day, week and the mountain of work waiting for me. I stopped worrying he was around every corner. I was able to focus. I didn't think of him until the end of the day. There was freedom to the day. I got an insane amount of work done without concern over what I looked like or being witty or spiteful.

Day two Josh-free was funny because I watched him dart away from me a couple of times. He might have done it for comic effect, but I appreciated it. It was a calm and centering day. I went to yoga with Sarah, and it was amazing. My mind stayed focused and sharp. I got a lot accomplished. I only thought of him as I drifted off to sleep. Unfortunately, it was the thought of his hands wandering all over my body.

Day three Josh-free was again unexpectedly productive. There's a lesson in this. He was a ghost today. Not even a vapor hanging around.

Day four Josh-free was different. I started looking for him. I listened at doors hoping he wasn't hiding. I kinda miss him. I thought of him often, but only because I wanted to talk to him. Something I hadn't felt like doing in a while. I didn't see him at all. Maybe I'm getting clear of him.

Day five Josh-free and I should not be left alone with my thoughts after consuming way, way too much wine. I might have thought about him too much last night. Especially while coming in the middle of the night all by myself whispering his name. But then suddenly, the universe gave me a gift, and it's a pinhole opening to move forward. A hint of possibility with someone else. And I welcomed the time that I thought of only that. The rest of my day was delightfully full of hope and not regret.

Day six Josh-free. I drove the gondola thing carrying the grapes to the tank room today and wanted to tell him, but I can't find him. He's not that good at hiding. Sam's here today helping Alena out with the tanks and transfers. I'm going to head over to the tank room to get a giant Sam Langerford hug and maybe some answers. But I must be sly about it.

Sam's supervising his own family's harvest as well as helping with LaChappelle. The Gelberts, the parents and my friends, David Gelbert and his sister Becca were here picking yesterday with their cousin Poppy. I adore how the Five Families have each other's backs.

Everything is going well for harvest, and the systems I put in place to get all the other stuff done is working. I have Bax and Poppy on a permanent loan for those reports I don't understand. I just email Bax, and he does them from DC. And I get to drop off and pick up the rest of the paper stuff at Poppy's restaurant. I get to see her at least a couple of times a week, and her food is always remarkable. She's become quite the fixture in my life. She's so positive and bubbly it's infectious.

Bax is also doing his own family's reports. He likes paperwork, and in exchange, I proofed and fixed a bunch of the marketing stuff for their new label. All of Josh's wine generation have put into motion a new label that's just theirs. I'll be the point person on branding for a little bit on it, a little pro bono work. I love how this entire world of "The Five" as they call themselves works. It's never, "what can you do for me," it's always, "what can I do for you." Except for Josh, who does what the fuck he wants whenever the fuck it suits him

I stare at Sam, Josh's best friend, and I mean to ask him one thing, but another slips out of my mouth.

"Where's Josh?"

"Where's Josh? Is that what you just asked me? I was under the impression he was not part of your day-to-day right now. And I thought we were talking about winemaking today there, missy. Hmm."

My chest and cheeks flame because I'm flustered. "I meant, where's Sammy?"

"Cuz those names sound so similar. My place sleeping and LA."

"What are you talking about?"

"The answers to your questions."

"Sammy's in LA?" Sam walks away from me, throwing his hands up. Then I get a little put off Josh didn't tell me he left me again. But why would he? He doesn't usually tell me when he leaves. When the hell am I going to learn? Jesus. "What the hell is he doing in LA? I assume we won't see him again for months. No. Don't tell me. It doesn't matter. I don't care."

"Okay. But if you need any more information that doesn't matter, ask the source. I'm out of the middle of whatever the hell you two call this *sitch*. The two of you are fucking exhausting, and I've got a lot of shit on my plate right now. I' don't need any part of your fights."

"We're not fighting."

"Don't you have a date tonight?" Sam looks at me, accusatory.

"I did not know you knew that," I say matter-of-factly. I'm a bit shocked.

"I know everything. And seriously, don't trust Sammy. I'm way too good with my tongue for her to hold onto any secrets."

"I'm glad someone's getting some." I turn back to Sam. "Did you tell Josh?"

"No. And again, I'm out of the middle."

"Understood. Sorry." He hugs me and walks away.

I'm having dinner with a wine rep at B&V Whiskey Bar, but I haven't told anyone but Sammy. In the middle of my Josh-free week, an opportunity presented itself to move on. It's forward momentum that will pull me out of his gravitational pull.

You can't fight with someone you don't even see. We are, most assuredly, not in a fight. Suddenly, I realize I didn't ask Sam the right question. I asked him if he told him about the date.

"Sam. Wait. Sam. Please, Sam."

"That's a little pleading. I will not like this, but what?

"Only one more middle question. Does he know?"

"Yes."

I gasp. "How?"

"Will has a big mouth. Take note. He can't hold a secret to save his ass."

"Huh?"

"He was behind you in line at Whole Foods when it went down yesterday morning. When the dude asked you out."

"Fuck. Fine. Sam. I'll be back in a little bit. I have to…" I don't want Sam seeing me text Josh. I need to yell at him for leaving and head off any anger about the date. Even though it's none of his business. Maybe now we are fighting.

"Text Josh?" Sam says with a smirk, finishing my sentence.

"No. I am not even thinking about him. And I thought you wanted out of the middle?"

"Here's how I get out of the middle. Unclench your jaw and get on with it. The two of you need to get laid," Sam yells after me as I stomp towards the Farmhouse.

"Working on it!"

*ELLE: Again, you leave town and don't say a word to me. I shouldn't be surprised, but there's shit to be done here. But that doesn't matter to you, I'm sure. Do your parents even know you abandoned them again? Never mind. Why would you tell me?*

*JOSH: Seriously!? Woman, answer your own damn question for me. Why should I tell you? How is it your business that I was going out of town? I'd be happy to check in with you if you wanted me to. If we were together or even friends right now. But you won't talk to me. You literally keep me at arm's length. And you asked me to leave you alone. WHICH I DID. So answer your own damn question.*

I was not prepared for him to answer so quickly. I'm going to ignore him. I'm also not going back to the tank room with Sam. I need to be in a better headspace. A shower is calling me. I've been sweaty in the fields all day, and harvest has claimed my formerly white Madewell t-shirt. I've always hated the boot flair at the bottom of my Guess jeans so, yesterday I cut them off. But my cutoffs are crazy filthy right now too. I'm pounding the dirt out of them as I reach the top of the parking lot and my phone dings again.

*JOSH: I'm waiting.*

I'm smiling because he's irritated, and now it's a battle of wills. I finger the screen where a picture of him pops up. I slow my walk to the Farmhouse as my phone rings. I send it to voicemail, but he texts immediately.

*JOSH: Elle. This is ridiculous. You chastise me and then disappear. Answer your damn phone.*

I laugh at my phone knowing I've annoyed the hell out of him.

*JOSH: Ms. Parker, if we were sleeping together, I would swat your ass so hard you wouldn't be able to sit down for a week for ignoring me.*

Holy shit. I'm instantly wet. I hate my body and my mind for letting it be so affected by Josh. I'm standing just north of the parking lot, almost to the Farmhouse. I have a huge problem. I need to tell him to stop flirting with me like that. My chest and face are beet red with desire thinking about the idea of spanking. I need tonight's date to go well.

*JOSH: That's right, Cosmo. My handprint would be the color of your chest and cheeks you're currently displaying in that way too low cut-shirt that you shouldn't have worn around the vineyard workers. You do know they all looked, right? Just like I am. Can't look away. Only your stems in those cutoffs can distract me from your chest.*

Now my whole body is flushed and surging with energy as I frantically spin around looking for him.

"Here." His voice booms from the porch of the Farmhouse. Tie loosened, sleeves rolled up, and blue suit jacket tossed over the front railing. He's beaming his mischievous smile at me, and his teeth are so white. I look disgusting covered in grime. I have a random, messy bun, and my maligned white t-shirt, but I have to own it, I guess. I put my hands on my hips.

"That was a dirty trick."

"Ready for your punishment?"

"Hell no."

"Your chest and face say something entirely different."

# 9

## JOSH

Sure, I've dreamed of ripping that Halston dress off her, but this get-up tops that fantasy. Fuck me. With her ratty white t-shirt, cut-offs, no makeup, and Adidas classic shell tops with the black stripe, this is my favorite version of Elle. I desperately want to bend her over my knee right now. I don't care who's watching. I made myself hard by watching her. Fight with me, Elle, tell me something. Let me know where your head is at in all of this. Fighting is so much better than the defeated, apathetic conversation we had at Starling's a week ago.

I know she's going out tonight with some wine rep. My dad made sure to tell me, hence the flight back this afternoon instead of tomorrow like originally scheduled. There's no way this date will go as she plans.

"Why did you leave? Why LA? Never mind. I need to stop expecting you to tell me why you keep leaving me and saying nothing," she bellows, not coming a single step closer.

"I didn't leave. I went on a work trip and came back in a reasonable amount of time. This was different. And I can absolutely tell you why I didn't let you know I was going out of town."

"Why?" She pops her hip again in defiance. I wonder if she thinks this is a power move. She's too fucking cute when she does it for it to intimidate me. She's so beautiful in this light. The dirty get-up and her hair loose around her grimy face. Her green eyes shining at me with gold flickering in them take my breath away. She does that often. Not just her beauty, but her strength, resilience, her humor, and her drive. All of it breathtaking.

I say to her, "You told me to leave you alone. No contact. Give you some space. And now you're pissed at me because I did as you asked?" I stand up and throw my jacket over my shoulder. I don't care if she sees I'm hard. She knows she's the reason. She's always the reason.

"But you never listen to me."

She's so fucking wrong. She's the one who never listens. Me, I can be patient if it's going to get me what I want. It's why I'm so good at making tough deals. I can wait out anyone and let it seem like I've lost. I can do it without ever really giving up control of the situation. Settle, woman. I got you.

"That's where you're wrong, Cosmo. I've heard every single word. I just don't always choose to follow your directives." I make sure she knows this.

"I don't give directives," she says with a sexy-as-hell, haughty tone. I just want to be inside her right now. I want her submission so we can talk. Maybe the only way is to fuck the anger out of her. Is that a thing? I'd like to make it a thing. That could be a thing.

"Back it down, girl. I'm not looking for a fight. But if your blood's still up, perhaps you can insult Mrs. Dotson's coffee cup system again. She's got a fiery temper when stoked. But I'm tired, and I have shit to do tonight."

"I'm sorry. I wasn't sure which Joshua I was going to encounter," she says to protect herself, but I want to disarm her.

I make the distance between us disappear and pull her into my arms for the first time since that night. I can't wait any longer. My jacket drops to the ground. She doesn't resist, but she doesn't wrap her arms around me either. It's a step forward. I caress her cheek, which is less red and now a sweet pale pink. She sighs. I catch it and smile. I run my fingers along her delicate jaw that has smears of the vineyard on it. She closes her eyes while I do this, her eyelashes fluttering. I press my lips to her dusty forehead, and she gasps ever so slightly.

"There's only one Josh now. Just the one and he's not going anywhere. I came here for my parents and the winery, but I'm staying for you." My LA trip released me and it's time for her to listen, but I need her full attention. Sal is working with the Feds and we worked out a system where I'm not longer his bitch. He's moving forward knowing I have his nuts in a vice. I can tell her everything now, but I'll wait until she's ready. I'll wait but not long.

She breaks free of me, and I let her go. Hell, I'm going to let her go on her date. But I'll be there too. I know this woman. She'll change the location to Poppy's for the home-court advantage. She craves control. It won't look strange that I'm there because I'll be there first.

"I have to change. I have to go...um."

"Get ready for your date?"

"Yes." Her cheeks are red again, but this shade means she's flustered, not sexually excited like the color from earlier. I know all the shades of this woman.

"If you want the date to go well, I'd wear that. Don't change a thing. Go on and change, but know that those cutoffs were made for your legs." She rolls her eyes at me and disappears into the Farmhouse.

*JOSH: Plans tonight?*

*TABI: Not a damn thing. What's up? The pilot canceled on me.*

*JOSH: Are you still on that?"*

*TABI: Sex in a cockpit. Hells yeah. And someday I'll get to mark it off my 'Fuck it List.'*

*JOSH: Poppy's 6:30.*

*TABI: Cool. I need to get drunk. Costas is driving me fucking insane.*

*JOSH: Your father has always driven you crazy.*

And there's like four more texts with emojis. Apparently, she wants to get drunk with teddy bears. Tab's a mess of herself. So funny and blunt. But I just need my senior prom date for my little game tonight. Plus, I've missed Tabi, we've all been way too bogged down in harvest. And I was mired in Santa Barbara for far too long.

Her dad, Costas, put her on paperwork and annoying shit for harvest. Although she can handle anything he could throw at her, she wants to run the vineyard. Sadly, her out-of-touch Greek father sees it as man's work. And since she doesn't have a brother, he keeps trying to get one of her hundred male cousins to get interested in the winery. He's always missed who she is. She's more capable than most men I know.

Goldie, her mom, stopped putting bows in her hair at around four years old, but Costas still sees her through his traditional family lens. It's a cultural thing, but Tabi keeps trying to change the way he sees her. She could leave but Tab loves the winery too much. And a challenge. She loves a fucking challenge. She helped us rotate some of the workers from Stafýlia, her vineyard, to ours. Dinner is the least that I owe her.

Her vineyard's name is my favorite. It means 'grapes' in

Greek. People think it's exotic, but it actually says exactly what's there. There are two original gates onto their property one says Stafýlia, the other Eliés, which means olives. Originally in the '70s, when the Aganos family started their winery, it was so the workers could tell where to go; they try and use lots of a Greeks. Some picked olives and some picked grapes, and the name of the vineyard stood.

I may have gone over the top with my date outfit. But I wanted to feel pretty. I'm standing outside of B&V Whiskey Bar, which is delicious, but I need a friend around. I'm a little nervous. I text Cam to change venues and have him meet me at Poppy's. I am going to focus on him, not whatever the hell that was with Josh today. His caress was so sultry and seductive, but I can't think about how much I wanted him to kiss me. I can't trust him or myself. I need to remain protected. Internal walls are safely back up, and it's time for a fresh face to entertain me.

I hustle to Poppy's wearing my canary yellow long sleeve chiffon mini dress. I bought it online from Sachin & Babi Noir. I don't usually buy things online because I like to feel the fabric, but everything they do fits me like it's custom. I adore this dress because it makes me look tall, well tall for me. There's no skin revealed up top, but it skims above the knee, and I paired it with gorgeous light brown leather strappy stilettos that wrap up my leg a bit. I'm wearing coral pink NARS, *Beautiful Liar* lips.

The dress is technically a cocktail dress, but I don't give a shit. And the look on Cam's face says that he doesn't mind at all. He's on the shorter side with broad shoulders. It's nice to look directly into his chocolate brown eyes instead of craning my neck. His hair is blond like Baxter's. I'm excited this isn't Asher or Josh. Clean slate.

"Wow. I am the luckiest man in Sonoma." He kisses my cheek. No stomach flip, but it's early.

"That's kind of you."

"Seriously, that is a killer dress, and you wear the heck out of it."

"Thanks." He kisses me on the cheek again then holds out his arm. We sit down near the front window. Poppy comes out with big hugs as Cam makes a mildly funny joke about being too intimate too fast. Poppy laughs as if he's funny like Sam.

He crooks his eyebrow at me. "Now, I understand the venue change. You wanted back up in case this all goes terribly, huh?"

"That obvious?"

He laughs easily. He's easy. Isn't that nice? We order off the specials board, and he brought wine for us and Poppy. It's an Albarino. A crackling dry white wine with Spanish origins.

I've not entirely stepped out of the Valley in terms of understanding different regions. But it's super dry and tart. I like learning from him so far. He says it will be the perfect complement to steamed mussels and Hog Island oysters. I'm on a date. And it strikes me that I haven't thought of Josh in like twenty minutes. Dammit, that realization means I just thought about him.

Back to Cam, who is telling me about his job, his dog, and growing up in Ohio. After forty-five minutes and two dozen oysters, this man is sharing all the things. Just saying. I know about his parents, his past relationships, and his thoughts on cilantro. I have an excellent sense of who he is and who he wants to be. He's so open. I wish I were.

My head dips towards the bar area. There are only six seats, but Tabi's at one of them. I wave her over.

She hugs me as she says, "This the guy?" I adore her, but she's so freaking blunt.

"I'm the guy. Cam Bauman."

"Tabitha Aganos." She looks to me. "Why are you so yellow?"

"I rather like her dress." Cam defends my dress, but Tabi puts her hand up.

Cam tries to address her directly. "Ah ha. I know you."

"No, you don't."

"I know of you. Stafýlia makes great wine."

"You're some kind of wine rep, right? Do you sell our stuff?"

"Alas, I only work with larger production wines. Not yours." I smile at him.

Tabi responds, "Okay. That's enough from you." She turns towards me with her lips pursed and head cocked, "Seriously? This guy? He used the word alas. Come with me back to the bar." My eyes widen, and now I'm determined to have a fantastic date with this man just to make it up to him. She's terrible.

"Go away, Tabi."

"In a sec. We'll chat later. Call me when you get home, in like an hour or so, I suspect." I roll my eyes at her. Then she turns to poor Cam. "Hey distraction, I wanted to say thanks for the Albarino. My date and I are enjoying it."

Cam gets a bit biting, but I don't blame him. "Then stop talking to us and pay attention to your date. Possibly he'll improve your attitude." I giggle. I glance at her date, and my fucking stomach seizes up. Fucker. Tabi returns to a seat next to Josh.

I turn my head before we make eye contact. I am curious if Tabi meant 'date date.' I know their history. They lost their virginity to each other but never dated after it. And now, he mostly thinks of her as a cousin or a sister. Josh headed down to Stanford. Tabi went to Berkeley, eventually ending up at Georgetown. But why are they here together? Focus.

"She's..."

"Blunt. I know. So sorry."

"As long as our evening can be ours without your friend, I'll be a happy man."

"Of course."

"And I'm sorry I got a bit snippy." Cam touches my arm. He just apologized without being prompted or scolded. He's a nice man.

"No. Tab always deserves it. No worries." I hear Josh's laugh, big and bold. I don't turn. My neck seems frozen in place. Does he have a hand on Tabi? It's fine. I'm here with Cam. Cam. Cam is the future.

He takes my hand across the table, and I stare at it. He weaves his fingers through mine, and it should feel nice. "Let's have an amazing date to spite her." He grins, and I feel suffocated by this moment. Fuck. I can't breathe. Josh's damn scent is in the air.

"Can you excuse me? I need to run to the ladies' room." Our entrees arrive as I stand.

"See you in a minute then. Do you want more wine?"

"Yes, please." I kiss him on the cheek and squeeze his shoulder. Quickly walking to the kitchen, I fling open the door. Poppy looks up and then back down to the food she's garnishing on the line. I glare at her.

"I know. Not my idea. I told Josh to leave. I told them to go anywhere else. I offered to pay for their dinner elsewhere when you called."

"What the fuck, Pop?"

"To be fair, you weren't supposed to be here. They were here and a bottle into their night an hour before you switched locales. I thought they'd be gone by now. And you know neither of those hardheads would listen to me. No one can tell them anything. They're perfectly matched."

Fuck. Are they matched? He thought I was going to B&V, and he's here with Tabi? "I thought Tabi was seeing that guy from Delta Airlines."

"I think that's just a sex thing."

"Does she have lots of just sex things?"

"Oh, hell, yes. Have her share her 'Fuck it List' with you. Types of men, situations, public places, etc."

No. No. No. Tabi and Josh. My stomach is churning, and the thought of food is now a risky maneuver. I bolt from the kitchen and duck into the bathroom. I stare at myself in the mirror. There's no reason he can't be on a date. I'm on a date. We're not together despite whatever that sweet thing in the parking lot early was. I get a text. It startles me and I spill my purse. Most of my items are skidding across the floor as my phone bounces into the sink. It's Cam.

CAM: *Are you okay?*

It's the same thing Josh asked me at Starling bar. My heart sinks a bit that it's him. I become quite aware that I'm not being fair to this lovely man. I slide down the wall to sit on the bathroom floor with my skirt hiked up to keep it clean. I sit here for a while, the tile cold on my thonged ass. I regulate my breathing and attempt not to cry.

Turns out my protective walls are not in place, they're cracked. I'm fooling myself, and poor Cam got caught up in my foolishness. I suck. Poor guy. He's good-looking, charming, clearly into me, and I'm sitting on the bathroom floor contracting some rare filth disease through my ass.

I collect my scattered belongings and put on some more *Beautiful Liar* lipstick. I'd like to text him that I left, but I know I have to be a big girl and face this. Going back to New York will help heal the cracks. As long as I'm around Josh, I won't ever truly be free. And whether Tabi is a date, a fuck, or a hangout, I can't screw up his life anymore either. I hoist myself up and smooth down my dress. It's time to go home.

---

CAM WAS KIND AND UNDERSTANDING, but I could tell he was pissed. I slipped back into the kitchen to pay Poppy so at least he got a dinner out of it. I snuck out the back door, never making eye contact with Mr. Whittier. Someone should enjoy their date.

There are millions of stars tonight, and I have one of the Albarinos to keep me company up here on the roof. I'm still in my dress. I just love it so much. I didn't want to take it off. I ditched the heels at the base of the ladder. I have quite a bit of thinking to do, and I want to drink up my last Sonoma moments.

I'll tell Sarah and Will that it's time for me to go. I'll work my ass off for the next week to get them ahead on specific projects. I can do some of the paperwork from New York. I'll fly back for the sale if they want me to, but they don't need me anymore. It's all moving forward as planned. The Five are going to be marketed like that, and I think that's a fitting tribute to this tight circle of people. It was fun pretending I was one of them for a while.

# 11

## ELLE

I avoided him all morning. I don't want to see his stupid happy face. I don't want to know if he got laid. I barely slept thinking about him kissing Tabi. I barely slept trying to figure out a way to either be with him or get over him. The thought of him licking and having her in any variety of familiar ways turned my stomach. I'm so angry that I'm jealous. I'm wound tightly today. I'll bet she's super experimental. I'm walking towards the parking lot when I hear his annoying bellow.

"Cosmo! Cosmo! Where are you going?"

I need to not be around this Neanderthal barking orders at me. Fucking go away, Josh. I don't want to know if it happened. It's so hot out, and after spending the day swilling gallons and gallons of water, I need something else. I need liquor. I hear him run up after me. He's covered in a sheen of sweat that I refuse to find sexy as fucking hell.

"Cosmo!"

I turn to him and say, "Don't call me that."

"Elle. Where are you going?"

"Town. I need a minute."

In a forceful voice, he continues, "I need you to go to the warehouse and sort wine club orders."

I pat the dirt off my cargo shorts and pull them down a bit. "I don't think so."

He approaches me swiftly. He's so close I can smell the scent of hard labor on him. It's not his usual sexy cedar but a more animal scent. That fucking scent is turning me into another person. Someone who can forget for a moment he's a jackass who fucked an old friend last night. My panties are history. It's turning me a bit carnal. I want to eat him when he smells this manly. I would genuinely like for us to stop talking and climb on top of him and release all this tension from the past couple of months. But then again, he's trying to tell me what to do, and my lady boner begins to dry up a bit.

"What did you say to me?" he commands.

"I said no. I'm not doing that."

He roars at me, and I don't fucking care. *"Jesus Fucking Christ.* You're such a pain in my ass."

I remain completely composed, knowing it will irk the shit out him. "Sweet talk won't work either."

"Just fucking do what I say, one goddamned time. One time."

"I did. Once. Well, several times. But got fucking burned pretty badly. Never again, asshole."

His eyes flash hot, and his lips go straight as he presses them together. He runs his hands through his damp and floppy hair then he balls his fists and releases them. He starts again. "I need you to do this. Please. I have no one else to go out there."

"Tabi busy?"

Electricity flickers in his eyes and his mouth curls slightly, "Maybe she can head out there with Cam. What's he doing today?" He knows his name. Tabi must have told him.

"I wouldn't know. I don't even know if Cam finished his dinner."

He exhales deeply as I admit I didn't sleep with him. "And I wouldn't know about Tabi." And then my body relaxes a tiny bit. "This is work. Don't make this personal."

"Trust me, Josh, there's nothing personal between us."

"Stop being so fucking mad at me. Stop. I'm not leaving you again. Trust *me*."

I turn to him and unload. "It's just I've been out in the blocks since four this morning. I went to bed well past midnight, catching up on my real job. You know, the multi-million-dollar business I run in New York? Don't you have one of those to run?"

"If we're being petty, mine's billions. And were you actually worried about Tabi?" I maintain my stance and shrug at him, keeping my chin up. He laughs at me. "Silly Hellcat. She's a bit extra for me. But our priorities *have* to be here right now. We can always fix what blows up at work later. We can figure our shit later too. But this is a timing issue. This winery crap has to be done today. Just do it. Get your sweet ass to the warehouse. And do what I say."

I step to him with rage in my eyes. I speak succinctly, so he doesn't miss my meaning. Our faces are so close I can feel his hot and angry breath ruffle my eyelashes.

"You seem to be forgetting. I don't work for you. I'm not part of this winery. I am a volunteer, and I'm fucking fried. So is Sammy. She and I are going for a drink right now, Mr. Whittier. She's about to crack. All of them are."

He snaps at me, "Don't you worry about my employees. I can handle them."

"They're not you. They will crack. You can't drive the staff as hard as you're driving yourself. Even you need a break."

"They *HAVE* to work as hard as me. We don't have a choice. They'll do what I tell them to do for as long as I tell them to do it. Unlike a certain fragile city girl who can't handle the pressure. Get in line or get the fuck out of my way."

We're both out of breath as we look at each other, nose to nose. The blue of his eyes piercing every part of me. Both of our chests are heaving, and my breasts keep brushing up against his hard, warm pecs. I don't think I've ever wanted or hated anyone more.

I say in an even tone, no anger, "Fuck you. You need some sleep. You're cranky." His lip curls slightly at my joke. I raise an eyebrow, but I don't back out of his face. I will not back down.

"I'll tell you what I fucking need."

I lick my bottom lip as I respond to him. An involuntary response. "What?"

"This." He swiftly tangles his hand in my hair and yanks me to him in one sudden motion. I don't resist. Our lips smash into each other as our tongues collide in chaos. He's drugging me with his tongue. It's sweeping so deeply, and I welcome it. I taste all of his desire and story. The story I'm not ready to hear, but he's trying to tell me this way.

We move our hands in a frenzy of groping. I can't stop myself. We're like two powerful magnets with the opposite polarity snapping us together whether we want to or not. We have no choice but to submit to each other. We're helpless against this lust.

We move together as I arch my back and grind into him. He's so hard. He grazes my ass and then grabs it in full. I begin to overheat with desire for him. Tension builds between my legs and in my low belly. He moans into my mouth, and I move my pelvis into him. I can feel him thicken, and I want him just as much as he wants me. His running shorts hide nothing.

Our heads keep thrashing back and forth. If we weren't in the gravel parking lot in hundred-degree heat, we'd already be fucking. I moan loudly with my tongue so deep into his mouth. I want him inside of me despite everything.

"Yes. My god. Elle. That fucking sound."

I dig my nails into his shoulders as I mount him. I hitch my legs around his waist, and he catches me. His hands move to under ass as I begin to slowly ride him up and down, giving us both an instant jolt of fulfilling friction. There's nothing delicate or romantic about the moment. This is pure lust. He's moaning in my ear. I am about snap and take off just enough clothes to get this done. I reach for his waistband. I'm over the edge with desire. There is no one and nothing except us. We live in a vacuum of lust in this dusty parking lot.

"Fuck. Yes. I've missed you so much, Elle. The taste of you, the feel of you, and just you," he whispers to me. It's everything I want to hear.

As I open my mouth to respond, I see Sammy come around the corner in my peripheral. I slap Josh's insanely gorgeous bicep and jump off of him. He removes his arms from me and runs his hands through his hair. He turns away from her. I back away from this powder keg, both of us breathing heavily. He walks towards his Jeep.

He says over his shoulder, "Sammy. Be back by five."

I take on an official tone to my voice. "Oh, and for your information, Mr. Whittier..."

He doesn't turn around. I know he's burning to turn towards us, but he doesn't want Sammy to see his insanely hard dick through his running shorts. I'm happy to be wearing shorts because if it were a skirt, we would have been mid-fuck when Sammy found us. Close call.

"...Randy shipped all the wine club stuff out yesterday. We already took care of it. You handle you, and we got the rest."

I turn and jump into my car while Sammy slides into the passenger side.

"What the hell was that?"

"Closure."

# 12

## JOSH

THAT WAS NOT THE WAY I WANTED THAT TO HAPPEN. I was working towards an evening where we could reconnect, but that was so blisteringly fucking hot. Jesus. It's as if it were an out of body experience. I was not in control of the guy who did that to her.

I need an outlet for this extreme sexual frustration. I'm speeding up the hill to Lookout cottage with a raw, rock-hard cock to again try and get her off my mind. I'm barely in the door when I grab myself and release what she started. I've never masturbated this much in my life. Until that lava-hot-as-fuck woman. Any desire I ever had since high school, I'd just go out and find someone to release it into. But now I only want her.

I picture her moving up and down after she wrapped her legs around my waist. Holding her supple ass as she found a way to make me forget all the bullshit panic around this harvest and the Sal shit. In that moment, I was free of stress and anxiety. Just the two of us suspended in peace and bliss.

As I imagine her lips on mine and that loud moan emitting from her, I let go into the shower and rinse off. And I'm left vaguely unsatisfied, with the taste of her still on my tongue. I'm annoyed at her for making me want her so badly. New goal. Make her want me as badly as I want her. But first it's time to find a release of a different kind. I need to unburden.

---

SAM'S MANNING the crush pad tonight. Alena needed a break so I asked if my overworked friend would manage this part with me. I sent a bunch of people home around four after we sorted and loaded the destemmer. It's hot, and they need to shower and gear up for the next phase of picking.

We've moved to a night-harvest, and I promised them if they come in at 2:00 a.m., they can leave by noon tomorrow. I have no idea what day it is. She was right, I *am* tired and cranky. I grab a six-pack from the cooler in the tasting room and join Sam in the tank room. He's racking our Sav Blanc juice that's tasting really good. We need to get the Chard pressed and in the tanks like yesterday. Tempranillo is on deck, and if we have to pick early, we might have to crush them at Langerford. We'll get the barrels ready and move them to the cave in the morning. Well, I'll have huge men with machines move them to the cave.

"Did you fuck Elle in the parking lot like an hour ago?"

"No. We were interrupted."

"Sammy says otherwise and that she can't get any intel from Elle."

I shrug at my friend. "There's no intel to get."

"That's what she *said.*" Always with the joke.

"Ha, Ha. Ha."

I hand him a beer and sit down on this old faded green and blue plaid recliner that's been in the tank room for years. It's probably riddled with diseases, but it's so damn comfortable. Almost everyone one of our vineyard crew, including myself and my dad, have slept on it at one point. I lean back and imagine she's on top of me. Man, I have to stop.

"Moment of weakness. We're both exhausted, and we were fighting. It was strictly hate lust. Nothing more."

"She called it an angry, passionate lapse in judgment."

I laugh easily. Sam sits next to me. "What else did she say?" I shift in the chair, hoping that might calm my dick down.

"That she was thinking with her clit and not her head." Sam continues, "You gotta stop making yourself crazy, man. I see it on your face. Be with her or don't. But this undefined angst is tearing both of you apart."

"It's not that easy. I need to tell you a story. I need to tell someone."

"About her clit, no thank you. Got my own glorious, gorgeous clit to contend with."

I wince at the thought of Sammy's clit. "Nah man, about why I left." Sam rounds the tanks and starts spraying down the pad. He sees my face and nods to me.

"Go ahead, Josh. You know I'm listening."

I tell him about Sal. I tell him about the money and my business. The story of how Sal staked me when I was starting out. I tell him that Sal basically told me I had no choice but to sit in my office and invest his money and be at his beck and call. I tell him about the threats and the security I have in place at his winery.

"Fucking Lou is a ninja security dude? He's awesome. Works like a demon and has a crazy good palate. He's a sweetie. Who knew?"

"Glad he's helpful then. Ironically, he used to be a Sal guy. I didn't know who he'd threaten, and I knew Lou would know what to look for."

"Did Sal do anything?"

"Lou took down two guys and beat the shit out of them when they were sniffing around the gas lines at your back-barrel room. One of our security dudes pummeled a guy who was trying to install a camera in the Longhouse. And we found one hidden in the Lookout. So far, the sweep of the other buildings is negative. But we haven't swept Langerford or Tabi's or..."

Sam interrupts me, "Are there plants at all of The Five?"

The Five. I smile thinking about the good part of growing up. Not the fields with my overbearing grandfather, Lucien, but pickup basketball games at Schroeder's or epic Nerf gun battles at Gelbert's. Tommi Schroeder always kicked our asses. She'd deck herself out in camo and then put leaves and shit in her hair. We never saw her coming.

"Yes. The Five. But there are people here round the clock. I don't think Sal even realizes past Langerford about the others."

Sam sits down next to me with another beer. "What the fuck, man? Thanks. I mean this is why you left her?"

"He threatened her the day after the Members party. He stalked her in the city and let me know how close he could get. He also threatened Mom and Dad if I spoke about him or why I left to anyone. Sal didn't want anyone connected with me to be a liability to him. I owe Bax an explanation why I had him bolt over to the Ritz that day. Sal proved his point, and it scared the shit out of me."

"Get the fuck out of here with this shit."

"I know. I'm not sure if he'd actually hurt her. We used to have a really great relationship. I never felt or saw that other person until he flew up in the copter. Suddenly I saw the man everyone fears. He was also desperate, something else I'd never experienced before. I was an idiot to think that I alone wouldn't be tangled in his shit. He demanded I get back to Santa Barbara right after the Members party and tell no one why I left. He flew me home and had me delivered to my house. I've been on house arrest basically. He had a shit ton of work for me. He was frantic to put large sums of money in legit businesses."

"Have you told Elle all this?"

"No. You're the only living person who knows this story except for Mark and some random white hat hacker I needed help from."

"Shit. Mark. Damn, love that guy. But you got the FBI involved?"

"He told me to tell you to shut the fuck up." Sam laughs loudly."

"Tell him he needs to speak up."

"It will be quite a while until we hear from Mark."

"Why?"

"He's part of Sal's outfit now. You can not fucking tell Sammy. That shit stays right here."

Sam whistles for effect. And the I tell him what Mark and Melissa independently discovered, and he asks a million more questions. I can't blame him. But then I tell him the resolution.

"And you're good?"

"I'm prepared. We have a truce. No one can blink. I evened the playing field. I don't want to hurt him. I like the fucker. He stays away, and I show no one what I have on him. I won't be fucked with. The truce was why I went to LA. There are legitimate reasons for his behavior, but for now, he's the fucking enemy. I had to show him how big my balls are. Just took me a while to find them. Mark's got it for now. We didn't walk away with good feelings about each other but he can't fucking come at me right now. There are things we'll still need to discuss but for now, you're all safe."

"Aren't your balls something Sammy and Elle should be discussing?"

I slap my best friend on the back. Even though I've saddled him with this knowledge, I feel lighter.

"I have Mark's thick file on him and illegal activities, pictures files, and voice recordings. It will bring down a lot of his business and set him up for racketeering. Sal has two more years on his plan to be completely out of the gang world in LA. And he's agreed to work with Mark. Mark is working towards a much bigger score if you can believe that. There's some power puppet master or some shit. I'll step back from my firm and handle his investments into legit businesses privately for three years, and I'm finished. But I don't want his name associated with my firm. He signed a nondisclosure agreement as well as some documents for Mark. That's why I went to LA. "

"Does this mean you quit your job?"

"No. I mean. Kind of. I'm stepping away from the firm while I sort out this Sal bullshit. I have more than enough money. And I can work from anywhere."

"Like New York."

"If she'll listen."

"Damn bitch. There's a lot to unpack there." I smile widely at my friend.

"No more threats and the statute of limitations, even if his businesses are clean, will still be in play. I'm out, but I'll finish the job."

"Make her listen. She needs to know that you didn't leave her by choice. Cuz that's the shit that girl is carrying around her neck. But that woman is in love with you, and you're in love with her."

"She's so fucking complicated."

"Doesn't mean you're not in love. I've never seen you in love for real before. But she's it. Look, here's the thing. Sammy is easy but complicated. She's maddening and perfect. Every time I'm with her, there's not enough time. I can't fathom a moment when it will be enough. She still holds secrets. I don't know much about her life before Sonoma, but I don't care. All I want is more. More of her all the time. Sex is one thing, but I want all of it from her all the time."

I look at this man who seems changed by a woman as well. "You're in deep."

He sighs. "That I am. But so are you."

His words punch me a little bit in the gut, and I attempt to not react. He tips his beer towards me and then drains it.

"There's so much. We're so complicated. It's not just that I left."

"I know. But figure that shit out."

Sam climbs the catwalk to the top of the tank and keeps hammering at me. Elle gave me back the joy of this place and my family. Hell, I love Sonoma, but it's not real life. Elle somehow healed all anger and animosity that my grandfather left behind. He wanted to force me into having his life instead of building one from the ground up by myself. I wanted to create my own legacy instead of being spoon-fed one that had to be run by some set of standards laid out in precise terms by him long ago.

I guess the sale will be a new start for all of us. I don't know where that will be for me. A clean slate can't be wrong, especially after she realizes she's mine. I grab a couple more beers and hoist myself to the top of the tanks to help with the juice.

# 13

---

## ELLE

We're so busy, and I don't think I can handle anything else. Certainly not dwelling on the insanity that happened in the parking lot today.

I'm bone tired but also in desperate need of fancy, sophisticated cocktail. There's so much beer around the winery right now. Sam told me that it takes a hell of a lot of beer to make good wine. I'm desperate for the Hibiscus Paloma at Starling Bar. I'm hot, every part of me is covered in grime and the animal scent of a sexy jackass.

"How are you?" Sammy asks pointedly.

"Fine. Why?"

"You're kidding, right?"

"I mean, who the hell knows, right? He was with Tabi last night."

"Come on. You know Tabi would never hit that. Despite breaking girl code, she's not one for repeat performances."

I admit something. "I still don't like him, but I have missed the Rootstock."

"You call his dick Rootstock?" Sammy laughs uncontrollably. I giggle too. "You know that's not what that word means, right?"

"It does to me." And we laugh harder. So hard that I have to wipe tears from my eyes.

Sammy sees another couple sitting at the bar and waves. "Sorry. We'll get back to your soap opera in a moment. I have to say hi. I just worked with Meg at the film festival when we poured for her."

The couple approaches. They hug and greet Sammy. Then she introduces them.

"Meg Hannah and Wade Howell, this is Elle Parker."

The curly-haired beauty speaks first, she reaches her hand out. "Hi! We met briefly at the Whittier Members party."

"Right. And you're that fabulous writer, right?" I turn to Wade, joking.

"That I am, Ms. Parker. You sly minx." Meg hits him. They seem together but not. I stand, and Wade embraces me. His dark long hair flopping into his face as he smirks and his eyes light up.

"I finally read the book."

Wade winces as I tell him I finally got around to reading his novel. "And?"

"It's terrific. Are you working on another one?"

"My dear, why can't one novel be enough in life? Why must there always be another project? More. Everyone wants more."

Meg laughs. "Otherwise known as writer's block."

Wade shrugs, and we laugh at her joke.

I take Meg's hand. "It's nice to see you both again."

"How's harvest? Sammy said it's seriously stressful. Like nutty pressure. You have no one to hire. Do you need me to pick?"

Meg certainly is chatty. She just blew a wayward curl out of her face and kept on talking.

"We're managing. And it's all hands on deck. But now that you bring it up...what are you doing tomorrow? Want to pick a Pinot block?" She laughs loud and easily. She's kind of cool.

"Nah. Gotta, I don't know, sleep." I giggle at her. Wade pulls her arm, and they say their goodbyes.

I turn back to Sammy as they leave, resuming our conversation about Josh. "I know. I know. He admitted that he didn't sleep with Tabi."

I recount the fight that led to my ill-advised but well-received jumping on him. Sammy tells me she's thinking of pursuing a career in wine. She feels as if Sam fits in her life without judging, anger, or evaluating what they are to each other. They're happy and together, and that's enough for her. I need to get the hell out of Sonoma and back to New York so I can find what they have. It's not here.

Yet as I sip the second cocktail, I realize that leaving Sammy, who seems to be my only true friend, will be devastating. As well as this whole place. I'm annoying to myself with all the flip-flopping emotions.

All my New York friends like my posts or occasionally text a picture of food I should be eating with them or an ex they spotted at some club. But none of them call. None of them have reached out to see if I'm okay. Only Evan. I didn't realize I'd created a lifestyle but not a life. I also don't miss them.

Randy, Sammy, Sarah, Poppy, Will, and hell, even Mrs. Dotson will all be sorely missed. I want to build a community when I get back to reality. I don't really like any of my friends. None of them know my parents are dead or that I grew up on a farm. But here people ask about my past and I know they care what I have to say. I feel open and embraced.

I'm hosting one more marketing dinner tonight at Swiss Hotel with the buyers. Then I'm done. It's going to be casual. I want to sit out back on the patio, despite the temperatures. But it should be cooler at night. The Whittiers, Bax and his dad, Adrian Schroeder, are coming. I'm forcing Evan's new boyfriend and Sam's brother, Jims Langerford, to tag along because Sam blew me off. Jims has been flying to New York whenever he has a spare moment to spend with Evan. I'm so happy for them. Tabi's parents, Goldie and Costas Aganos had to back out of the dinner tonight, but Asher will be there. I'll get to say goodbye to him in person. It's been a long time since we've had contact.

---

I'M SIPPING A YUMMY VIOGNIER, my new favorite white wine. It's from Stafýlia, the Aganos' vineyard. I'm wearing my favorite royal blue dress. Asher's seen it, but I don't care. I love it. The dress is short and floaty enough to help combat some of the sticky lingering heat from the day. Asher's pouring wine and the soft light that's all around us is making me remember the first night I met him. He changed my life. Not the way I thought he would, but I'll always be grateful. I smile at him.

"You are dazzling, my darling Noelle."

"That's sweet. Thank you. Thank you for all of this."

"I had no choice but to whisk you away to this life. You're were my missing piece."

He's cryptic but complementary. The buyers that Asher brought to the table, the Vino Groupies, will make their final offer next week. They came out of nowhere with a ton of cash. I can't even believe that they want all five wineries and have agreed to all the terms we're proposing.

Despite what everyone thinks of Asher, he brought a lot

of power and money to the deal. And this is one more dinner to get to know these people who will take over the management of the other wineries and ownership of LaChappelle/Whittier.

Jims is stoned out of his mind, but no one's noticed except Baxter and me. We exchange glances while Jims eats from the breadbasket on his lap. Sam better have a good reason for his absence. He's never let me down.

Bax is playing with his calamari and just staring down. He looks like he's the strait-laced good boy with prep school blond hair, but he has a wicked sense of humor. His translucent, sea-glass-blue eyes are the only similarity I see between he and his sister Tommi. Tommi's uniquely herself, shaved head or brightly colored. She's as tall as Baxter, but conversely, to his slim muscular build, she's built like a shit bCam house. All curves and sass. She's the winemaker at Schroeder and a damn good one.

The evening is winding down when I hear a clatter out in the alley behind the Swiss. Nothing materializes from it, so we all go back to our wine. Will, Sarah, and Adrian say their goodbyes. The buyers bid their farewells.

There were tons of laughs, and my last working dinner was actually fun. Asher was fun tonight. I might have judged him too harshly. He seems more misplaced in the world than the bad person Josh makes him out to be. My head is swimming with way too much wine, and my thoughts are all over the place. I shouldn't have had cocktails with Sammy this afternoon knowing I was headed to a wine dinner.

"Pssst."

Jims guffaws at the loud sound and waves but never gets out of his chair. Then there's another second loud whisper.

"Holy shit. That's Bax! Bax, man, hi!"

Baxter turns his head. The matriarchs and patriarchs have all left, so it's just Josh's friends, Asher, and me still around.

The waitstaff is done for the night, and after a large tip from me, they're letting us sit back here in the open beautiful patio. We could head to the street side front bar if we want more. Can't imagine drinking more.

Asher scoots a little closer. I think nothing of it as his arm comes to rest on the back of my chair. I assume the whisperers are locals.

"Bax. Come here. Bax. Bax, it's us."

Baxter turns towards the darkness and says aloud, "I'm well aware of who you are. Gentlemen. Come sit down." The loud whisperers laugh in high-pitched boyish squeals.

I drain my glass, and it's instantly full again. I should not drive home. A deeper, urgent, loud fake whispering starts and is now directed at me.

"Elle! Noelle Parker. Over here. Elle. Oh shit. Elle. Elle. Fuck. Elle stand up now. Stand up. Go to the bathroom anywhere. Go. Get away. Fuck. Elle. Come here. Come here. Come to me now. Stand up. Now. Before he sees. Before…" And I realize it's Sam. I'm confused until I hear a primal drunken growl erupts at full volume. Sam was trying to stop the next thing from happening.

"Asher muthafucker Bernard." My heart sinks. His raspy and possessive voice continues. "Whatcha think you're doing with that arm there? That's not yours. That's not where your arm goes. Your arm doesn't deserve to go there. It's too close to that."

Out of the darkness, he appears with David Gelbert flanking his right side, trying to calm him down. They're swaying and super drunk. Asher stands and faces them.

"I wasn't aware this thing was yours either."

"Hold up! Am I the thing?"

Sam answers me in a loud whisper even though he's right in front of me, "Yes. You're the thing. Go with it." I let my feminism slide for a moment to see what goes down.

Asher curls his arm and pulls me to him. "If it isn't Sonoma's best and brightest viticulture minds."

"Oh, snap!" It slips out of my drunk head. Sam and Jims giggle at me. Stepping behind Josh, Sam motions me over. Waving quickly. I place my hand on Asher's arm to steady myself to get up. Josh growls again. Sam pulls him back.

"Asher, if you'll excuse me for a moment. Please let me up." I say in what I hope is a kind but authoritative tone. But pretty sure it just comes out drunk.

He never turns away from Josh as he speaks to me. "I thought he was just a passing fancy. Noelle, you do not need to cater to that alpha male. I'm right here for you, my angel."

As Asher says it, Bax is up and blocking Josh's lunge. I turn Asher to me.

"You have to stop. We're not anything, Asher. I'm not your angel. Please don't do this tonight."

"I'll stop only for you, Noelle. I have no need to get violent with these men for comeuppance; it will happen soon enough."

He kisses my hand as Josh yells, "Hell no." And is again subdued by his friends.

Asher returns to his seat. Baxter's still blocking Josh's path.

Josh crosses his arms and stares. Sam and Baxter hug. I hear Bax shout. "It's just Asher. He's not worth it, Josh. He's harmless."

Asher simply laughs. "You have no idea. I may seem harmless. That's fine. But what I am is patient." I hate this moment and want it to stop.

Bax says, "Asher, excuse my friend, but it might be time for you to go. I can guarantee you that I'm not strong enough to hold him back much longer."

Josh commands loudly, "Fuck off."

Josh sits down directly across from me. He drains a

random glass of wine left on the table without breaking eye contact. Those damn possessive eyes. They're telling me that they own me and I'm not sure I want that to be any different.

Sam pulls Bax to standing and tugs on Josh's shirt to get him to go inside. "Come on little brother. You too, weasel." Sam nods at Asher. "Everybody to the front bar. Let's go."

"I'm fine here. In fact, can we raise a glass to Baxter getting engaged? He's good at love." Josh sits back.

"One of us should probably get married and per usual, I'll be the responsible one. Now, let's go Ash." Baxter smiles at us and we half-heartedly raise a glass. There's still too much tension for us to celebrate him. But I've met Shawna and they seem well suited. I guess. She's kind of cold, and they've been on and off since college. But good for him for plunging forward.

"I am fine here as well," Asher says.

Then Josh crosses his arms over his chest again. His black t-shirt tightening around his biceps. I begin to rush below and blush above.

Bax negotiates. "Both of you stand down. I'm in no condition to drive to the hospital if there's blood."

"I'm merely making sure my darling Noelle is safe," Asher says smugly. I need him to go away before I can never return to the Swiss Hotel. They won't let me eat here if I've brought a brawl to their patio.

Drunk David stumbles from the darkness. I assume he was pissing somewhere in the bushes. He hugs Bax while looking at Asher. "Trust me, the girl can handle herself. Congrats."

"Thanks, David." Baxter turns his attention back to Asher.

Asher stands. "I trust that the gentlemen present will watch over my precious angel." Josh instantly stands, and Sam pushes him back into his seat. Asher turns to me. "I'm going to take my leave. Noelle, I'm always captivated by you.

I will contact you tomorrow. Sleep well, my angel. I know you don't think that you are, but you'll always be my angel." I roll my eyes. Josh launches at him but gets caught up by a chair and almost trips and then tries to carry it off.

Asher knows he's outnumbered. And he's being kind of an asshole. He exits as Sam stands behind Josh with his hands pushing his shoulders down.

I stay seated at the table. My eyes never leave Josh's lips. People should write songs and poems about those lips. They're such good lips. I want those lips. I want to taste them again. Too much wine is a bad idea. His lips are a good idea, though.

The boys exit the patio and head to the street side bar out in front of the building to snag a table. I saunter around the table towards Josh. His gorgeous lapis blue eyes possessing me with every step closer. We have unfinished business from this afternoon. I want to own his tongue, and I need his lips on me now. Everything in my life fades away as I get closer to him. The left side of his mouth curls up.

I take Josh's hand, which is strong and commanding. He tries to pull me into his lap, but I pull him to standing. I'm too drunk to muster self-control. I guide him back towards the shadows of the courtyard and away from the dining area and towards an empty secluded seating area.

"Cosmo, this is your blue dress. The one you like. Your favorite. It's hot, girl. Hi there, Elle. Sam and I had a long talking. And it's time to tell you things. All the things."

"Def later, but right now, I don't care." I go up on my tiptoes and pull him to me, his mouth immediately slanting over mine. I hear him drop an empty bottle at our side. His hands are instantly on my ass. And I moan into his mouth as he pulls me closer, and our tongues explore each other. My body is curling and twisting with mad desire.

# 14

## JOSH

I NEVER GET THIS DRUNK AND OUT OF CONTROL. I CAN BARELY stand it as she swallows my tongue. Fuck yes. This feels so good. I need to tell her about the mob hit she avoided. Who has to say that to their woman? That they avoided a possible mob hit? What the hell has happened to my life? It's insane. I slide my hand up her porcelain thighs and under her skirt. She's dripping for me. She's so wet and softly moaning as I put my hands on her bare ass. My finger circling and teasing her opening. Goddamn, I love a thong.

"Josh. Josh. I'm so drunk."

"Then, no sex. I'm just going to get you off. I want to taste you. It's been too long, Hellcat. I need to refresh my memory." I kiss her with intense passion. "I'm going to lick the hell out of you and make you come. Okay?" She moans. "I need your words, beautiful."

"Yes. Do all of that."

I instantly go to my knees on the concrete patio with no pretense and guide her skirt up to her hips. I pull her thong to the side and kiss her sweet soft blonde hair that lives in a perfect 'v.' Her breath catches. Not too much, not too little. I hate a landing strip. I hate bald. Give me a fucking well-maintained but full bush. It's gorgeous.

I take my hand up her thighs and pull her thong down. She delicately steps out of it. I show her that I'm placing it into my pocket to add to my collection. She nods, and I thrust a finger unexpectedly into her. I lift her leg to my shoulder and wrap my hand around her ass to brace her. She gasps and pushes my head towards where I'm desperate to be.

I spread her with my fingers, exposing her clit to the elements. I lick then blow on it. She moans loudly. And as always, I could come just from her sounds. I continue touching different parts of her. I lightly slap her clit, and her knees buckle as she emits a sharp gasp. Then there's a deep throaty growl. Fuck, she's hot.

I suckle and pinch, tasting her as she coats my face. She can't be wetter or taste better. I've craved her tart sweetness. I thrust a finger in her while I continue to work her with my tongue. She's moving into my finger, and I add a second one. The two working together curling inside of her. Her breath gets shallow and quick. I don't think I can handle how beautiful she is. She's moving in rhythm with my fingers as I fuck her with them.

I let her guide how fast she wants to come. I nip her clit and put pressure on it when she stills for a split second. I don't remove or stop my fingers. I want her cunt to clamp down on them. I want to feel from the inside as her vibrations rip her apart.

I keep moving my fingers but back my head out and say, "Come on, dirty girl, let all of this hotel and the plaza know you're coming. Let me hear it. Come for me. Come on me." I intensify what I'm doing to her. I feel her body still for again. Then I put my thumb on her clit with intense pressure, and she's gone.

"Josh. Fuck. Oh. Fuck. Josh. Please. Josh, make me come."

She screams my name, and it's the most magnificent fucking sound. My fingers feel like they're in a vice grip. It's like she wants to keep them. She can have everything. I stand quickly, kissing her. I keep my thumb in place, pulsing on her clit. I'm on her mouth before she's even done with her pleasure aftershocks. Tasting all of her goodness on my lips. She responds like a wild animal. Clawing at me and scratching my shoulders. I pull her hair back to jerk her face away from mine. I look her in the eyes.

"I told you we weren't done. We'll never be done. Elle. You're mine, Hellcat. And I am yours." I attack her mouth again. She pants and regulates her breathing. Her smile is so broad. I haven't seen a moment of pure happiness from her in a while. I know she just had an orgasm and we're both ripping drunk, but right now we're just grinning at each other like idiots.

She reaches for my pants. As much as I want to bury my cock up to the hilt in her, I'm not sure I wouldn't get whiskey dick in the middle. I want this to be it for tonight. I want it to be a conscious choice the next time my cock is deep inside her where it's supposed to be.

"This was all about you. It's always about you. Until tomorrow, Cosmo."

She simply says, "Goodnight, Suit." She pecks my lips again and squeezes my hand. She collects her purse from the ground. She turns towards the parking lot and away from me.

## 15

## ELLE

I can't sleep. I've tossed and turned most of the night. That wasn't enough. I need more. I need his dick, and I don't know how to get up to the Lookout in the dark. But I don't want him to think I want more than sex. Because that's all I can allow myself. That release was epic last night. I haven't had that in so long. But I won't be hurt. I can't be left again. But apparently, I can be finger fucked.

My alarm is going to go off in like ten minutes. Time to harvest while it's still dark. I click on the nightstand lamp. I can't stop thinking of him and that damn orgasm last night. His tongue is sublime. My nipples are hard and pulling upwards. I reach under my tank to circle them with a wet finger. I drag my hand through the wetness that's accumulated below as I try not to think of him.

What did that mean? Was it drunk or more? I can't ever trust him. Or me around him. He'll leave me again. That's what he'll do. That's what people do. They leave me. I'm always the one left behind. I won't invest so I can't be left. I'm so confused, I'm rhyming. I increase the pressure and speed of my hand, arch my back, and gasp. I reach down further to finger my...

"You know I can help you out with that."

I freeze, remove my hands from myself. My chest and face instantly turn mortified red. I flip over onto my stomach and up onto my elbows. I turn towards my bedroom door where he's leaning on the frame with a sly sexy grin on his face and his massive arms crossed. He came right into my room. I didn't even hear him.

"I'm *so* embarrassed."

"Don't be. That was the single sexiest thing I've ever witnessed or probably will ever witness. And now I get one of my favorite views." My body's humming in his proximity. I do have my ass in the air like I'm presenting my butt in my little cheeky sleep shorts. Good lord, I need to get fucked. I must maintain. "What? Why? Oh my god."

"I came to give you a ride out to the Tempranillo blocks. We're going to the back of the property, and you didn't answer your phone."

"So, you just came in my room."

"No, you were about to come in your room. Don't let me stop you. We have a couple minutes. Pretend I'm not here." He grins madly at me.

"You just walked in?" I sit up and pull the covers around me.

"Hey, genius, your door was cracked."

"Oh, god. Your parents?!"

"They're downstairs. No worries. Only I know that you were about to make yourself come undone. How close were you? Were you to that adorable panting stage, just before you tip over the edge? Was it me you were thinking about? Because I know we were drunk, but damn that was a good time on the patio last night."

That smile. The lip licking. Killing me. "None of your fucking business what I was thinking about."

"It's *so* my fucking business, Hellcat. Given the flush on your chest, I'd say you were about three minutes out from detonation." There's no way he can read my skin like that. "That's right. I know what each shade means. Come on, let me help. I'll bet I could get it done super quick. I know the exact angle to push that swollen and waiting button for you. Just one friend helping out another." He licks his lips again and rubs his hands together.

"You did quite enough last night."

"Apparently not. Someone's not quite satisfied. And it's one of the things I adore about you. You're an orgasm hoarder. Always looking to add one more to the collection." My entire body is tingling. I am a hoarder. I didn't used to be that way. Not until him.

"Get out!" I throw a pillow at him.

"I'll go. But know that I'm not going anywhere. You, on the other hand, appear to be packing. Were you going somewhere without telling me?"

I look at his face, and it seems a bit crestfallen. I speak softly as I sit up on the bed to face him. "I was going to tell you. Home. New York."

"You seem pretty much packed up. It doesn't feel good to be left out of that decision. I get it. I understand what you think you're doing but no. The answer is no." He smiles smugly at me.

"What? No. What?"

He scrubs his sexy stubbled face with his hands. "Give me the chance to say what I never gave you the opportunity to do."

"What is that?"

"Stay. I'm asking you to stay. Don't go. I never gave you the chance to say that to me, but I'm taking this opportunity.

I'm sorry I took that decision away from you. But listen to me now. Stay with me."

"Stop saying that."

He quickly moves to the edge of my bed and takes my hand. All traces of the silly grin have vanished. In its place is a serious and softened look. He stares straight into my eyes as I pull the sheet up over my super hard nipples.

"Never. Do you hear me, Noelle Parker? I'm not fucking around. And when you're ready to hear my story, I'll tell you. But know this, I'm not leaving. The longer I'm near you, the more I know I'm staying. You'll see that you truly are mine."

"It's like you're on some quest to win me. It's just because I have a good moan."

I try to take the piss out of the moment. I'm not sure I can handle what he's saying. I sit up on the edge of the bed next to him. His face is gorgeous and giving, but his tone is direct, not patronizing. He's raw and honest. I feel every thread of his vulnerability, and I want to weave it into a cohesive narrative. I want it all to mean something.

"Fuck that. Don't trivialize what I'm saying to you right now. Although your body was made for mine, it's not just that. You'll see. I don't like being without you. I don't like who I am in the world without you. I don't like not telling you about my day. It used to scare the shit out of me, but now it pisses me off every fucking second you're not in my arms."

Tears sting the back of my eyes. They fill as he says these things to me. I wish I were the girl who could simply crumble into his arms and be past all this. I want to be her so fucking much, but I'm not. I can't let it all go. And I'm terrified that by the time I figure out how to let him back in, he'll be over me.

"Elle, I want to be with you all the time. Both feet, no hesitation. I'm happy when you're near. I'm silly, stupid happy even thinking about you. If it takes the rest of my fucking life to prove to you that I'm not leaving, it will be time well spent. This means you don't get to leave either. You don't live in New York. You don't belong there anymore. It's time to stop hiding in that city. You unpack your fancy Louis suitcase and settle in for the long haul right the fuck now. We belong to each other. You stay with me. I am yours, and I'll wait a little while longer while you get right with that."

The tears stream down my face, and his thumbs wipes them away. "I don't know how to get past being left. I don't."

"Woman, I'm not running back to Santa Barbara, LA, or off to New York. I'm not going to ass fuck your assistant. I'm not going to give you a mediocre relationship or unsatisfying sex. I won't dismiss you or mansplain. I don't want to teach you anything. I can last longer than twenty minutes, and you won't ever be bored with me. And listen up, this is the important part. I'm not dying in a car accident or any other way without you by my side. I will defy the natural order of existence if it means proving to you, *I will not leave you.*"

I can't breathe. I can't deal with this.

He continues to talk. "Joshua is gone. I love making deals. I love conquering and winning. I will always have that cutthroat nature to me, and I'll find an outlet for it. But I don't want to win you, I want to earn you."

His thumbs catch my tears as they fall. I'm a mess. "I can't."

"Not yet, you can't. But I'll wait." He stands up and kisses the top of my head. He pauses at the door as I try to get myself back to normal.

I look up at him as I dry my face with the sheet. "Can we table all of this for a minute?"

"Sure, Cosmo. But in the meantime, I'm available to get you off whenever we have a free moment."

I'm glad for his innuendo and lightening the mood. "Can we focus, please?"

"I am very focused on your lips, your pu…"

I interrupt him, "Enough." I pull my lips into a small smile.

"Fine. Tabled. Now, get your attractive ass dressed, we've got grapes to pick. Wanna drive the gondola again?" He raises his eyebrows at me. I smile at him through my glassy eyes. I've never been more confused in my life. He leaves, and I feel the absence of him in my space. I don't know how long I will stay, but I can stay for now.

# 16

# ELLE

WHILE PICKING GRAPES AND DRIVING THEM TO THE CRUSH PAD, my head is buzzing. I don't know what's next, but Josh is right, it's not New York. As I was making plans to leave, I dreaded going back there. He broke something loose in me this morning.

Plan B time. My dad would say what's the plan B you can live with, the one that puts you in charge. The one that makes you happy. San Francisco perhaps. Maybe I'll be a decorator with my old friend. Or go to school and become a sommelier. Or maybe I set up a West Coast outpost of Parker & Co, soon to be Parker & Bixby. I know that my heart's no longer in Manhattan.

New York helped make me become who I am, but I don't need it anymore. And now it's time to let it go. This revelation makes my entire body relax into a smile. I've lifted a weight off with this decision. Even though I still need to get Josh out of my system before I can make a fresh start. Maybe I can fuck him out of my system? Is that a thing? I want that to be a thing.

So I don't second guess myself, I instantly text my lawyer

to officially give Evan controlling interest and make him CEO. And all of this happens while I'm happily driving farm equipment. Which really should have been a dead giveaway that New York is truly behind me. I have lipstick on though. It's a fuchsia pink, Gucci's *Love Before Breakfast.*

I'm involved in all aspects of the winery deal. I even created a marketing strategy to build out an overall ladder of price points for distribution using the five different wineries, the Chapel label being the ace in the hole. The cash that can be made from Chapel, LaChappelle/Whittier's everyday label with mass production vineyards in Lodi is tremendous. The vineyard is jointly owned with Schroeder and they produce an everyday label called Bellamy's Ghost. There's too much juice for their collective facilities to keep up with production so they sell about half of the juice off each year. But the new distribution company can create facilities to use all the juice internally and expand both labels. Because Sarah and Will have a significant bargaining chip, they ensured the deal for the rest of them. The other four estate wineries will be distributed as high-end products. The other wineries remain in control of their production and their land, just get a wider distribution. And the boost in capital will be enough for the 'boys' to start their organic boutique label. Tommi, Sam, Bax, Jims, Tabi, and David are dying to put their own stamp on something. They'll have enough startup capital for acreage and a small facility and possibly a warehouse.

It's been too long since I felt a part of things. When this deal is done, I need to find something to be a part of. My company is wonderful, but I'm in charge, not a part of it. Not a cog that helps it go. I'm the force that pushes it forward. I'm the one who ultimately has to, or it will fail. But here, I've become more myself than I've been in a decade. Regardless of what Asher is or isn't to me, I am grateful that my innocent Valentine's dinner in New York brought me to Sonoma. Time to take my daddy's advice and get on with my plan B.

---

I'VE BEEN all over the property today, and now I'm pouring for the people. It's so hot outside, and the tasting room is cool and has all the Rosé I can drink. I relieve Sammy, knowing she wants to track down Sam, whose helping with juicing today. They're inseparable after only three months.

"Randy says he's out smoking."

"Go have tremendous sex with your man. I got this. I mean we close in twenty minutes." I have no right to excuse Sam, I'm not management. I'll apologize for my actions if someone calls me on it.

Suddenly there's a steady stream of people. I'm in a faded blue ringer LC/W t-shirt and cutoffs pouring wine for the people when he walks in the swamped tasting room. It's just me behind the bar. He jumps back here. My basement floods remembering the last time we were behind this bar together. Push it from your mind, Elle. I can't help thinking about the way his hands caressed down my arms, as he pressed himself up against me, pinning me to the bar.

He puts his hand on my back. My chest flushes, and my skin reacts to his touch. Dammit. Stop it. Stop it. Stop. We still haven't discussed what he said this morning. I'm not ready.

"I'll take the left side. You take the right." He jumps on the bar and then raises his voice to all folks gathered. "Welcome everybody. What are you having? No tasting fee today, just belly up and try some damn good wine."

I grin and return the ten-dollar bill someone just handed me. "You heard the man. What would you like to try? We have seven open to sample."

The two of us pour wine and dance around each other in the confined space racking up a shit ton of sales. Josh never fails to smack my ass or graze my fingers when he needs the bottle I'm holding. I don't hate his touch. I do the same to him. He grins each time.

Randy never returns to close, so we lose track of time. It's nearly an hour and a half after closing time when we kick out the last taster. I hop up on the bar and pour myself a glass of Rosé while Josh sips some Sauvignon Blanc and counts the cash drawer.

I've already run reports in the back and stocked the racks. Josh said he'd grab a palate in the morning to restock the cases we went through. I'm staring at his ass when he turns and catches me. Josh winks at me while he continues counting.

I finish stocking merch and head to the courtyard. I slide into an Adirondack chair. I'm soon joined by Josh who's just locked up the tasting room. "Truce."

"Truce." I return the sentiment.

He turns to me, and his blue eyes are blazing in the end-of-the-day gloaming. They look more natural and approachable in his well-loved gray Stanford t-shirt and khaki cargo shorts. His shirt is popping up just a bit, and I can't look away from that solitary strip of tanned flesh just above his waistband. He breaks my trance by speaking.

"Can I explain?"

"Please don't, Josh. Can we just let it be what it was?" I plead with him. I don't need it anymore. I just want to enjoy this moment.

He reaches his hand out. "Then let's begin again." He puts his hand out, and I shake it.

"Noelle Parker."

"Joshua Lucien LaChappelle Whittier."

I smile at him. "Is that how you always introduce yourself?"

"No. In the real world, I'm Josh Whittier."

"Funny."

"What is?"

"To me, this is the real world."

"Are you thinking of staying?" He sips his wine, and I don't have a real answer for him.

"I don't know."

"Wow, Ms. Elle Parker without a plan in place? And without directives to give or quips to snap at me."

"I'm too tired. Tell me about Santa Barbara."

"What about it?"

"What does it look like for you?" I want to talk about something that has nothing to do with the winery or us. He starts talking about his assistant John.

And suddenly we've started again. Our connection and the ease with which we're talking I guess that never went away, I just buried it.

He continues, "It was work. Lots of it. And the rest of it you're not ready to hear, according to you."

"Sam said you have a new girlfriend. And may I point out that I'm done being the one you cheat on her with."

17
———

JOSH

Oh, fuck Sam needs to shut his mouth. I need to get past this. I will tell her the truth. "Yeah, I did. She was going to visit soon."

"Was? I'm sorry. What went wrong?"

"She wasn't you, Elle. I thought you got that." She looks away from me and sips her wine, and I see the hint of a smile. Progress.

I ask, "Why was Asher there the other night? Are you interested again?"

My mind is burning, even asking the question. I hate that weasel. I have never trusted him. I hate that he scammed half the Valley and yet he still seems to be everyone's favorite dinner guest. But mostly I fucking hate that he was near her. Touching her. I don't trust him at all. Then Elle laughs, and my chest eases a bit.

"Look, you might have been a mistake, but at least I didn't have to get myself off quietly in the bathroom after sex."

I say to her matter-of-factly, "Do you need a reminder? My tongue is always motivated and at your service. It was just telling me early today how much it wanted to feel you come on it again."

"OH! I thought we were starting over?"

I crook my left eyebrow at her. "That was our start, remember?"

She smirks and pushes me away. "Change the subject."

"Television, art? What's your choice?"

"You pick." She snuggles down into her chair and turns her face to mine. We're staring at each other. Her eyes capturing me all over again with their sultry sweetness. She's sweaty, no makeup, hair's a frizzy wreck, and she could not be more beautiful.

"How about hungry?" I finally say. Our gaze is broken by my words.

Elle sits up in her chair, and her hair falls over her face. "Yes. I am. Was going to head up to the house and see I could scrounge something there."

"I have a better idea. Trust me?"

"Only if I can drive."

She winks at me, and I know that as those green eyes hold my gaze, I'm going to let her drive the Spyder. I nod, and she squeals. I think we might be becoming friends. Step One.

———

"WHY HAS no one ever told me about this place?"

"Probably thought you were too fancy to sit at on the turquoise diner stools of Juanita Juanita."

"This is the best burrito I've ever had. Oh! Carne Asada Burrito! You told me you craved it the night we met."

"I did. I can't believe you remembered." It was a throw-away comment on my way to conquering her that night at Steiner's, and she cared enough to tuck away that information. Off kilter. I never have equilibrium around her.

"I remember everything."

"Good." I smile and turn back to my dinner.

The burritos are the size of my forearms. This place is a little out of the way, and it's not on the tourist radar. It's sublime, and I can't believe I've never taken her here. She attacks the burrito and salsa squirts out all over her face. She's laughing her giant guffaw, and she charms everyone around us. She can't put the jumbo food envelope down, so I wipe the mess from her cheek. I'm laughing now too, and then I slam a beer. I turn to her and feed her a sip of her beer.

"I don't know how to put this down without it falling apart."

"Just keep eating, Cosmo. I'll wipe your face and make sure you get some beer down your gullet." Her gorgeous gullet.

"Why are you being so nice to me?"

"You know why. Why do you think my parents want to sell so badly?"

"You know why. It's time. They want to see the world before they can't."

My semi hippie parents have always been a carpe diem sort, so it does make sense. I haven't asked them because every time I do, it comes out as an asshole statement. I'll try again. I do want to know the story from them.

She talks with a mouth full of Carne Asada. "Tell me some more Lucien stories."

"Lucien? He was a great vintner and a great man."

"Bullshit. Your boys think he was the ultimate ass, and it's where your jackass side comes from." She says with her mouth totally full of burrito.

"My boys are talking? Hmm. I need to ban you from Wednesday nights."

"You can't. They've claimed me."

I will joke with her to get off this Lucien topic. "You do hear the main descriptor there, right? *Boys*."

She begins mocking me. "Tabi, Poppy, Becca, and Tommi aren't boys."

"Yes, they are, you just don't know them well enough."

"No, you don't know them well enough as grown-ups."

"True." I take another big bite, relieved that we've moved on from Lucien.

She turns to me, and I wipe some guacamole from her cheek. She continues, "You're not mad that I know your friends. You're pissed off that I know more about you and Lucien. I know he hit you and the vineyard was supposed to be yours."

Give it up to Elle. Stop pushing. I snap at her, "And that's all you need to know. I'm not taking the vineyard, and Lucien is dead."

This isn't what I need to discuss. The flicker of fire in those emerald eyes will be my undoing. I see her winding up to push way too far. Hell no. There are actual things I want to tell her, but she won't let me. And now, she wants to hear about shit I don't talk about.

These are things to be shared if we're together. She hasn't earned the right to know all my pain yet. Show me you'll let me in, and then you can know all this shit. I need to tell her about Sal, not discuss my baggage. God forbid we're not on her agenda. Stop controlling things, Elle.

"I know you were bred for the winery. You ran away from it the first chance you got, leaving your parents stuck with it. A business they weren't even sure they wanted."

This is too far. Hell, just eat your burrito. Now I have to defend myself? Come on. "He shoved them into this business, not me. He forced them, and they went along for the ride. They never stood up to him so now they're vintners. Not me. I stood my ground, and I'm not a winemaker."

She stands up, getting into my face. But she's still holding onto her burrito which is now in shambles. "And you kept them in it. You left them. That's what you do, leave. You leave when shit gets intense. It's a bit self-serving. They stayed to provide for you. Lucien was going to cut them off from all money when Sarah was pregnant. Did you know that part? Or that your dad was offered a job in Boston writing for a scientific journal? Lucien knew you were a boy, so he held them hostage, to get his heir. She told me that story. I didn't ask to know any of this. But you left without ever asking or telling them anything. And that's a rather familiar scenario."

Enough. Of course I know that shit but she shouldn't. And she's certainly skewing it through her own lens. I grab her burrito and throw it back into the basket. It splatters all over me and the counter. She looks at me a bit stunned, but what did you expect, attacking me about my family.

"Good lord, Elle. Shut up. You can't equate me going back to work and stepping away from whatever we were beginning to be with my entire family history. That you, by the way, aren't a part of at all. I care about you, but that's a pretty bold and blanket statement. You know facts, but you didn't live through either situation. And you didn't know Lucien. Stop drawing parallels to fuel your righteous indignation. It's my family's history you're bending and cherry picking information from to justify your own fear of relationships. Shut the hell up. Stop discussing my family. You don't belong in this conversation."

"Like I said, I didn't ask to know all of this, but how can you want me to get to know you and I'm not allowed to talk?"

"Come off it. You won't let me explain anything about our situation. And you don't talk about your own shit. I don't know about your childhood except for snippets that slip out.

But how come you get to pass judgment on my life choices? What the fuck, Elle?"

I speak too forcefully. I had to go back to Santa Barbara. Shit. I'm trying to convince her to fall in love with me, and this sitch isn't helping. She's flaunting my intimate family secrets at a taco place. I look away from her. Wait. Did I just think about love? Sex. Whatever. Now I'm pissed that I had that thought. Fuck.

"Take me home. I'm not hungry anymore."

My blood is boiling. She should back the fuck down before I eviscerate her. I need to calm myself down. She's put me in the red zone. I need to breathe. I'm fighting to prove my feelings for her, but I'm desperate for her to stop talking. I'm hostile and vulnerable. She drives me to the brink of insanity. I wish I had something to pull me back, to tether me to reality. Instead, I snap at her.

My voice is much louder than I intend it to be. "We will go when I'm fucking ready. Sit your ass down."

I turn away from her, and she walks out of the restaurant. I see her blonde ponytail swinging in a huff in my peripheral vision. I let her go. We're miles from the winery. When she doesn't come back, I realize she called an Uber. Infuriating. Another fucking thing I have to apologize for. Goddammit.

# 18

## ELLE

AND I THOUGHT WE WERE GETTING SOMEWHERE. I AM GOING back to avoiding him. In fact, I'm done giving him the time of freaking day. Asshole. I am stomping around the Farmhouse trying to process what the hell just happened.

I don't want to be around people, so I grab an open bottle from the tasting room and climb up to the roof. I'm sipping and cooling down. He's got me all hot and bothered. And I mean bothered in an annoyed way, not in an *"I want to fuck him way."* He claims I'm his, but he can't share any of himself. Fuck that.

Whether I want to admit it or not, just knowing and dealing with Josh has opened me up. And now I'm pissed at me as well as him. I swallow a big swig from the bottle. I sit down in a huff and stare out over the vineyard. My friend the owl hoots in the distance. I listen to the vineyards sounds as they all start to settle into their nighttime symphony. I exhale loudly to join their chorus. Then it hits me: perhaps I overstepped. And perhaps I might be a wee bit of a hypocrite.

I deflected from my pain and doubts and demanded he open about his. I don't know where to put him. I don't know what to do with all the stuff I've hidden away for years that I'm feeling all the time these days. I miss my mom. I wish I could talk to her about this or anything.

Sarah's fantastic, but I miss my mom. I never let myself miss her, but here staring at the stars, a habit I picked up from her, I let the tears slide down my face. I'm not sure I've cried enough for her. I've cried for lost business, or love, or leaving Kansas but not for all of the *"could have beens."* All the things that my mom will miss. The advice she doesn't get to give, and I need. That's why I'm crying. The wedding she won't see, the business success or the grandchildren she'll never meet. I swore I wouldn't have children because I didn't think I could bear the pain of them never knowing their grandparents. Or the giving them the pain of losing me. The pain of losing my parents is still the very depths of sadness. I've spent the last decade, making sure I didn't love anything that couldn't be lost. Then he cracked open my fucking walls, and all this stuff keeps spilling out.

I'm so tired of being an army of one and making every decision and facing all the consequences alone. I'm ready for someone to be on my side, unconditionally.

I hate Josh for teasing me with that possibility. I wipe the tears from my eyes and take a swig of wine from the bottle. I forgot a glass. Then I hear the ladder thud. I'm trapped. I didn't hear him come home. I glance over to the edge, and his deep blue eyes pierce the inky night around us.

"Not very proud of myself. I'm sorry I reacted that way. I shouldn't have used that tone of voice. And you know I don't apologize."

"Yes, you do."

"No, I don't."

"You do to me."

"Then you get what a big fucking deal this is, Cosmo."

I'm still hanging over the edge looking down at him. "I'm sorry too."

"Really?" He smirks at me.

"Yes. I shouldn't have pushed."

"It's what you do, Hellcat. Push me past my limits and expectations."

My checklist from the morning after our one night stand flashes in my mind. I realize he does that to me too. He pushes me past all limits, rules, and boundaries.

He yells up to me, "Now that you're sorry you ruined our dinner, can I come up?"

I laugh at him and sit back up away from the ladder. "It's your barn and spot."

"I bring reparations." I glance back down. He's holding up churros and another bottle of Rosé.

"I'll agree to those terms."

He throws a pillow at me from the ladder, and it hits me in the face. Then he throws a second one. They're the new merch I ordered with LC/W on them. He climbs up and lays down next to me. I'm too exhausted from life to hate right now. And I'm hungry. I didn't finish my burrito.

"I don't like to talk about my grandfather."

"Duh. Yeah, I got that." I roll towards him as he moves towards me. And we face each other like little kids at a sleepover.

Josh says, "I'm sorry I snapped. But you do realize that you don't share those dark places with me either. It's not fair to demand it from me, and you get to hide behind your walls. You get to run away, but I get chastised for protecting myself."

I reply, "I shouldn't have pushed. You're right." He tucks a piece of hair behind my ear. "I can't help myself sometimes."

"Duh. Yeah, I got that." He winks at me and rolls back onto his pillow.

"I'll forgive you if you tell me one thing about him. Your choice of story. Good or bad." I know I'm pushing again, but I want to know. I actually want to know why he never brings up his mother's Parkinson's. But I'll save that for another time.

"In exchange, tell me about the man who hurt you so badly. And not your dad dying. He didn't want to leave you."

My breath catches as tears well up instantly. He squeezes my hand. I welcome it even though I hate needing his touch. I vowed never to love anything or anyone that couldn't be lost. I have to leave before he becomes all of my reasons and all of my feelings. After sitting for a good five minutes, not moving, my breathing resumes to normal.

"Tell me a tale of the dude who made you mistrust all of us."

"You mean you?"

"Touché. But I believe there was someone there first. I wasn't treading new territory when I supposedly left you."

I think about the words he's saying. It's only fair that if I'm going to make him unearth some nastiness, then I should too. "Deal."

He quickly retorts, "You go first." I hit his arm gently. It's easier to talk about all this stuff while we face the stars and not each other.

"Gavin Durang."

"Dumb name. Is he the one who screwed your assistant in a certain location?"

"Yes. Dumb name Gavin. When I moved to New York, I sold my parent's assets and had their life insurance money as well. I finished college, paid for it, and brought the rest of the money to New York to start a marketing firm."

"After Bali."

I'll be damned, he remembers things too.

"Yes. After Bali. I didn't really know how to open my own

shop, so I went to work for one. I was at McCann New York for two and a half years. Gavin was my boss and quickly became more. I was vulnerable and alone in New York. He was charming and insanely good-looking."

"Permission to be jealous?"

I smile a big smile without him seeing. "Granted."

"But in my mind, he's a troll who never laid one finger on you. Just sat in a corner telling you how beautiful you are all day."

I laugh. "He did have good fingers." He hits me in the face with the pillow.

"Let me live in my delusion please."

"What delusion?"

"That I'm the only one who's ever finger fucked you. Except you."

"Go right ahead and believe that."

"Thanks." I laugh at him.

"Eventually, I confided that I had the startup capital for my own agency. He jumped on board with the idea. We'd been together for about a year and a half. I moved into his place, and we found a space for the new firm. He stole clients, and we hung a shingle."

"What was it called?"

"It's still called Dragonfly."

"You were Dragonfly?"

"I was. I named it for my childhood pet bunny."

"Heartwarming." He squeezes my hand and laughs a bit. "Pet bunny. That is freaking adorable. No dogs?"

"No. Which is odd. I mean there were lots of animals. And a shit ton of cats but no dogs."

"Okay, back to the story of the dude who never ever finger fucked you or violated you in any way."

I laugh at him. "Almost two years into the business and an engagement ring later, I found him screwing our assistant. In the ass. On our partners' desk. Here's what you don't know. *He* left *me*."

"Wait, do you not like to be left?" I sit up and toss my pillow at his face. He grabs my wrist pulling me down to him. We're as close as a whisper, and I retreat quickly. My body is all tingles and excitement.

I sit, pulling my knees up and face him while he remains laying there. He uses my extra pillow to prop himself up. Then he puts his hands behind his head, and it's like he's flexing his biceps for me. Damn, he may be an asshole, but he is so freaking hot.

"He disappeared with her for a couple of months, leaving me to clean up his mess."

"Ow. Damn, that's cold. Did he ever get a crack at your crack?"

"Not the point. He didn't cheat on me because I never let him in the backdoor."

"No backdoor, check. Good info. I am learning a lot tonight."

"That's not info. Just something Gavin didn't get."

"Noted. Don't be like Gavin and all doors might be open to me. I like an all-access pass. You would too. Trust me." He raises his eyebrows, and his lips curl to the side.

I slap his legs. "Stop it! He was also screwing our clients and some wives of clients. Then overcharging them. I did damage control when he left. Eventually when he resurfaced, married to the ass hoe, I had him buy me out."

"Damn. That's cold. Wait. You fixed the business and then handed it over to him like a gift."

"I never told him that I'd only invested a third of my money into our business. And that I knew he'd tank without Evan and I. That way he'd have to give away pieces to new partners and he'd end up making a living wage but nothing more with in a year."

"No shit. Shark."

"My daddy was a very shrewd man. He used to tell me all the time you make your own plan B. So, I pulled the rest of the money from t-bills and bought a rundown old brownstone in Murray Hill. Evan and I did a lot of the labor ourselves. I lived in the falling down building up until three years ago. Evan, my art director extraordinaire, genius creative, best friend and my new CEO, is the only thing I took from Dragonfly. We started out together at McCann and have stayed together. And I'm thrilled that the New York shingle reads Parker & Bixby now. He can handle anything, and he's the only person I truly trust."

"Evan's your plan B?"

I take in a deep breath and exhale some truth I've been afraid to voice. "No. I think it's this."

"No shit. Sonoma?"

"A west coast office for a start. I took all the money I made over the past year and stuck it into a fund with the idea of opening a branch somewhere other than New York. Or to buy a house upstate somewhere with stars. I thought it might be Miami or LA, but San Fran is looking pretty good right now."

"You should let me invest it."

"I already invested it and have found myself with a quite a tidy sum."

"You're a shark."

"Damn straight, I am."

I stretch my legs out while looking at his chiseled face. It looks so angular and strong in the moonlight. He's giving me a little glinting blue side eye, and it sparks like a diamond catching sunlight. He runs his hand up my calf, and it's familiar and comforting. His hair is back to being a little shaggy and is flopping to the side.

He asks, "And that's why you're afraid I'll leave? This Gavin asshole?"

No. I mean, partly. But it's also because my parents died. I pause. I can't tell him that directly. I just can't. But I feel as if he might understand a bit of it. "No. Not just him. I miss my mom." That last part did not go through my internal editor, it just came rushing out.

He sits up immediately and holds my face. My eyes go glassy, but I pull the tears back. He strokes my cheek and says nothing. Which is perfect.

He arranges a pillow next to his and we both lie back down, staring at the sky.

# 19

---

## JOSH

"Lucien was two people. He fiercely loved his family, but honor, prestige, and power were what fucked him up. His only balance in the world was my grandmother, and she died way too early. His ego went unchecked for years. *The legacy must live on* was a lot of pressure for a five-year-old. I always heard my only obligation and duty as a LaChappelle was to the land. Never recognizing that I'm a Whittier."

"Go on." I shift to look at her as I begin these stories. She props up on her elbow to give me her full attention.

"He lectured me about how I was the steward of the legacy. That my place was tied to the success of this farm. It was constant psychological warfare that my father rebelled against. My father tried to get between the two of us often, as did my mom. They didn't want me saddled with this. I didn't abandon them, they told me to go."

"Still not fair to dump this life on them when they didn't want it either." There's no malice or judgment in her voice.

"Perhaps the sale is best for everyone," I say resolutely.

"I never thought I'd hear you say that."

"Lucien was the man I looked up to, rightly or wrongly.

He was the dominant master of his world and my young life. Just as I am a master of mine in Santa Barbara. He was strong, and this business wouldn't have survived without him. He saw trends long before they came to fruition. He saw growing opportunities and bottle niches. He lived and breathed this business that was handed to him by my great grandparents. He'd be shocked at how good my parents are at this whole thing. He'd also be pissed because they aren't doing it the right way. The 'Lucien' way."

I sit up to face her and sip some wine. "After my grandmother died, he shut part of himself off. He became married to duty and legacy. He was also a ruthless bastard. He was ultimately disappointed that my mother was a girl. He never got over the heartbreak of my grandmother dying when Mom was just an infant. He could never hide his disdain that she didn't have any business acumen. She was a constant reminder of his heartbreak. Not the healthiest way to grow up, but look at my mom. She's the most caring, open, positive person in the world. Mrs. Dotson was her nanny and eventually caretaker. Mrs. Dotson's the only mom she ever knew."

"Hold up! That's why Mrs. Dotson is still here? Was there a Mr. Dotson?"

I laugh at her reaction. "There might have been, but the rumor is that she added the Mrs. part to avoid a scandal while she kept time with Lucien."

"OH MY GOD. Mrs. Dotson's a hussy."

"Hey! That's the only real grandmother I have."

"Wow, I never thought of that. That's a hell of a granny. You know she hates me?"

"She doesn't. Well, she might. Just put the mugs back the way she likes them already. I know, you're doing it wrong just to needle her now." She laughs really hard. I'm not wrong. She reaches her hand for mine. She threads her fingers in and out of mine. What the hell is she doing? She's touching me first. I want to fucking cover her with my body right now. Instead, I'm going to try and not react. I don't want to scare her off. I want her to keep touching me.

I continue the story. "Look, he gave me confidence and an opportunity to be strong. He also underestimated my mother and father, and so did I. Here's a story about Lucien that explains him in a nutshell."

"Give it to me."

"Maybe later, but right now I'm telling a good story." She laughs easily.

"Not tonight, Suit."

"It's almost midnight. I'll bring it up again tomorrow."

She grins and licks her lips, thinking I can't see her in the darkness.

"There was a time when I was super young," I say, "like three or four, and the CFO was his best friend. The only actual partner he ever had. My dad told me they were inseparable, and it was the only time Lucien truly relaxed or laughed. He was utterly devoted to his friend.

They ran the company for almost a decade. Absolutely thriving and dominating the wine world together. Until Lucien discovered that not only was Barry Marcus skimming, he was stealing barrels of juice and selling them to low-rent wineries to bottle under their name. He attempted to sell the LaChappelle name out from under him. He used one of the low-rent wineries as a shill to cover the money trail by trading on the winery's name for distribution dollars."

"That's complicated."

"It is. That was just the business stuff. Barry and his family lived on the edge of the property. LaChappelle paid their bills and kept a roof over their heads. He had a great salary, and my grandfather thought that maybe Barry's son might become the heir apparent. My mom told me that

Barry's son was Lucien's constant companion for like five years learning the business. He'd come home from school and work late into the night with him and before he'd go to class in the morning. I think he was like early teens. This was before I was truly in Lucien's crosshairs."

"Your life is so much more colorful than mine."

"Bali," I state plainly.

She smirks and raises her eyebrows. I want to ravage her. "Someday I'll tell you the stories."

"I look forward to them. And again, no one finger fucked you in that year, right?"

"Correct. I was a finger fuck virgin until you. In fact, thank you, Josh, for taking my innocence in all things."

She's pulls her hand back and readjusts to sit and sip. I feel like all the light has drained from the stars as she lets go of my hand. I fucking hate débourbage.

I sigh and continue speaking. "That kid was always around my grandfather learning the business, or so I've been told. When Barry's misdeeds were discovered, Lucien threw them out of the house, sued them, and ran the family literally out of town. He boarded up their house so they couldn't even get their stuff. It was broken into years later and emptied out. Lucien blackballed him to anyone who would listen in our Valley and beyond. Barry couldn't get hired anywhere in California."

"Holy shit."

"Lucien had no grey area in him. I forget the kid's name, but he wasn't welcome back here. I heard this story a lot. Lucien's parable about 'trust no one.'"

"What happened to Barry?"

"The Marcus family became infamous after my grandfather sent him to jail for embezzlement for three years. You don't fuck with Lucien."

"Did they have any stock in the winery?"

"Whatever they had got revoked to pay for what he stole. Barry killed himself about five years after all of this happened. I was nine almost ten. We went to the funeral. My mother brought a noodle casserole, but my grandfather didn't utter a word to anyone. He stood in the back with his arms crossed."

"What kind of noodles?" I hit her again with a pillow to the face, and she giggles.

"The son, at this point, is like seventeen and threw a giant tantrum when we arrived. He called Lucien a murderer. We paid our respects and left. But as we got to the car, the son came charging at my grandfather. I mean, full-on fucking charging at him. My father stepped between them. Although my grandfather was like seventy-two, he would have torn that boy from limb to limb. The kid was screeching things like, 'I was the one. I was your heir. LaChappelle was supposed to be mine. It will be. You killed my father, and I will take your winery. I will take what's rightfully mine.' I mean, it was some delusional shit."

"Holy shit. That is a lot. Oooh, do you think Lucien was really his father?"

"Now you're making this into more of a soap opera than it needs to be."

"And Mrs. Dotson's his mom?" I can't help but belly laugh at the thought, and she continues, "But it's an interesting thought, isn't it? Poor guy. Hope he's found some peace, wherever he is. And Lucien hit you?"

"Why are you fixated on that?"

"Why aren't you?"

"He cuffed me on the head or the arm. He was tough. I did love him. But the way he force-fed this place to me made me bolt."

"He still beat you, no matter how you rationalize it away. It wasn't your fault. You were just a boy. If you condone what he did to you, do you think it's acceptable to do it?"

"Are you asking me if I'd hit or spank a child?"

"Yes."

"Why are you bringing up children?" She says nothing. Interesting. We stay in this suspended state for a second or two. "Answer me, Hellcat."

"Um…" I love making her tongue tied.

"What do you think, Elle?"

She grabs my hand and squeezes. "No. I don't think you would do that at all."

"You, on the other hand…..

She lets go of my hand before I can finish that sentence. I glance over to see if her cheeks are flushed at the thought. And there goes my dick again as I imagine my palm on her perfect peach ass. But for now, I'll have to settle for lacing my fingers in hers. She's not quite ready yet. She needs to settle just a bit more.

We lay there in our revelations. Both pushing past who we started out to be and settling here instead. She breaks our silence.

"Can I ask you another question?"

"Nope. Not another question from you tonight, missy. Not unless you're willing to hear why I left? I have answered quite enough."

"I'm not willing to hear it just yet." It hurts that she still won't listen to that, but she'll listen to everything else I have to say. I think she knows it's a valid reason and then she'll have no excuses and nowhere to hide. "You're right, Josh. You've answered enough for tonight."

"I'm sorry, did you just say I was right? Can you repeat that?"

"Nah. One time thing. Enjoy it."

Over the next half hour or so, we sip our wine and eat

our churros in silence, absorbing the universe and all the shit we just said about ourselves. I lean up on my elbow at one point to look at her face. I could stare at her face forever. I see all the answers to all my questions in her green globe eyes. I hope she can find her answers in mine. I kiss her forehead, and that's the most restrained I've ever been in my life. I want to give her space to find her way to me, but I can't help but want to push.

# 20

## JOSH

I SEE THE PRINCESS DRIVE UP IN HER LEASED CHERRY RED C 300 Cabriolet Mercedes and she parks in my space to annoy me. She's been doing it all week. That car is choice. The woman does have good taste in automobiles. But she's had this one for almost six months, and it's scratched all to hell. She'll never drive the Spyder again.

She's been very short with me since that night on the roof. Pissing me off. We're almost to the tipping point where she either admits her attraction to me, or I'm fucking done. I'm not this much of a pussy. Débourbage. I'm just letting her sediment settle. Hopefully, she's getting more clarity every day. There's been no stargazing, nighttime run-ins, or drunken oral sex lately. I'm sure she's trying to put her walls back up again. She's angry at me still. I'm sure it's because of the things we revealed to each other. I know it's her stuff not my own, but it's hard not to shake her and make her listen. She seems to need space from me, so that's what she'll get for now. Besides we're so fucking busy that it's for the best.

I have to concentrate on this fucking equipment, the sprayers have gone to shit. It's sweltering out, and grapes are dying for water. I'm desperate to get someone out here today. We've done all we know how to do, and it's still making a horrible scraping noise and not working. I don't have time for her today. We've said all we need to say, and she still won't trust me. I feel like Charlie Brown kicking the football, never learning that Lucy's going to leave him flat on his ass.

Elle walks by me, and unfortunately, her ass looks spectacular in her flowy cream skirt and lightly colored delicate floral silk blouse. I know she had Apple to contend with this week, and things were prickly. But all I see is the blouse unbuttoned just enough that when she strolls by me, I can see a hint of her coral bra. Coral. She's an asshole. It's the matching bra to the thong I have tucked away in an open envelope in my desk in Santa Barbara. She told me I destroyed it that night.

Now I'm fucking twitching down below. My dick and my head are not on the same wavelength. I need to tell my cock that we don't have time today. I nod to her as to not give away my thoughts. She walks right by. "Hey, Cosmo!"

She doesn't break stride as she heads over to my dad but calls back, "Don't call me that, Suit." I smile. I do enjoy annoying her. It's like a slight respite in this shit day. She floats by, leaving her scent wafting towards me, and I have to turn away so she doesn't see me straining against my zipper.

It's so hot out here, and we need to cool off the Zinfandel before it starts getting dried out. Alena and some of the others are doing punch down on the Merlot. We're going to have to haul hoses or something to keep the Zin cool. We don't have a place to put the fucking fruit if we start picking it now. As cold as August was, it's now blazingly hot and brix in the fruit is rising way too rapidly for us to keep up.

My dad and Elle are talking, and he's pointing to the equipment. My father and I are covered in filth and dust. We look like real farmers, and she looks out of place. Off-kilter. I need to get away from her again so she can't invade my mind. I've stayed at Sam's house for the past couple of days to avoid her. Give her room. Sam thinks she's the greatest thing to happen to me. I felt so too, but her new silent treatment is starting to irk the shit out of me. She even blew off Wednesday night. I'm sure it was to avoid me. Something's gotta give soon.

Now, what the hell is she doing? She's heading out to the vines. Probably to set up more promo shots of a working winemaker. My dad follows her out to the vines. I turn back and walk to the other side of the tasting room, blocking my view of her. I shift my phone while I'm still on hold.

"Any luck?" The most reassuring smile in the world looks at me, unconditionally.

"Nah, Ma, still on hold and nothing's budging. Where you headed?"

"Randy called in sick, and they're down some help in the tasting room. Just going to do a couple of vertical tastings for some wine club members. I don't have time, but there's no one else. Then back to scheduling and payroll."

"Are you going to the cave?"

"No dear, I'll be in the tasting room."

"I'll take over for you when I get off the phone. That way, you can get back to the fun paperwork."

"Oh, goodie!" She kisses me on the cheek. She deserves a break. She's taking on too much. The rest of the desk jockeys are in the fields, or racking, or punching down, or in the tasting room.

I haven't even asked my parents where they're moving after the sale. I wipe my brow and go to take a sip of my fruit punch Gatorade when a voice startles me. I spill the entire freaking bottle down the front of my shirt. I toss the empty bottle and my shirt to the side of the path.

"Thanks for waiting. How can I help you?"

"Hey, Suz. It's Josh Whittier. We need help today. The sprayer's screwed."

"Joshie! Sorry, hon, we can't get there until at least tomorrow afternoon."

"Shit. There's nothing you can do?" And with that, I hear the sprayer come to life. I see water spritzing as I round the building. I listen to cheers erupting. My dad and the workers must have figured it out.

"Scratch that. Looks like we got it."

"Great. Take care, hon."

I hang up the phone and walk towards the vineyard as the team emerges. My jaw drops because her cream skirt and face are covered in black grime and grease. She's holding a ratty bandana to her hand.

She walks past me, bends down to the hose and rinses her hands off. I walk up, and I can't help myself, I smack her ass. She stands immediately, unflappable. She crooks her left eyebrow at me, and it's sexy as hell. I wonder if her ass cheeks are as flush as her face is right now. She ruined her outfit doing manual labor without flinching. And that's hot.

"What voodoo did you do, Cosmo?"

"Stop calling me that."

There's no way I'm letting her golden pussy walk out my life or stop calling her Cosmo. This shit ends right now. "Fine. What did you do, Elle?"

"I fixed it. And the catalytic converter on the front tractor is only going to last another forty miles or so." My jaw is slack as she reaches around and smacks my ass. "You might want to make a note of it, Suit."

How did she do that? Snarky and haughty. She stomps off, still holding the bandana to her hand. My dad smirks at the whole thing and wanders into the tank room.

One of the workers motions to her and says, "I think she cut it on the edge of the hood. It looked kind of bad."

Running after her as she crosses the courtyard to the cave, I call out. I panic because I see blood dripping. "Hey! Cosmo!"

"Fuck off."

I keep following her. "Elle!"

"Leave me alone." She almost enters the cave, and I follow.

"Stop. Truce!"

She slowly turns around. Her hair sticking to her cheek from sweat and mud. But under the grime, her scent makes its way to me. Lilacs and orange blossom fill my nose and break down all my defenses. She cocks her hip and pastes on a defiant look. Her emerald eyes dancing in the sun. Then I see there's some blood on her blouse and skirt as well.

I remove the hair from her cheek. "Let me look at that."

# 21

## ELLE

MY HAND FUCKING HURTS. I DON'T WANT TO BE VULNERABLE in front of Josh. I need him to step away from me. It was too much the other night. I can take care of myself. And why the fuck is he shirtless? Who can look away from that? That's not fair to anyone. Anyone, except maybe his parents, would want to hit that. Good god, this man. How am I supposed to concentrate on anything but his glistening biceps and the pecs that are literally assaulting my eyes like he's a sculpture? Don't get me started on the six-pack. He must work out every spare moment. He's downright yummy, and now my hand is throbbing as well as other parts of me.

I'm only mean to him because I don't think I can stop myself if he stands this close to me half-naked. I can barely contain myself as I come face to face with the most perfect pelvic V dipping into his jeans. That damn V that seems to be inviting me to find its point. I attempt to stop looking.

He's fixing my hair for some reason, and his touch is gentle, but his new slight calluses feel prickly on my cheek. His hands are becoming less venture capitalist's every day.

We're standing face-to-face and closer than we have since the Swiss Hotel where I orgasmed for the whole city to hear.

I'm staring up into those Caribbean sea-blue eyes. They look deep and vast. There's a moment where the world falls away, and there's only us. I'm hoping he doesn't see my pulse quicken. I need the flush in my chest, that's creeping up, to stay put. I break our gaze by looking back at his pecs. Stupid move. Now I want him more despite the bloody injured hand. I keep stealing glances at his pecs that are damn close to perfect. I have a growing need, and my nipples are pulling taut.

"How did you do that?" His voice is low and rumbling through me, making my body come alive.

"Caught it on the edge of the sprayer motor housing."

"No. How did you fix it?"

"I can fix anything."

"This, I know. You are indeed a fixer, but really, anything?" He raises an eyebrow, and I'm about to fucking swoon. He says, "Come with me."

He takes my uninjured hand and pulls me further into the cave into one of the side rooms. He lifts me up, placing me on the edge of the long table set up for tastings. He walks away from me. I take in several large breaths trying to maintain control. My mouth is watering at the thought of his taste. If he keeps touching me, I'm going to slide right off this table.

I'm not caring so much anymore *why* he left but if he'll leave *again*. Perhaps I need to get out of my own way. He swears he's not going anywhere, and I don't see him packing a bag. I see him coming back to his roots. He shows up to Wednesday nights. He picks up Mrs. Dotson's groceries at Sonoma Market even though Whole Foods is more convenient. She insists she doesn't trust a chain market. He washes all the cars in the parking lot regularly. He was twitchy before, one foot out the door, but now he seems rooted. Sammy told me he was talking with Sam about that label he wants to start. Maybe he's coming up with a plan B as well.

Oh god. His back is just as good as his pecs right now. He's turned away from me to get a little tub of water, broad shoulders sweaty and glistening from the sun. This is the asshole who gave you the most fabulous orgasms of my life and then disappeared for almost three months. Fucking shut me out. Hold on to your anger, Elle. His abs are toasted brown, and I wonder how often he's without his shirt. Focus!

"Where did you learn to fix anything?"

"Kansas. Morris County." I have no cause to hide anything from him.

"Internship?" He laughs at his own joke.

"Seven hundred and twenty-two acres of premium soil outside of Council Grove with the name Doyle on it." He turns quickly back to me.

"Relatives?"

"My last name is Doyle. Parker was my mother's maiden name."

"I thought you grew up in New York. A farm was your parent's asset when they died? You sold the family farm."

"Yup. I'm a farmer's daughter. Or Brittany Noelle Doyle was." And my deepest secret and regret is revealed. I too ran away from the family business. I ran from my legacy and destiny. I ran from them to college far away, and they knew I wasn't going to come back. They let me go too. I reinvented myself in another place and launched a business. Who am I to judge what this man's done with his past?

But I wasn't there when they died. I had to be told by a stranger. I'm not sure I'll ever get over that. That may be why I've been so angry at Josh. I'm pissed that he cut his parent's out of his life. I don't want that for Josh. I don't wish that on anyone.

The three of us were all we had. An only child of two only children, like Josh. But he still has his brothers and sisters of the five families that he grew up with. He just forgot they were here. I had no one, and now I have them too. I have Evan. And I don't want to believe that I can have all of this because I'd perish if it were taken away from me.

I buried Brittany when I buried them. I shut the door on my childhood. I was afraid it would be too painful to open any part of it.

"Oh, sweet girl, you're not cosmopolitan at all are you?"

"I told you."

"You did, beautiful, but I didn't listen. It won't happen again. Let me take care of you. I want to hear all about your parents and how you'll justify your hypocrisy. I do, but I'm worried about your hand, and we have business to discuss."

He strides to me with a first aid kit in his hand. The air shifts around us with my revelation. He surrounds me and places the kit on the table. My breath hitches when his musk hits my nose. It just makes me want to spread my legs. But mine are pinned between his legs, so I submit.

"Take these."

I swallow a couple of Advil and a sip of water. He has a wet soapy washcloth in his hand as he removes the blood-soaked bandana. I imagine what it would feel like to soap up his chest, and suddenly it hurts. "Ow. OW. Ow."

"I'm sorry."

There's a moment when I don't know whether he's talking about hurting me or leaving me. I stare at him and look for clarity. He's focused on my hand.

"Let me see it. I'll be gentle." He looks into my eyes while holding my hand, and I smile as he winks at me.

"I know."

"Elle."

"Yes."

"I'm done waiting. I'm taking the burden of decision away from you." I'm literally trapped, pinned between his legs. I can't run, but that's all I want to do. Screw my hand.

"It's fine. Don't. Please don't. It's not necessary. I told you it's fine. Ouch."

"It doesn't have to be fine. Dammit, Elle."

His voice shifts. There's a hard edge to it. No more caring but truly angry. His eyes narrow, and I'm a little nervous.

"It is."

"No!" Now he's yelling. "THIS SHIT ENDS NOW."

I plead with him, "No, please. Stop."

He stops yelling, but there is a sharpness to him. "I am done letting your fear rule us. If I make sense, then you have no more excuses to push me away. I know you're afraid that if my excuse is valid, then all your reasons to be alone fall away."

I spit back at him, "Reasons for what?"

"To protect yourself. To deny us. This." He gestures between the two of us. "This. This connection, this soul-fulfilling connection between us. But what if there's not pain on the other side of your fear."

Tears tease the back of my eyes. He needs to stop. He can't tell me these things because I don't know how to stop the floodgates of emotions. I'm holding the last shred of myself hostage, away from him. Tucked away so no one can get to core of me. I can't feel this much for someone else and not crumble when they're gone.

"You are so fucking scared to care about me without limits because you'll lose me. You're terrified because you know I care about you without limits already."

"You can't say things like this and not expect me to fall apart. I don't know if I'm strong enough for any of this." I don't know how to do this. I don't know how to let him in and protect myself.

"You're kidding, right? No one is stronger than you. I'm terrified that when I'm done telling you my story, you'll be done with me. I'm scared shitless about what's on the other side of this moment for us. But mostly, Elle, I'm petrified of becoming Joshua again. I don't want to lose me. The 'me' you found and opened up. He can only exist with you. And I sure as hell don't want to lose you. I know, babe. I know you're so afraid of being devastated that you live in a constant state of nothingness and anger right now. But if you fall apart, I'll be here to help you pick up the pieces."

He's saying all the things that should logically make me leap into his arms. It's like a Hallmark Christmas movie finale, but I'm paralyzed. "There's always devastation. I can't tumble into that abyss again. Leave it alone."

"I see the flashes of us, and you still feel them too. Time to cut the shit. It's time to listen because I'm done waiting. It's not fair to either of us. You're already a part of me. Gather up your denial. All your reasons are bullshit, they're laughable in the face of what we already have. So, with all due respect, shut the fuck up my beautiful, stubborn, infuriating, Elle. Listen."

His voice crescendos into a giant booming reverb echoing through the cave. I can't help but laugh at his power. He kisses me on my grimy forehead while I laugh at him.

"You do love to hear yourself talk." All those times I had to decide everything and all those times I complained that I didn't have anyone and here he is deciding for me. He's begging to be with me so that I'm not alone.

"It was a dick move not to trust you with this information. But know that what I did was for your safety and protection."

"What are you talking about?" This is not what I expected at all.

"There were threats. We'll go into all of it later. I put you in harm's way, and I had to leave to keep you safe. I needed to keep you safe like I need to breathe. I was desperately trying to make sure nothing would touch you. Especially because it was my fault. Despite the fact that I was told not to tell anyone, I knew if I shared it all with you that you'd do something stupid. You would have followed me or demanded I let you take care of it. I couldn't risk it. So, I left. I left to fix it. And I came back not just because my dad called. But because of the possibility of you. I've never felt anything like this before, it's bigger than both of our bullshit."

I'm incensed as my world and thoughts flip upside down. "Fuck yeah, I would have followed you. Who did this to you? Fucking helicopter man? That piece of shit." A realization comes over me like a sudden chill. "Holy shit. The Ritz Carlton bar." He grins uncontrollably at me.

"Yes, my brilliant girl. I sent Bax to run interference, but you thankfully went upstairs. The man sent me a text threatening you. It was a picture of you at the Ritz bar."

"That rather formal Italian-looking man. Fucker. Is that why we all of a sudden have a series of brawny men working for minimum wage who tend to sleep in their cars at the entrance of the Emma Farm? And follow me to the Basque for coffee?"

"You're too smart." He tucks my hair behind my ear.

"Are you safe? Are we all safe? Do I need to protect you? Can I kick his ass? I will cut a bitch. Brittney Doyle doesn't fucking play."

He laughs, heartily, and kisses my non injured hand. It's as if a door burst wide open ushering in all of my possessiveness and caring. Every emotion I hid and buried away cascades over this moment. His eyes soften as he takes in my contemplation.

My adrenaline is still surging at his explanation and how pissed I am at this mystery man. I speak a little too loudly.

"How did you stop him? What did you do? Are you okay? Did they threaten Sarah or Will? I can rewire or hot-wire anything and used to be pretty handy with a shotgun."

He speaks with an even tone, "Slow it down there, Bonnie, no need for me to be Clyde. No one needs a sawed-off in this scenario. We're safe because of the understanding he and I have. And there are other forces that we'll talk about later in place to make sure we stay safe. I've invested a lot of money for him. Never dirty money. But it's a long story. You don't need all the details."

"The hell I don't. If it affects you, it affects me." Well, that came out of fucking nowhere. A broad smile blooms across his face as he keeps working on my hand and never looks up.

Then he pulls my overgrown bangs back behind my ear. "Babe, it's over for the moment, and that's why I left you. It tore me in half to hurt you. To not be able to reassure you that I was never really gone. It was a dark time. I didn't know how long it would last so I set about trying to move on. But I couldn't. I was despondent. I missed the feel and smell of you. But I also ached to know what you ate for lunch or how much more you grew to hate that ginger barista at Peet's."

"A whole hell of a lot. He's a smug asshole who thinks he's some kind of god of coffee. It's a freaking drip roast, asshat, get over it. Him and his pour-over bullshit. Shut up, ginger."

Josh drags me to him and kisses me quickly. It's a light peck of affection, and I just want more.

He has more to say while he works on my hand. "I didn't know how to get out from under him. I didn't know how long it would take or if I would ever get out. I couldn't handle the fucking pain of it all. I decided to get over you so that I never put you in danger again."

"Claudia?"

"Claudia. And I need you to know I would fucking shred

and kill anyone who hurts you. Then Dad called and I didn't hesitate."

"And you came back." I flatten my good palm to his chest and feel his heartbeat.

He exhales as he looks at me. "And then clarity."

I ask, "What do you mean?"

"Being near you gave me clarity."

I wince in pain as he finishes cleaning out my cuts and putting peroxide on it.

"I've got you. Almost done."

Do I trust him? Do I throw myself at him? I don't know what to do with this information. He didn't want to leave. He wanted me. I want to forgive him for that. I'm scared, but I also want him to eat me out until I can't see straight. But if I'm sincere, I also want him to be here tomorrow. And take control away from me sometimes. I want someone on my side.

He cleans off the blood and discovers a small sliver of metal. He reaches behind me to get tweezers from the first aid kit, and I close my eyes and inhale him. His skin is so hot as it brushes mine. He reacts as we come in contact like he's surprised to touch me. As he eases the sliver out, it hurts intensely, and then there's a rush of relief from the absence of pain. There's a flip side to pain. I always forget that.

He looks at me, still holding my hand. I try to take it back, and he won't let it go. He bandages it and then pulls it to his face. I stare at him as he kisses my bandage.

"There. Now it's all better."

"Thank you." I attempt to scoot off the table. I'm trapped between his legs, and now I can't stop staring at his lips. His nose is slightly pink from a day of saving the fruit. He's dirty, sweaty, and smells like the bed after a good shag. Our breath quickens and gets shallow as we stare at each other. I look down to try to break this spell. This man that I hated more than anything, apparently wrongly so, looks so fucking good I can hardly contain myself.

"Time to trust me. I'm not going anywhere. I will fight the grim reaper off to prove it to you. Let's be scared together. Be with me, Elle."

His hand, warm from the sun, lifts my chin. I take in a sharp breath and part my lips to speak. To tell him I need to go. I have no sound. I'm frozen in place. Then his lips are on me, and I let him make this decision.

My whole body is full of his warm summer heat. His tongue is delicately exploring and licking into mine. He's gentle, but I am not. It's like a dam has finally broken. I flood into his mouth, all of my rational thought, excuses, and decorum are gone. He pulls me closer, and his kiss takes all that I have. All that matters are those large hands on my back and sliding down to the top of my ass. His touch. His breath. His noises. He's flirting with the top of my thong. I feel for his pelvic V.

"You're so hard."

He reaches under my skirt and says, "And I can smell it. You're as wet as I dream of."

# 22

---

## JOSH

My Hellcat is bewitching me. I may have emotionally redeemed myself, but right now, I'm going to eat her alive. I'm going to fuck her until there's only me in her memory. We can chase away each other's pain. I'm not sure I'll be able to stop. Maybe we'll spend days and months just she and I exploring everything about each other. Everything is different. This kiss is so much more.

I can't think of anything that would make me walk away from this woman ever again. All the shit I've shoved down for years bubbles up around me because of her. The history of the winery, my role, my friends, my family, and her. They're intertwined now. All the bullshit I've held onto for far too long has broken loose in this kiss. In her forgiveness and in her trust. A life is possible here. Ten minutes ago, she hated me, and now she's mine. I intend to keep it that way.

I reach under her skirt to the top of her thighs and then back out again. She moans in approval. That's now the soundtrack to my life. Her moan will be my ringtone, my alarm clock, and my doorbell. This cave room has no doors, and the sound gloriously echoes. I move my hands back up and graze her thong just to hear it again. She satisfies my unsaid desire.

I want to taste her until she screams so loudly, the casks uncork. I slide my hands around her to the top of her ass, and she leans into me. I need to rip this woman open and own her.

She reaches for my shorts, and I need her to obey me right now. Like she would never do in the real world. But here, in my cave, moving towards sex, I need her to obey. I pull back, and she clutches at me with her good hand.

"Tell me how wet you are?"

"Very. I can tell you this..."

"Only answer what I ask." I rub my finger over her lips, and she licks it. She grins as she gets my game and nods in approval. I lean forward and move my now wet finger inside the top of her bra. I want to get her so turned on she explodes. I want to draw this moment out. I dip in further to find her perfectly hard nipple. She reaches for my zipper again.

"No, Hellcat. We're just touching you right now. I'm not sure I have time to redden both sets of cheeks, so do as I say." I step to the side so I can spread her legs and step back between them.

"Scoot to the edge of the table. I want you to feel my hard cock. But not with your hands." She rubs herself on me with her legs wrapped around my hips. The moment of contact has us both gasping at the friction. Her hands are caressing my chest. Like she did that day in the parking lot when we got interrupted. That will not happen here.

She's moaning in my ear as I make my way to her neck, grazing it with my tongue and teeth. She's furiously kissing and licking my shoulders with an occasional nip like she's snacking on me. She's rocking forward, and her clit is searching for my dick, even through her panties.

Elle's driving me and my cock to tear off our clothes. It's pushing against my shorts and needs to be set free. I move against her, and her body responds in kind. Her good hand begins to move, and I slap it. She pouts.

I snarl. "Then tell me."

She leans to my ear while I'm between her breasts, still sheathed in the coral bra. She gasps. "I want you right now. I need you more than anything I've ever wanted in my life."

I look at her face, almost smashing my nose into hers. "Tell me again. No games. This is everything. Tell me now, Elle. Words." We're locked on each other's eyes. I flatten my palms to the table on either side of her.

She doesn't flinch or blink. "I want you."

"Not just my cock."

"All of you. No games." Her softened eyes cut into my soul. Trust. Finally, débourbage. There's no filtering or fining needed, just clarity. Submission to the idea of us.

I cup her face and pause. "Where you go, I go from now on. I won't leave, and you don't pull away. Got it?"

"I do." Tears fill her eyes.

I ask again to make sure she knows this is it. "Do you? Do you hear me? Say it."

"Josh, where you go, I go."

I'm super serious. "I mean it. No running. No leaving. Together. You and me. This is it. This is everything. We face everything together. Things will get hard, but no more separation. I am unable to be without you from now on."

She speaks really sarcastically, "I do. I totally get it. I'm super happy about it, but right now I really need your insanely large and throbbing cock inside of me."

"There's my dirty girl. I have a great desire to make you keep moaning, so you guide me to that sound." I capture her lips, and she moans quietly.

"Louder."

"There are other parts of me that like to be kissed as well."

I move my hands up her thighs, dipping into her thong. I begin to trace her folds, and...

In the distance, we hear a tremendous crash. Both of our heads jerk apart, and she immediately sits up straight. She attempts to get off the table. I lower my voice, "You can't leave me, remember?" I grab her wrist and pull her back to me. She attacks my lips, smashing her tongue into me. Then my body goes cold when I hear a detached, weakened voice.

"Help! Is somebody there? Please. Somebody help." My dick instantly goes limp as her eyes widen. We bolt towards where we hear my mother.

# 23

## ELLE

"OH MY GOD, Sarah!" I didn't mean to scream so loudly, but there's so much blood. Her eyes are closed. It appears that his mother dropped a couple of bottles of wine but then fell on the broken glass. There's broken glass everywhere. The smell of Merlot and the copper of her blood cloud everything. She must have had a tremor or a moment of weakness.

"Mom. MOM! Can you hear me? Elle! Call someone!" I'm already on my phone, but there's no reception in the cave. I bolt to the house phone in the tasting table room. I call 911. I alert everyone, and we're whisked away in an instant from the cave and the moment I just shared with Josh.

---

THE WORLD IS a bit upside down as I deliver coffee to everyone in the waiting room. She's been in surgery for about an hour now. They felt it was better to sew her wounds knowing she won't twitch, so they put her under general anesthesia. Apparently one of the cuts was super deep and dangerous. I sit down next to Will, and he turns to me. "Did you hear anything else? Did you see anything?"

Josh responds from across the room. "Dad. We were at the tasting table. I was cleaning out Elle's wound, which by the way, you need to go get a tetanus shot while we're in a hospital. We heard nothing until the crash."

I smile at him, and under his veil of concern, he smirks at me. My hand is throbbing, but I'm hoping the volume of Advil I took will help. Then my eyes flick back to his face, and I sigh. We're both sharing the memory of us on that table. I don't know what the hell any of that means. My heart does a little flip as he looks at me and does that lip curl thing he does. It undoes me and makes me want to mount him right here. My phone pings a text.

*JOSH: Thanks for being here.*

I look over at him and smile a bit of a toothy grin. Feels oddly intimate to be texting in front of everyone.

*JOSH: I'm sipping this coffee, but I only taste you. I should be thinking about my mom, but the only thing I can think of is how the heat from my hand can pebble your skin instantly.*

*JOSH: And the only thing I hear is that gorgeous fucking gasp from your too perfect lips when I touch you. I'm almost hard thinking of making you sound like that. Tell me you don't sound like that for anyone else. That it's just for me.*

Dammit, now I'm wet again. My nipples will give me up under this destroyed silk blouse in a minute. Oh my god, this man. I can't believe that by hearing his story, it unleashed me from the bubble of loneliness I was living inside.

*JOSH: Tell me that no one makes you moan like that.*

*ELLE: No.*

*JOSH: You won't tell me. What if I demand it? As your boss.*

*ELLE: First off, that's sexual harassment. Second off, the answer is no, no one has ever made me sound like that.*

*JOSH: You're mine. Not sure you're getting this concept.*

*ELLE: Honestly? That was the only reason you left. This isn't bullshit?*

*JOSH: That wasn't enough? Come on, I have no other secrets to share. And you have no more secrets. We're clean and open now. I told you everything. What's that face about?*

*ELLE: Are you leaving?*

Now he's angry at me. He's texting aggressively, and I'm a little worried.

*JOSH: Listen to me right fucking now. I will tell you this over and over until you get my point. Until we're old. Like early-bird-special old. Mall-walking old. Until our last breaths, which I've decided have to be at the same time when we're like a hundred and twenty. But even that won't be enough time with you.*

*ELLE: I'm listening.*

*JOSH: Where I go, you go, and wherever I go, you go. You need to be in New York, I'm there. Plan B is San Fran, I'm there. My house in Santa Barbara, you're with me. I was without you around me for three months and a lifetime before that. You're my OPT. Your body, your heart, your unfounded fears, your mind, and your annoying way of correcting everything. You have no out. And neither do I. I trust you.*

*JOSH: Do you trust me?*

My eyes well up as I look up to him. He stares at me and points to his heart. My whole life turns on a text. I've just decided, I never want a day that doesn't include him. From now on. I don't know how to slow myself down from falling this hard for him.

*ELLE: OPT?*

*JOSH: One Perfect Thing.*

My breath catches as my eyes glass over. I place my hand on my heart at his sentiment. The one born directly from his parents' happiness.

*ELLE: I trust you.*

*JOSH: I want all the strings attached.*

*ELLE: Me too.*

He takes my breath away for a different reason now. I wipe my tears with my good hand. He hears me gasp, and the look of adoration in his eyes is something I'm ready to have forever. I pull us back to flirting. Now that I know how he really feels, and he knows I'm all in as well.

*ELLE: What's his name?*

*JOSH: Who?*

*ELLE: The man that kept those words from me for almost twelve weeks. He fucking owes me.*

*JOSH: Salvatore Pietro. But you'll never meet him.*

*ELLE: He's in big fucking trouble if I do. Making me believe I was alone. That you rejected me. Made me doubt the connection I'd never felt before in my life. Robbing me of my sanity and you for three months.*

*JOSH: What's three months against a lifetime, Hellcat? You'll never be alone again. As your boss you're going to need to take me at face value here.*

What is he promising me?

*ELLE: You're not my boss.*

*JOSH: Maybe not in the paycheck realm, but I am in control of you right now.*

*ELLE: You think so?*

*JOSH: My tongue wants to rim your tits and slowly sip and swirl down your body and suckle your clit until...*

I am dying. I'm dead. I need him so badly. And he knows he has me.

*ELLE: Until what?*

*JOSH: I did that to your chest. See that flush of red. That's me. See...I'm in charge. I'm the boss of your blushing. I'm the only one that makes you sound like that. I'm now the only one that gets to make you come. Well, you can do it too if you like.*

*ELLE: You know there have been others, but they weren't as good. And I believe you've seen me try to get myself off but was interrupted.*

*JOSH: We've been over this, there were no others.*

*ELLE: That's right. I forgot.*

*JOSH: I do want to watch and study your technique. That image has been burned in my brain, and soon I'm going to need you to finish that performance for me.*

*ELLE: Right now?*

*JOSH: Tempting, Hellcat. Tell me again that Asher never made you sound like that.*

And now I need him to know that I can control him too. Whatever sexual desire he's opened in me, it was like Pandora's box, and everything else came out with it.

*ELLE: Not him, not anyone has ever made me sound the way you do. Asher, Gavin, and all the men in Bali never made me lose my breath like you just did when you mentioned touching me. And I'm not talking size, although you win there too. I see you. I want you. My body needs your glistening granite. Your text made me wetter than any man ever could dream of.*

*JOSH: Good. FUCKING Christ. You're perfect. Sexy as fuck. I need my mom to be okay. I want to be fucking you right now.*

I read it and look up at him. He's staring at me. Not with the same hunger that was in the cave but with a new desire. I want to go over and hold his hand and comfort him. Is that who we are? Am I allowed to do that? Then I'm distracted again by his body. He grabbed a LC/W t-shirt from the tasting room that's a size too small. His pecs are outlined, and the bottom of the shirt keeps popping up. I realize that I don't want him to be with anyone else either.

*ELLE: Tell me Claudia didn't make you feel the way I make you feel.*

*JOSH: I had to think of you to get through it. I imagined your tongue, pussy, hands, mind, voice and heart. She and all women are nothing compared to you, Cosmo.*

*ELLE: That's nice hear.*

When Sarah wakes up and we know she's okay, I'm going to tell him how I feel about him. I could be wrong because what I feel for him is so much more than what I have ever felt. I'm afraid to put language to it. Now that I'm letting myself feel all of it. I didn't know I could care this much. I didn't know if this part of me still worked. I'd shut that part off when my parents were killed.

*ELLE: Sarah will be okay.*

He nods at me.

*JOSH: Then will I get to continue playing doctor?*

I can play that game too.

*ELLE: I think I can keep that appointment. What are you doing to me, Suit?*

*JOSH: Hopefully making you feel even a portion of how badly I want to fuck you. I want you right now.*

I close my eyes and throw my head back, biting my lip even thinking about it. When I open my eyes, he's staring at me hungrily. My hand is throbbing but I'm trying to ignore. Texting hurts a little.

*JOSH: I want to make you scream. I need to hear it. I need you to beg and moan my name. And to make you come so hard you lose all track of time and space.*

*ELLE: Let's find a dark corner so I can feel all of you. I want to feel your shaft in my hand, my mouth, and in the deepest part of me.*

*JOSH: Fuck. Elle. Fuck. I need that. I need you.*

*ELLE: I can smell you from here, and that's enough for me to want to tear into you. How about you bend me over the nurses' station. Will you make sounds for me too?*

*JOSH: That I can do. My balls have never been this blue.*

*ELLE: As blue as your eyes?*

*JOSH: Yes. Are your nipples the same shade as your cheeks when you blush? When you're thinking of my chest?*

*ELLE: Yes. Maybe a little darker like when I'm thinking of your cock.*

*JOSH: You do talk pretty.*

*ELLE: LOL.*

*JOSH: You know I can see that you didn't actually LOL. I mean, I'm sitting right here.*

He waves to me, and I giggle. His father and other assorted vineyard workers are all looking at him looking at me. I go back to my phone. Oh shit. My hand is bleeding.

*ELLE: Asshole.*

*JOSH: Yes.*

*ELLE: I'll be right back.*

*JOSH: Scoping a dark corner so I can devour you?*

*ELLE: Nothing quite as sexy. My hand opened back up and is bleeding. I'm headed for stitches or at least that glue stuff.*

He stands up and exclaims, "I'll go with you."

"No, stay here."

I'm touched by his attentiveness. It's the chemistry of more. Pushing beyond what we physically want to do to each other. There's a look between us as I shake my head no and he knows he should stay here with his dad.

24
———

JOSH

WHEN I GET THE WORD THAT MOM'S ALRIGHT, I'M GOING
directly to Elle and whisking her away to a beach to have her
for the next several days. Screw harvest. They can handle it
for a couple of days while I take her in every way possible. I
won't let her escape without coming many, many times and
in many different ways. Just her. I want her whole body to
flush under my touch. I need more. I need to possess her like
she owns me. We'll say all the things we haven't said. We'll
reveal all things we've been afraid of saying. All of my
thoughts, all of my heart, and all of my life is now filled with
Elle.

I trust her with my heart, with the Vineyard, and for the
moment, my dick. She's never lied to me. She's completely
open with her intentions and actions. She may hide what's
going on inside, but she's never faked anything. I get that
Sam thing, there's not enough time together. There will
never be enough time with Elle. Dear lord. I'm consumed
by her.

My mind shifts to the doctor exiting the door and

removing his mask. My father rushes to him, and I'm fast on his heels.

"She's lost a lot of blood and needs to stay here at least overnight. We had to give her a bit of a transfusion. I'd like to move her to UCSF when she's stable and get her looked at by a specialist in the next day or two. I don't think there's any permanent nerve damage, but it can be tough to tell in these situations."

The color finally returns to my father's face as he says, "Thank you so much. I understand. Can I see her? Is she awake?" I release my father's hand that I've been clutching, and we hug deeply. My father releases his tension into me. I'm so fucking relieved she's okay. I wasn't sure why she had to be whisked into surgery. But there was so much blood.

"She's coming around, but we're going to give her a sedative soon. It would be best if she slept. Not just rest. But we'll give her something to really give her some deep restorative sleep. She has a lot of sutures and some glue. We need them to hold through the night. We wrapped her up pretty tightly so that nothing will come undone should it happen again. But for now, she needs to stay put—"

I interrupt the doctor. "Happen again? That she slips and falls again?"

The doctor puts his hand on my shoulder and says, "Exactly. She's on her way up to 1401."

I'm entirely at a loss as to why this doctor thinks my mom is a klutz. But I don't care. I want to get to Elle. The doctor leaves as I quickly text Elle that I'm coming to find her. "Dad. Are you okay?"

"I am if she is."

"I know, Dad." He hugs me again and won't let go. He sniffles for just a second, and my heart warms at how much the two of them are in love. "I want to check on Elle's hand

and make sure she gets a tetanus shot. She went to the emergency room to have it looked at. We'll be right up."

"Okay. It's better if I see her first anyway. Go check on Noelle. If she needs anything, you let us know."

I kiss my dad on the cheek then bolt to find Elle. She's all bandaged up and has found my mom's surgeon. I approach her from behind.

Elle sounds concerned. "I'm worried that this will delay her trial start."

I had no idea that Mom was in some kind of legal trouble. What the hell is she talking about? I hang back to hear more. The doctor nods, acknowledging me, and he's well aware that I'm listening, but Elle is not.

"What about the medication she's on? Will that affect the healing?"

"It's why we need her to go to the clinic. They'll be able to deal with this a lot better than we can. She bled so much because of the blood thinners, and clotting was a nightmare. It's such a multi-layered disease."

My heart stops as well as my feet. Disease. Is the doctor talking about my mother? Or Elle? My mom? And why is Elle getting this information? Is she on her HIPA list? What the fuck is going on?

"I had a great aunt with it, but there wasn't much hope for her once she was diagnosed. It was so long ago and she was way advanced. I'm so happy that Sarah has so much support and many options ahead of her. Thank you so much, Doc—"

"What the hell did you just say?" My voice booms way too loudly and sharply for the hospital hallway. I can't help it. Elle whips around and looks at me, surprised. Her face lights up when she sees me. What the fuck? She's acting innocent, but she's guilty. She's totally shady right now.

She steps to me, and I back away. "I was just discussing your mom's condition in regards to her disease."

Her green eyes that I'd found so enchanting twenty minutes ago are now filled with betrayal for me. "Why the fuck would you be discussing it? What do you mean, *disease*? My mom is sick? You knew she was sick and didn't tell me? You kept this from me?" I stomp closer to the two of them at my full height and full asshole stance.

I raise my voice and say, "You knew my mother has a disease. You knew why she fell and yet you stayed fucking silent?"

The doctor looks at me quizzically. "Don't worry, her Parkinson's is totally under control right now. It's simply the blood loss we need to deal with. We had to give her some blood during the procedure, and now we monitor."

I sputter out, "My mother has Parkinson's?" It's like being punched in the gut. I have no breath. She has Parkinson's. And Elle kept it from me.

"Josh? Are you okay? There's no way you didn't know about this. What's wrong?" She moves towards me, urgently, her voice pleading. I step away from her. What the hell did she think she was doing? Hiding this? Is this a sick game? Distracting me with sex and never telling me my mother has Parkinson's disease. This is something I won't ever get past. Who knew I had a deal-breaker? But betrayal, secrets, and lies about my own mother seems a pretty solid reason to cut her instantly out of my life. That was quick. I'm done.

I take a flat and icy tone. "No. Not okay. Everything's wrong. Leave. Get out of our lives. Get your shit. Get out of our Farmhouse. Take your lying conniving, untrustworthy ass back to New York. We don't need you. Pack. I don't want you anywhere near my family or me again. Get the hell out of my life." It's cutting my heart to hurt her, but this is too much. Too much of a betrayal. My mom is sick and Elle knew. They were selling the winery and Elle knew why. She kept me in the dark.

"Josh. What? You're making no sense. What are you talking about?"

"We're done here, little liar."

"I never lied. Listen to me. Josh. Josh!! Please!! How could you not know?"

My voice takes on a stronger, deeper tone, and it even scares me a bit. "Shut up, Noelle. Shut up. Get out of my sight. Forever. This is it. Our will they won't, they dance is done. Are you fucking kidding me? You've got to go. All this time and you said *nothing* to me. I can't with you. Why the hell was the doctor discussing intimate medical details with you and not *me*, their actual child?"

She's instantly crying. I turn my back as she pleads. "I don't get this. Josh. Josh, you have to listen to me. Don't do this. Listen to me. I never…I didn't know."

I roar at her. "No. *I* didn't know! Apparently, all this was a fucking illusion. Am I part of your lying? Fuck you for making me feel something. And fuck you for being a lying—"

"Don't say that word. Don't you dare."

I turn away. I'll give her that. I won't use the word bitch to her face, but she knows I'm thinking about it. I run down the hallway to the stairway and the slam of the door silences her. I'm not sure what I'll do if I ever see or hear her again. I've never been this angry or deceived. How sick is my mother? And how long has this stranger known about it? It doesn't matter. Noelle Parker didn't ever really belong to me.

## 25

## ELLE

I PACE AROUND SOBBING AS THE NURSE BRINGS OVER MY release papers and tissues. What did I do? Good lord, that's a lot. Did he really not know? How? How could Will and Sarah do that to him? How could they do that to me? They're so open about it. Was he not seeing his mom's decline? Maybe his mind has been making up stories to explain all of it away. Now he thinks I lied and kept this from him. They have to explain to him. Oh god. He was so angry. But this is just a misunderstanding. They'll tell him.

*ELLE: This is silly. Josh, listen to me. Please, we need to talk about this. You don't understand. Talk to your parents. You're not really mad at me, are you?*

*JOSH: Give me a minute.*

*ELLE: Josh.*

I dial his number and it's sent to voicemail. I don't think I should go upstairs, but I want to. I'm baffled. I sit down behind a curtain and try not to bolt upstairs. I sit there watching shadows for close to twenty minutes when my phone rings.

"Josh."

"I'm asking one question. I need you to answer completely honestly."

"Anything."

"Did they tell you not to tell me?"

"No. I—" He interrupts me.

"No more talking. I can't. I don't care what you're answer is. I can't pretend. All this shit is in my head right now. That means you thought you were in on something against me? Even if you didn't know, I didn't know. How could you never bring it up? Do you think if your mom had Parkinson's, I wouldn't be all over that with you? Clearly you don't care. This is all a fucking joke. I can't be with someone like you."

"Josh, I don't know where to begin. You can't think that of me. I thought you didn't want to talk about it. I was giving you space to process."

"Fuck, Elle. You probably knew I was in the dark. And you thought telling me would ruin the sale, right? Pop your perfect bubble? You can control everything, even me, huh?"

"What are you making up in your head?"

"Go. Get out my home. Pack a bag or two and leave the Farmhouse tonight."

And he hangs up. I call back immediately, but it just goes to voicemail.

*ELLE: Josh. Really? This is all over?*

*JOSH: I can't wrap my head around any of this. Really. It's over. Get away from us. This is a time for family.*

*ELLE: Josh, please. Don't do this.*

My texts bounce back. He's blocked me.

I sit down on a chair in the waiting room and sob. The first thing I tried not to control. I just let it happen, and now I'm devastated by one moment. Never again will I let anyone in. I'm headed as far away from Josh as possible. Walls will be repaired.

# 26

---

## WILL

She's my wife and my life. I need her to wake up. She's my world. They said she was okay. They said it was just cuts. Cuts heal. Please don't take her yet. It's all I can think of. We were told we could manage this for another twenty years or more. We caught it early. There's still tests and meds and trials. I thought we'd still have time together that might have to be a little slower than others, but it was going to be just us. It would be us. I'd sell a hundred vineyards just to keep her with me a moment longer.

She's so pale. The pink to her cheeks is gone as is her ever-present smile. Whether it's one of disdain, disgust, or joy, she's almost always wearing a version of it. I'd like Elle to come up here so I can tell her a whole bunch of stuff that needs to be done. I need Sarah to wake up and give Elle a to-do list like she does every day for all of us.

I need her to go get Sarah's meds so we can bring them to the clinic. All of them, even the ones she stopped taking because of nausea or dizziness. She needs clothes. The yoga pants she likes and pajamas. I can't leave her to go get these things. And the dogs need to go out. Her eyes flutter just as I think of the dogs, and I hear Josh running in down the hallway and into the room. I rush to her bed.

"I'm here, my love. Your arms are restrained, don't pull them. Let the nurse untie them. Don't be alarmed."

They were restrained so that if she had a twitching fit, she wouldn't pop a stitch or fling her arm into a solid surface. They're loose restraints.

"Nod if you can understand me, my One Perfect Thing."

She contorts her lips into a version of the smile I crave and nods at me. She looks to the door and begins to silently weep. I turn. Josh is in the doorway, arms crossed and tearing up. He wipes away the evidence that our little boy still lives in that angry and confused body. I get up from my chair to give him access to his mother.

"Mom. You scared the crap out of us."

Sarah tries to smile again. I leave to get the nurse.

## 27

## JOSH

MY MOM LOOKS SO SMALL. SHE'S FORMIDABLE IN MY MIND. She's a giant in the world, but here under this fuzzy gray blanket, she looks as if she'd fit into a rabbit warren. I touch her cheek, and she leans into my hand. I need to know everything about her and what's happening.

My dad reenters the room. I'm still furious at Elle and them, but I have to compartmentalize. I need to bury my anger for my parents. I need to stop replaying the cave tasting table scene. She's a fucking liar. She saw me as vulnerable and took advantage.

The nurses remove her restraints, and after she's had a sip of water, she speaks in a whisper.

"Where's Elle?" That's her first fucking thought? How about an 'I'm sorry' to your only son?

"Why?" I cross my arms and feel the blood rise in my neck. My dad puts his hands on my shoulders.

"Son. What's wrong? Where's Elle? Is her hand okay?"

"It's fine. I sent her away. I fired her."

My mom whispers, "Why?"

"She can't be trusted. Mom. I don't want you to worry

about this right now. I want you to get better. They'll be right back to give you something to help you sleep."

She nods weakly, unable to respond right now. I'll confront them about the Parkinson's later. I hope I can keep my temper under control for a while. I need to bury this pain as well as any feelings I have for her, everything simmering right under the surface. The duplicity is stabbing at my stomach and heart. Why not just tell me that's why you're fucking selling the vineyard? It kills me that Elle knows their complete motives, and I didn't.

I help my mom sip some more water. Her best friends, Theresa Langerford and Tina Gelbert, step into the room with flowers. I slip to the hallway. I can still taste Elle on my lips, and I need it to stop. I unblock her. Was a dumb move, but I wanted to get my point across. There are fourteen missed texts and calls. All Elle. All within thirty minutes and then nothing.

*ELLE: I'm not sure what's going on.*

*ELLE: I thought you knew and just weren't ready to talk about it. We weren't in the best place to discuss your mother. You bit my head off when I tried to discuss your grandfather and he's dead.*

*ELLE: I didn't know they didn't know they were keeping it from you. Your mom asked me to not talk about it in public. So I never did.*

*ELLE. FINE. Message received. BUT tell your Dad to call me. The doctors need to know that she didn't take her Levodopa today or her other medication. I just checked.*

*ELLE: Josh. Please talk to me. Tell me she's okay.*

*ELLE: Josh. Please let me know she's okay. Please let me know that Sarah is okay. Even if you never talk to me again. Please let me know if she's ok.*

*ELLE: Do you really want me to go? I will do what you want. But know that I do care about your mother and father and my work here. And you. I care for you. I can send someone from my firm to finish the project. You can fire me, but you can't fire my firm.*

I get pissed off all over again as she tells me about her contract and keeping Mom's secret. My mother wasn't the one kissing her hours ago. My mother hasn't been up with her late at night, sipping wine and listening to the vineyard and sharing our souls. My mother wasn't sharing things that had been buried for years. Fuck her.

*JOSH: She's fine. We got it. And yes, you need to leave the Farmhouse by tonight. Send the information for our new contact to myself and Chelsea. She'll manage the project from now on. Your person can do clean up from afar. We don't need anyone on site. ANYONE.*

Her response is immediate.

*ELLE: Thank goodness. I'm so relieved she's okay.*

*JOSH: Please leave us alone.*

*ELLE: I'll leave the Farmhouse tonight, don't worry. Please tell your Dad about the meds. And you need to tell them that you know. Don't fuck with them.*

*JOSH: DO NOT EVER TELL ME WHAT TO DO. ESPE-CIALLY IN REGARDS TO MY PARENTS! YOU HAVE NO FUCKING AUTHORITY OVER ME. MIND YOURSELF.*

*ELLE: Josh, don't speak to me like that again. Even if it is in a text. You owe me more respect than this.*

*JOSH: I owe you nothing. I'm sure you and my parents had a nice laugh at my expense, plotting for their future without including me at all. And I don't ever intend to speak to you again. So don't worry about my tone.*

*ELLE: Be pissed at your parents, not me. I didn't do this. Despite your childish response. They set their plans. All I did was innocently try to help them. Also your mom will probably need a new cane. The dogs found her old one and have been chewing it pretty good. I fed them.*

*JOSH: Still taking care of things that are none of your concern or business anymore.*

*ELLE: Someday you'll be less mad about this and you'll see it clearly. I'll miss you. I'll miss what might have been. Take care of them. And I'll take care of the sale.*

*JOSH: All about the Benjamins.*

*ELLE: I thought you were never speaking to me again?*

Fuck me. I handed her the last word and didn't even realize it. I storm into my mother's room, and it's cleared out except for my father.

Will stands and faces me. "Son. I need Elle's help."

"In managing Mom's illness?" Their faces go pale as I reveal I know. "You should have told me this was the reason for the sale. I would have given you all my money. You should have confided in your only son that you're sick. Not in a stranger who works for you. She lied to me."

Will rises to his full height and uses the 'Dad' voice. "This is a longer conversation. You weren't here. We did what we thought was right. Now, drop your anger. Especially at Elle. That's on us. And we own that. We owe her an apology for putting her in that position. We put her in a bad spot and she had no idea."

I drop my guard. "You're right about me. But I'm here now. What do you need? Tell me how I can help, and then tell me everything you've chosen to hide from me."

My dad nods, then offers up. "If Elle's at the house, she'll know where the meds are and have her pack a bag to bring it here."

"She texted the med information. The only bags she's packing are hers. I'll buy whatever you need, Mom. But you're not understanding me, Elle's gone. Gone from the house and gone from our lives. It's my final decision. I will not allow that deception in my life, my home, or business."

My father crosses his arms and shifts his weight back and

forth. I remain stiff and wired. "Son, you don't understand. I don't think she knew we were keeping this from you. We never told her to keep it to herself."

"You wanted the information leaked to me? Was this the smartest way to handle it? I overheard it from the doctor whose concern is Mom's blood loss and blood thinners. He was discussing *my* mother's sensitive medical issues with a blonde woman. Solid fucking plan, Dad."

He crosses the room in an instant. "Watch yourself, Son. You are on some thin ice with your words and tone."

I will not let up. "I think I'm entitled to figure out how to process this on my own here. It seems like something we should have dealt with as a family. Elle is not family. And you're missing my point. She's gone."

"Family? You have no idea how much she's become family. And you have no leg to stand on here, so again, back it down."

The tone of his voice shifted. So, I change mine. "It's done, Dad."

He gets into my face the way he did when I was caught sneaking out and pinching wine to drink in the square back in high school. His tone is something I thought we'd both outgrown. Well, I'm not in high school any longer. He can try and tell me what to do, but we'll see how that goes.

"You're kidding, right? That's not your decision to make. Don't be fooled into thinking that you're in charge here, boy. You walked away from all vineyard responsibilities and us. Hell, you walked away from us again a couple of months ago without an explanation. Just when we thought we could trust you with hearing about your mother, you left again. You wanted a different life in Santa Barbara. You got it. You created a world where you're master of your universe, a hard-hearted fucking businessman. I don't give a shit about that man. You made it very clear we weren't a part of that man's life. Your engagement, your business, your successes or failures were all yours. Message received. But I don't have time to fucking chase my son and beg him to be a part of our lives anymore. We have bigger issues now."

He paces but begins again. I let him rant. He says, "Even though it broke your mother's heart when she wasn't invited to celebrate your engagement, we went on. We went on, together, like we always have. Our world blossomed without you. It had to. WE know how to be happy together. We didn't sit around hoping you'd bless us with a visit or concern for our wellbeing. We got used to be just us."

I spit out my own sentiment. "It's not like you made a beeline for Santa Barbara."

My father leans back against the large picture window. "No, Son. You made it abundantly clear we weren't welcome. That hole where you should fit into our lives will always be raw, but we moved forward. Then, *we* got diagnosed. *We* came to the conclusion that the stress of the vineyard wasn't worth your mother's health. And *we* had no one to give the vineyard to, so selling was our only choice. *We* hired Elle and began to rely on her both professionally and personally. But know this, fuck all the money. Fuck yours and fuck the sale. Fuck it all. I don't want any of it, if it means I don't have her. I only want your mother and as much time as we can cobble together. And when it's done, it still won't be long enough with her." His eyes get glassy. He clears the tears with his forefinger and thumb. Then turns from me, but his shoulders stay clenched. He has more to say.

He doesn't face me when he begins speaking again. "We decided to sell the vineyard to salvage whatever time we have left together. But we need the money for treatment and to travel the world."

"I have money."

He rounds on me, and suddenly I realize he's not only

releasing a lifetime of anger at me but Lucien. He's taking his fury at the disease out on me. It's okay, I'll be his whipping boy. I can't imagine holding on to all of it. He needs me. I deserve all of this.

His eyes are laser-focused and almost cruel as he speaks again. "And how the fuck would we have known that? Our decisions, much like your own choices in Santa Barbara, were made without thought to you. We're all making decisions independently. I thought that was the plan. You have no say here. Son, I love you, but not only did you write the business off a long time ago, but you cast us out as well. We will always want you around, but we won't be treated as trivial or second-class citizens in our own life."

"When were you going to tell me?"

"Now that you magically came back again, after your mother started the clinical trial. Which I hope to hell this incident doesn't mess up her chances of staying in the protocol."

"How long have you known?"

He's still angry. He's defending Mom's feelings as well. She's staying quiet, but I know he's releasing all of this for her too. His tone doesn't soften as he speaks again. "How long were you dating and then engaged to a woman we had to be told about through winery colleagues? When did you buy a fifteen-million-dollar home that we learned about from one of Tina Gelbert's design magazines? When did your business land on the Forbes list? When did you become a player to watch on Bloomberg's list? Milestones not shared with your only living relatives. Just the media."

"It was all none of your concern." Now he's pissing me off.

"Exactly. I'm sure your life is one with lots of dinners out and cocktails in complicated glasses. That's fine, but you can't have it both ways. You can't be Josh and Joshua."

I lean forward and unleash at him. "I CAN."

"DON'T YOU ROAR AT ME, BOY. I AM NOT INTIMI-DATED BY YOU." I try to get him out of attack mode, but I can see that I woke the beast. Which isn't a easy thing to do. He says, "Back the fuck down, Son. Your mother and I are still the head of this family and this business! You will respect that. Who are you? Who do you want to be? Because this version isn't working. Take a look at the way your speaking to the people around you. You need to respect us or get the fuck out of our way."

My father has made his point, but I hope I've made mine about Noelle Parker. He leaves the room to cool off. It's a classic Dad move, and I'm glad for the moment with my mom. "I'm sorry, Mom."

"You better be. I don't like how your father spoke to you, but I support his words one hundred percent."

She takes my hand, and I can't look at her. She lets me take a moment. It's a classic cool down, Josh moment. "Perhaps we should have pushed you sooner to be here. It seems that you are turning into someone we don't even know."

"I wasn't ready to be part of your lives again, not until...well, recently."

"Elle."

"Let's not talk about her. How sick are you?" My voice breaks as I ask.

"Oh, honey, it's under control. But it's a reality, you'll have to deal with now. It pisses me off every day, but then I'm reminded of all the good things I do have. The Parkinson's isn't one of them. Someday I'll figure out a way to be less angry about the disease. It's a cruel disease that pops up at inopportune times like a bad haunted house. I never know what's around the next corner. Symptoms come and go. I didn't know the tremors would reappear when I was in the cave today. They'd been gone for a while. But for now, it's one step at a time." I hug her as much as I can.

"I love you, Mom."

"I love you too." Then she speaks in a different tone of voice. "I saw you."

"Where?"

"In the cave." She blushes a bit and looks down.

"Oh god, Mom. Tell me you didn't see too much."

"I got an eye full. But I also saw my sweet and sensitive boy taking care of her."

She smiles weakly as the sedative being pushed into her veins takes hold of her. She says, "I saw you with her. That's a good thing. It means my baby boy is still in there somewhere. That your heart is pure. Lucien's gone. He can't control you anymore unless you let him. Choose happiness." She drifts off as she says these words.

"Son." My father reenters the room. "We need to talk."

I take a deep breath and exhale. Then I stand and face him. I say in a calm tone, "We sure as shit do."

"I'm sorry. I'm pissed at the world. I'm pissed that the universe did this to the purest soul I know. I meant everything I said though, I just didn't want to say it quite like that. I try not to get mired in the 'why her,' but it's hard. I'd rather it was me. Ask me anything." My dad's voice cracks, and his eyes fill. "I didn't know how much I needed you to shoulder this with me. Thanks, Josh. Thanks for being here."

He opens his arms wide, and I walk into my father's embrace. One I didn't know I needed and haven't had in a long time.

FUCK HIM.

I shower and peel off my grime- and blood-splattered outfit. I deposit it into the garbage can in Josh's room. If I could get up to the Lookout, I'd leave it there for him to find. I hold my bandaged and throbbing hand out of the shower. I let the water do most of the work. Washing my hair proves difficult and drying it even worse.

I awkwardly dress with one hand. Thank god for Stella McCartney white twill jogger pants. Not sure I could handle a zipper or a button. I have to wear a front clasp bra as it is. Also so grateful for my JBrand chambray snap front-shirt. No buttons and I don't need to dig for a t-shirt.

I'm able to pull my hair back into a low wet ponytail. It looks a little severe, but it will do. Screw it, I need lipstick to match the severe look. I dig around and find my Chanel red with the best name, *Pirate*. I slide into my favorite leopard print espadrille mules. Now I feel more like me, less like the sucker who left the hospital alone.

I make my way to the kitchen, collecting my vitamins, hand lotion, and a tin of tea. The house smells like history.

The faint whisper of old books and unwashed crystal goblets permeate the Farmhouse. The stone gives off a mineral smell that mixes with the flowers that surround the house, and the grassy notes of hay that's spread over the lower fields. Somehow this has become a home for me without noticing. It just happened, and I'll miss it forever.

I keep packing. How can he possibly think that I'm responsible for keeping this from him? Like I'm the liar. His stupid face makes me so mad. His stupid smug beautiful face. I want to smash it.

It's not my job to inform the son of my employers about one of their life-altering illnesses. Maybe if you visited once in a while, they wouldn't have to keep things from you like the sale or Parkinson's. Maybe just perhaps they'd confide and trust in their son. Not the asshole but the guy who took care of me this afternoon. The one kissing me, holding me, and making sure I was okay. That guy deserves to know what's going on with his family. That other one, the jackass, can go fuck himself.

Also, you can mess with my heart but not my business. I thought he'd already gotten that lesson. These people have given me their trust and their money. They need this sale to remove the stress and responsibility. The one person who should have swooped in to do it all was too busy trying to fuck Kendall Jenner Instawannabes in SoCal for the past decade.

Asshole. You can't take these people away from me. They've cared more for me than anyone in a long time. But he told me to go.

I sit down on the bed and begin to cry again. I thought we were something. I hate him. A thin line between love and hate. Oh no. Do I love Josh Whittier? Please, god no.

It doesn't matter now. He's cast me out. In the light of day, his parents will always side with him. I hate that I have to lose them. There are little maternal things I'll desperately miss from Sarah. She figured out how I like my eggs. I didn't have to ask. I'd come down for breakfast, and she'd just make them. I'll miss the eggs. Who will make my eggs right? No one. I know I'm being melodramatic but it fucking matters.

Dammit. Now I'm crying more for leaving these two remarkable people rather than that jackass. These two people who folded me into their lives. I've been to doctor visits with Sarah and sat with Will at boring city council meetings. We'd joke back and forth about who we'd kick off the island first in our version of a tribal council. I know her meds and her routine. And they know mine. I know when he needs to be alone with her, and when she's so twitchy, she needs to plant something or has a desire to create something beautiful. I know Will hides ice cream in the office freezer over at the Cooperage. Lots of ice cream. And they know I forget to fill up my car with gas, so Will does it. And Sarah has even learned my strange laundry habits of hanging everything to dry. And now he's pissed off that I cared for his parents. He's dismissed me. My phone pings, and it makes me smile.

*WILL: You didn't really go, did you? You're not fired. Only I can do that. Well, Sarah would probably do it. I'm too nice. I'm beloved.*

*ELLE: You are beloved.*

*WILL: Girlie, maybe lay low for a minute, though. Josh needs someone to be angry with, and he chose you. But if this helps, I needed someone to be angry with, and I chose him.*

*ELLE: That does help.*

*WILL: Yeah. Look, all of this is on us. It was unfair what we did to you, but it wasn't intentional. But we are incredibly sorry you got into this web of nasty sticky webbiness. You have to stay around so we can gravel. No malice or deceit meant.*

*ELLE: You're incapable of that.*

*WILL: We had words. You would have seen my temper that I*

*don't let slip often. You really would have been proud of me. I told him he was being an asshole. And to be completely honest, we'd definitely kick Josh off the island first.*

*ELLE: The tribe has spoken.*

*WILL: My dear, he'll calm down. Thanks for the med info. Once I get Sarah to UCSF, I'll figure out our next move. No time now.*

I type a response that he's often given to me as I try and speed up a moment, a work problem, or a timeline.

*ELLE: Everything will take care of itself as the universe sees fit.*

*WILL: My darling girl. Thank you for everything. Sarah and I are indebted to you as is our asshole son. But he doesn't know it yet. Don't give up on us yet, or him.*

That was cryptic. But okay.

*ELLE: You're my client. I'll see that the job gets done.*

*WILL: Bullshit. You know we're more to you than that. You talk a big game, but I had no idea how much we both needed you. The sounding board and the distraction of your disastrous love life, always entertaining.*

*ELLE: Such a charmer.*

*WILL: Elle, your parents would be proud of who you are in the world. We love you despite you being a New Yorker.*

My heart explodes as tears splash down my face. The flashes of charming I see in Josh he gets directly from his father. I'll bet he uses it to secure money in his real world. I'll bet wallets and legs fling open with just one of his winks. The difference is, his father is sincere all the time. Question is, can Josh be?

And just like that, clarity. I wipe my tears, finish packing, load the bags into the car, and speed quickly south away from the Farmhouse.

# 29

## ELLE

I ENTER HOSPITAL ROOM 1401 TO A GLEEFUL SMILE FROM Will and a jolt of anger from Josh. I put Sarah's bag on the dresser then motion to Will.

"I packed one for you too."

He bellows at me, and I'm ready. "I thought I told you to pack a bag and get out of the Farmhouse."

He's in my face, and his cedar musk is threatening to break me. I don't want to back down based on his smell, but I need to turn my vagina off, she's getting slippery. My stomach is on fire, and I can feel my chest flush. My hands are super sweaty. I think I need to give myself a pep talk—I can do this. I can stand up to him. It's a good plan. He has to listen. You're right, Elle. You got this. I answer as innocently and annoying as I can.

"I did. I packed all your mom's necessary items and her favorite tie dye yoga pants. You know the ones, Sarah, they're the tight compression ones so you can feel in charge of your body. Also, I grabbed Will's favorite shampoo. The one that Madelene, his stylist, convinced him to buy because it will slow down the thinning."

Then I speak in a flat and even, almost a cold voice as I hold up a large bag of pills. Ones that I'm sure he's never seen or knew existed, but that was not my fucking fault. "And here's the multitude of medicine and supplements your mother needs to take every day. They need to be evaluated by the Parkinson's specialists at UCSF. Oh, and there's a change of clothes for you in Will's bag. I brought you a shirt that will fit better than that child's medium shirt you're sporting. I packed bags of things your parents need to feel human and left the Farmhouse to come here. Isn't that what you meant? As their caring and loving son?"

Sarah's awake and beaming a smile that I've decided to challenge him. "Thank you very much, Elle. I don't know what we'd do without you."

Will crosses the room and takes me into his arms and whispers in my ear. "I see we're going with a different plan than laying low. Good for you. And good luck." He kisses the top of my head and retreats across the room.

Josh stands. "Can I see you in the hallway, please?" I don't respond, pretending he wasn't talking to me. Then he grits out, "Hallway."

"Sorry. Were you talking to me? I thought you were never going to do that again. I was simply trying to do as I was asked. I'm here to please the clients." I curtsey in his direction and he growls.

He's looks like he wants to throttle me. His mother grabs his hand, and he softens while smiling at her. I'm not sure what they've told him, but he knows more now than when I left. I know he's hurting, and I want to take it away from him. But first, we need to get a few things straight.

All my anger towards him dissipates as he gets angrier at me. His hollow threats probably make him feel better, but I'm just going to throw it back at him.

"If you're here to please the clients, you do realize I fired

you. I told you to leave. Get far away from us. Especially me."
He steps closer to me, his scent, and intense eyes are going to
reallocate my feelings again. But I stay strong. I stare at him
directly in his eyes, getting up on my tiptoes.

"And when have I ever done what you've asked? I know
you think you fired me. But as I've told you many times
before, I don't work for you. You're not my boss. And you
know what else? You're not my friend. You're not my
colleague. You're not in charge. You're not my sparring partner. You're not my client. You're just mine. Where you go,
I go."

Will crosses his arms grins from ear to ear at my bold
statement.

Josh tries to intimidate me by placing his hands on hips
and staring. I mimic him with my hands on my hips, despite
me being much shorter. I stare right back up at him until I
think I'm going to break. Then I hurry to the door, my
adrenaline flooding through me. Please god, let me not have
misread the situation. Please let this get through to him. I
pause at the door, glancing back at him, he's slack-jawed and
fuming.

My voice is unshakable, even though the rest of me is
trembling. "Where you go, I go. You're here, so I'm here. You
don't leave, and I don't pull away. That was the deal. There's
no more 'out' anymore, asshole."

Josh doesn't move. He keeps his poker face intact. Will
looks elated, and I turn back to Josh. "Did you still want to
see me in the hallway or can I go get your dad a turkey sandwich? He looks starving. You didn't even think to get your
dad a turkey on rye with a smear of yellow mustard and
absolutely no tomato? No worries, I'll get it. I'll take care of
that too."

I walk away. I'm shaking. My system is tapped out from
confrontation, worry, and exhilaration. I can't believe I said

that, did that. I can't believe I found the strength to fight for
him. I was cruel but also made him realize that the time to
run is done. I hope it worked. He has to overcome his shit
and come to me. If he has to be at his mother's bedside, so do
I. He asked me to trust him, and that's what I'm showing him.
But he needs to trust me too. I feel as if I may throw up. I
breathe deeply. He can tell me one thousand times to go
away, but I won't. I won't hide anymore in solitude. I'm done
being alone. I finally believe him: I am his.

I bolt down the hallway as my stomach butterflies finally
subside. I don't know how long this is going to take until he
realizes he's stuck with me.

I run down the hallway having no idea where I'm going. I
keep walking. I turn another corner and lean up against the
wall, determined not to cry again today.

I am trying to maintain my pressure valve level. I've cried
enough. I'm exhausted from my day of simultaneously
wanting to bury him and fuck him. But now my over-
whelming ruling emotion is how I want to comfort him. I
want to tell him how strong his mom has been. I want to
share all that I've learned about Parkinson's and that it's not a
death sentence, more like a delayed one. I want to take away
his confusion and anger. I'll wait.

# 30

---

## JOSH

"Son, you have an apology to make."

"Don't 'Dad' me right now. She said some harsh shit. She said shit to make me feel even guiltier for not knowing you guys."

"Josh, she didn't say anything that wasn't true. And you just told me you want more truth. She also just affirmed everything anyone could ever want in life. She's got your back, always. You did hear that, right?" My dad's gift in life is lightening a room or a mood. He's very good at that. I'm just too stubborn to respond most of the time.

"I'm here for you guys. But when the hell did our marketing and branding expert become family?"

My mom chimes in, "Sweetheart, it just turned out that we didn't know how badly we needed someone, and the perfect person came to us. But she's no longer here for us."

"She's a shark."

No one speaks to me that way. No one cuts me to the core. I should want to scream at her, but all I want to do is thank her. I'm not sure how to back my ego down.

"It's okay to be scared, sweetie. We all are. Lower your defenses for a moment, dear. I've learned, quite recently, that when you're petrified, you learn to go forward anyway."

My mom has always seen me. She reminds me of things I should be instead of things I've become. "Don't be confused. She stayed. Even if you don't stay in Sonoma, how will you know she's not your One Perfect Thing?"

My breath catches because I already know she is. My anger, pride, and fear got the best of me. My mom has to be okay. This disease doesn't stop. I don't know how to process any of this, but I know who I want by my side as I navigate it. I let so many years slip by without being in their lives, and now I'm told there's an expiration date. I can't let another second go without them or Elle in my life.

My mom looks at my dad, and he blows her a kiss. They don't care where they are or what they're doing if they're together. They used to embarrass me with their affection when I was growing up. I know so many people from fucked-up homes, and here I am running away from a perfect example of what love should be.

My mom speaks again, "Can you give up control? And be happy?"

Give up control is exactly what I told her to do, and now here's my mom demanding the same of me. Can I do that?

"I can try."

My dad puts his hand on my shoulder and says, "Then you'd better go see if my sandwich is ready before she thinks twice about leaving. I'm actually starving."

I bolt out of the room and look down the hall. There's no sign of her, but suddenly it's imperative I see her. Touch her. No more distance, pauses or waiting, just moving forward. She cares so much she ignored me. No one ignores me, except her. No one goes against my directives. But she did.

She called me out. She challenges me like no one else ever has, in the best and worst possible ways. Thank god she never listens to what I ask.

I'm searching and finally, a nurse points around the corner. I guess if you see two people running in the same direction you can imagine that the second one is looking for the first.

I tear down the hall, and she's standing there leaning up against the wall. Her face is her hands. Her long bangs slipped from her ponytail and are covering her face. The silky rich blonde blending in with her creamy skin takes my breath away. She hears me round the corner and looks at me with those satiny green globe eyes, and I melt a little. I stand in front of her. Her lips are ruby red and luscious looking. They're parted slightly, and I want to taste them. Is she cherry flavored today like her lips?

She's not in the attack position that she was in moments ago. I see her the way she was this afternoon in the cave. Complete and open.

Her face is ruddy and her eyelashes wet. I did that, and I never want to do it again. I move to her, close enough to inhale her orange blossoms and lilacs. Her chest flushes. Earlier I knew the red blush meant she was angry. It's creeping up to her cheeks as it softens to a pink loving glow.

I say nothing but place my hands on her waist and press my fingers into her hips. The two of us are well aware of what's about to happen and quietly consent to the moment. It's a point of no return.

Then I lean down and gently brush my lips over hers. It's not the carnal crush of earlier today but a more profound, softer kiss. Elle moves her arms around my neck and caresses the back of my head. She melds into me, her body fitting into mine, and it's precisely where I want her. Just not in a hospital hallway. A tiny but distinct moan slips from her perfect mouth as I move my hands down her body.

"There it is."

She grins. "There's what?"

She goading me again. This woman. "The sound I've waited all day to hear again. The sound that feeds my soul."

She blurts out, "I'm so sorry." And I take my finger to her lips, pulling her to me so I can hold her. Her warmth reminds me that my icy bullshit heart has melted. Even though I tried to put it back into the deep freeze today. She weeps quietly, and I mold her body to mine.

I stroke her hair. "Shhh. It wasn't your fault. I never should have spoken to you like that. I'm the one who's sorry. I'll do my best to never do that again. And I owe you a giant thank you for taking care of them when I was too wrapped up in my own bullshit to do so. I'm so grateful they had you. But enough about my parents. I told you that you can never leave me, and you didn't. You came back to me. No need for sadness, Cosmo. You listened and trusted me even when I couldn't trust myself. And from now on, I intend to do the same."

She looks up at me, and she's still crying. It stabs at every part of me like a thousand paper cuts. It fucking rips me in half, knowing I caused her pain again. I tried to send her away.

Her breath gets stuck in her throat as she tries to speak. "I'm not sad." She squeaks out. And I'm confused. "I'm sorry that was cruel of me to play your parents against you, but I'm crying because you're holding me and I'm so happy about it. Sometimes I'm just so happy that it leaks out of me."

I stroke her hair and hold her tighter. I rest my chin on her head, and I know that I am hers. I know I'll hurt her again because, in my soul, I'm an asshole. But if she'll have me, I'll do my best to stay with her and be the best version of an asshole I can be. "Shh. Stop. No. I'm sorry. And you know that's not something I ever thought I'd say, multiple times. I don't ever want to have to apologize to you, and I don't want you to apologize to me again."

She kisses my chest and looks up at me to speak. I place my finger back on her lips. I rub my finger on the outline of her cherry red lips. Then she opens her top lip until my finger falls into her mouth. Closing her fiery pout over my finger, she begins to swirl her tongue around it and suck it until I moan just a bit.

"There it is," she whispers and grins.

I laugh at her. "What am I going to do with you?"

"Everything. All the strings attached."

I slant my mouth over hers and cup her perfect ass. We're going to need a secluded spot very soon. But we're waiting for the freaking transfer to the next hospital. The one that's the expert in my mom's disease. Relief washes over me that I don't need to go through this alone. Holy shit, I'm not alone. And I'm not thinking in terms of days or weeks but for a more intimidating forever.

She whispers into my ear, "We need to find a bed or couch or a table or back ourselves down and go to your mom's room."

"Well, my dick's pretty hard. I may have to wait for a second to go see my mom."

"Already? I'm so good." She reaches down and feels me through my cargo shorts.

"Woman! That is not going to help. And don't tell me you're not soaked for me." She shrugs and kisses me again while still keeping her hand on me. I back away from her. "Stop."

"Sorry."

I crook an eyebrow at her. "What did I tell you about apologies?"

"Sorry, Josh. I forgot. Shit. Sorry. Whoops. Man, remembering that is hard." She looks down at my pants and giggles again. "And so are you."

She reaches, and I take one step back. "Stop touching me."

"I don't have to touch you to keep you like that."

We're now standing on opposite sides of the hallway. I cross my arms and raise an eyebrow at her. "Unless you strip right here in the hall, you got nothing without touch."

She reaches up and unsnaps one snap on her shirt. I fall to my knees. I did not fucking realize they were snaps. I want to rip that shirt off her. Fuck, that's hot.

She walks around the corner, and I catch a glimpse as she pulls out her phone. I untuck the shirt she brought for me and set off to catch up with her. Finally, my dick seems to be obeying as I think of Mrs Dotson washing the bathroom. My phone dings in my pocket.

*ELLE: I'm so wet I'm shocked it's not seeping through my pants. You made me glisten with just your touch on my back. Can't wait to find out just how much more there is. Can you outdo the Members party? El Dorado? I DARE YOU to make me lose count.*

*ELLE: Oh, and this pair isn't so much a thong as something to highlight your favorite asset in a lacy pearl.*

She's walking two feet in front of me, and that perfectly round ass is tempting me too much. Fuck me. She's wearing cheeky panties. I can see their slight outline ahead of me.

"That's not fair!"

"All's fair."

"This is neither love nor war."

"Fine line."

She steps into the elevator. My heart is sinking. Is she leaving? "Where are you going?"

"Turkey sandwich." I jump on the elevator and grab her

unbandaged hand. We interlock our fingers together as we both lean back side by side.

"Does my dad really hate tomatoes?"

"Only on sandwiches."

"I have much to learn."

# 31

## ELLE

The transfer took most of the night, and we kept our distance from each other. But now at UCSF hospital, he's rubbing his thumb over my knuckles, and my skin is a tingle. We're too tired to pretend we aren't together. It's not like it's a huge secret. But as we enter his mom's next hospital room together, he's clutching my hand. As we step through the door, his father applauds. His mother, still all bandaged, is sitting on the edge of the bed with a Cheshire cat smile.

"It's about fucking time," Will calls out. I instantly blush. I break away from Josh as he heads to his dad for an update. I help Sarah to bed.

"Are you okay?" Sarah whispers to me as she attempts not to wince while getting into bed.

"I'm perfect. Apparently, I'm a 'One Perfect Thing.' As is he." Sarah eyes well up as she places her way too bandaged hand on my bandaged hand. "But shouldn't I be asking you how you are?"

She smiles and nods at me. "Fair enough. The next couple of hours and days are going to be rather painful, I gather. I don't want Josh to see that. There will also be a lot of tests with results that may scare him. We're going to learn specifics about what's happening in this phase of the condition. He can't handle that. Can you take my baby boy away from here, please?"

I stand up straight. I want to make sure she understands there's been an actual shift in my allegiance, not just a pretend one. "Sarah. I adore you. I would do anything for you but make no mistakes, I am not your secret keeper. He's the strongest person I've ever known. I didn't know how much you'd kept from him. And that wasn't fair of you to do to me. I forgive you because I don't know what I would have done in the same situation. But you and Will should know this. Over the last twelve hours, I've shared everything I know about Parkinson's, your condition, and why you're selling the vineyard. I am transparent right now and intend to stay that way. Josh deserves to know what's going on. I won't ever keep things from him again. No matter what happens in the future, I can't and won't do that to him."

She looks up at me. "He doesn't deserve you."

"No, he doesn't. But then again, I don't deserve him."

Then her eyes drift behind me as Josh puts his hands on my shoulders. He heard what I said. "That transparent thing, does that go for where you hid the remote for the TV in my room at the Farmhouse? I know it was you who took it."

I smirk. "I did. It's in my suitcase. But come on, you listen to the TV way too loudly, and we all needed some sleep. I did it for everyone here." He tickles my waist.

Will slaps him on the back. "Go. You two don't need to be here. We're just going to try and sleep. They even promised me a cot of some sort. Super psyched about camping!"

We laugh.

"I'll bring your pillow and big blue tomorrow." Will hugs me.

Josh asks, "Big blue?"

"His big fuzzy heavy blanket."

His mom finishes, "He can't sleep without it."

"Really, Dad? A blankie?"

"Don't knock it, man." Will smirks.

I tell Josh, "Seriously, I once napped on the couch, and your dad covered me with it. It's like the best sleep ever." I smirk at Josh. He rolls his eyes at all of us.

Josh crooks an eyebrow. "You do know that *I'm* your child, right?"

"Do we get to vote?" Will teases Josh.

Josh steps to his mother as she says, "I'm just going to sleep, Joshie. All details can be figured out in the next day or two. I promise, no more secrets. Go home, let my dogs out, then eat and sleep. Come back tomorrow. You still have Elle's and my dried blood on your shorts, for Pete's sake."

Josh kisses her on her cheek. "And if anything at all happens…"

Sarah doesn't miss a beat as she says, "Then we'll secretly text Elle and tell her what's going on and ask her not to share it with you."

We all laugh but no one harder than Josh.

# 32

---

## ELLE

I DOZED IN AND OUT IN THE PASSENGER SEAT OF MY CAR WHILE Josh drives us the hour home. His hand never leaves my body. I wake up just as we turn into Emma Farm, the land's official name. I rarely call it that. Maybe it's because I know the new owners will change the name and that breaks my heart a bit.

Everything I know about Josh's great-times-four grandmother, Emma, the 4G, is fascinating. She's was spirited, feisty, dedicated, and had an enormous heart and drive. She deserves this legacy, but it will be tucked away with the rest of the LaChappelles when the winery changes hands. The name will live on, and their souls will live in the soil, but the stories and purpose will get buried.

I smile at his exhausted face as he turns to me. He's so haggard and tired. There are slight worry lines in his forehead, but his skin is still the color of a golden summer day. I put my hand on the side of his face. He puts his cheek into my hand then kisses it.

He's lightly tanned, the pink of the day before yesterday's burn becoming the sexy sienna coloring of today. It's been a day and a night and a day, and we're spent from catching naps where we could. We're also worn out from us not being a couple, to deciding to become a couple, then breaking up, then settling on being together for the foreseeable future.

His blue eyes are shining in the twilight hour with his eyelashes, black and thick, almost brushing his cheeks when he blinks. I must look a wreck, but somehow, he's staring at me as if I'm beautiful. We pull up to the Farmhouse.

I ask, "Hungry? I'll call Poppy and order something."

He shakes his head as we get out of the car. He opens the backdoor, the dogs rush out and run around jumping on us. I continue to come up with suggestions. "Or I think there's some chicken in the fridge."

I start pulling leftovers and looking for pasta to boil. He puts Agave and Juniper's fresh water and food outside. Then he shuts the backdoor with his old school black Chuck Taylor high tops, shaking his head no.

"I can run into town and grab anything. What do you want?" Again, he shakes his head no. His eyes flash a darker blue, and his intense stare is almost more than I can handle. "You said you were hungry."

In a flash, his mouth is bruising mine, and my entire body is aflame. I blush from head to toe, and I'm sure that it's the fire he's stoking in me.

He nibbles my ear and says, "Yes, but not for food."

I reach down, and he's so hard. He scolds me and removes my hand from his cock. "Not yet."

"I like that you're hard instantly."

"I've been hard the whole way home. Super fucking painful. But you have to wait."

I wrap my arms around him and play with the tendrils of hair at the nape of his neck. "But what if I really, really want it."

"Not enough. You don't want it enough yet. And you're

not ready. You might need a reminder who's in charge here. And also, I need to smack that fabulous ass of yours until it's the color of your flushed chest right now for not telling about my mom."

My tummy flits and sparks shoot to the ends of all of my nerves at the idea. An idea that used to repulse me. The sting of pain that turns into a more profound pleasure that forces us both to be in the moment. All worries, concerns, and to-do lists fade in those moments, and we're just with each other.

We're still in the stone and wood-beamed kitchen. The modern island is black and white marble, almost as hard as he looks. I'm trying to read his roguish expression, wondering his next move. He removes my arms from his and backs up from me. He leans on the refrigerator and crosses his arms over his chest as his shirt pulls on his biceps. He really is delicious looking.

"Ditch the pants, Elle. Let me see those cheekies," he says in his booming voice with a low sexy tremor.

I panic. I don't know if I can take this leap of faith. I need to know that what's happened in the last day or so is real. That all of this isn't the result of exhaustion or concern over his mom. I need to hear that he's not going to take these parts of me and leave me stranded trying to cobble myself back together. I don't do anything but stare at him. He crooks that sexy eyebrow and a flash of dominance crosses his ocean blue eyes.

"Did you not understand me?"

My voice stumbles a bit. "I do. But I need to know—"

He interrupts me, "You already know everything you need to."

I say quietly, "I don't want to play right now."

The dominant look is erased from his face and smile sweetly, "Elle, I thought you trusted me?"

I shoot back at him, "Do you trust me?"

I'm asking a question, which is not what he wants. I see his expression change to puzzled. I've crossed to the other side of the kitchen. Putting distance between us for both his sake and mine. He's circling the island like a shark with his dinner. He stops. We now face each other across the wide kitchen island. I kneel on one of the milk paint white wooden bar stools and cross my arms over my chest. I'm ready to hear an answer.

He places his commanding hands on the counter and leans towards me. His massive body covering half the distance. I meet his stare. I won't back down from this question or this moment. I narrow my eyes at him. This moment will forever define me one way or another. I'm either getting fucked tonight and then walking out the door tomorrow, or I'm making love and staying forever.

"Do I trust you? Hmmm, let's see. Oh, woman, that's an awfully loaded question. You're tricky and full of surprises. And I don't see you giving up those habits."

Now he's growling at me in that sexy, throaty way he has. His hair is blonder from the sun and flops over his sapphire eyes. I nod. I need an answer. His face softens, but his eyes are still intense as if they see all of me.

He continues, "I don't know if I'll ever totally trust you, but I do know without hesitation that I completely and totally love you."

My entire body freezes and then a flood of heat rises. I don't think I can form words.

I throw my hands up and scream, "HOLD UP!"

He laughs a bit, and I have yet to blink. I climb onto the island, crawling towards him. My shirt floating down and revealing my bra. His lips curl up to the left as I get closer. He stands up at the edge of the island, and I kneel, bringing myself eye to eye with Josh. He's looking at me as if he'd devour me if I'd let him. Neither of us touches the other one.

I say very pointedly, "What the *fuck* did you just say to me?"

"You heard me."

"Repeat it. Right now." I demand.

"I love you, Cosmo." I used to hate that name, the one he called me to mock that I was too cosmopolitan for Sonoma, but now I would legally change my name to that. Tears threaten to leak out of me again.

He speaks again, "Despite my best efforts and your stubborn, annoying, controlling tendencies, I'm insanely in love with every single part of you Elle Parker, Brittany Noelle Doyle. All of you, inside and out."

I pause and smile at him, shaking my head. I feel the tension roll off him in waves as he waits nervously for my reaction. He doesn't need to worry. "That's super convenient because I love you too. Madly and completely."

I haven't said that phrase since Gavin, and I don't think I've meant it since my parents. And I know that I've ever really felt it from or for a man until now.

"Then stop dicking around and take off your clothes. It's the only way we're going to have epic sex. And I need to be inside the stunning love of my life. Now." He throws me over his shoulder. I squeal as he carries me up the stairs to his bedroom.

"Put me down."

"Nope. I'm afraid you'll run."

"No more running. Or hiding. Just lollipops, sunshine, and fucking." He laughs heartily, and I'm afraid he will drop me. I stick my hands down the back of his pants and pinch his ass as he smacks mine. "Oh."

"Later, love. We have a lifetime for me to redden that ass.

I need to feel you and see you right now. I want to make love to you."

He places me down on the ground, and I put my hands on his face. "I need that too. I love you so much, Josh."

"Say that again."

"I love you, Joshua Lucien LaChappelle Whittier." He moans. "You do know that your name is the most pretentious name in the world." I get an ass smack for that and I don't hate it.

He gets within a whisper of my lips and stares at me. Then gently he slants over my mouth, and I open to him. His tongue darts into me, swirling and dancing with precision and lust. Then with his lips on mine, he reaches down and rips my shirt from my body with a popcorn sound of snaps releasing. I gasp but hold back his moan for a moment. Then he pulls off my pants, placing me on my feet and turning me around, taking in the full view. I'm in my lacy panties, bra, and leopard shoes.

"Babydoll! These are hall of fame panties. Remind me to look at them more later." He smacks where the lace cuts across my cheeks and peek out from the bottom. I squeal.

Then he assesses me for a moment. He kisses my neck and works his way between my breasts. Then bites the front clasp of my bra, and it's the hottest thing in the fucking world as it pops open.

# 33

## JOSH

I KISS HER LIKE I'VE NEVER KISSED HER BEFORE. I KISS HER LIKE I've never kissed another woman before. Not just with passion, but now with love. My desire takes a slight back seat to wanting to experience this moment with her. We're tentative. She's soft and quiet in my arms and on my lips. I savor her as I run my hands up and down her body. She reaches for my shirt, and I help lift it off. She peppers my skin with light breathy kisses. The carnivorous lustful moments behind us for a moment. I back her to the bed and when her legs make contact, she sits on the edge. I retrieve a condom from my wallet as she undoes my belt and slides my pants down. I don't want to discuss birth control. I don't want to know if she's been with someone else. I just want to go forward in this moment. I've been ready for her for months. My dick spring towards her, and she rolls the condom on. Then she lays back, and I follow her down. Our electricity sparking with each part of our bodies that touch.

"You're the most beautiful and precious thing in the world."

"And you're sure about this?"

I kiss her neck and run my tongue on her jaw line as she throws her head back. "Elle, you can't joke this away right now. Feel this with me."

"Feel what? This?" She reaches for me and I let her make contact, but I keep staring directly into her eyes.

"No. Forever."

Her eyes soften. I mean exactly what I say. This is it for me. She's my everything. And I so don't know how that happened. I only know that I don't want anything different than this moment. I lean up and begin kissing down her body. Making sure I give each nipple a circle, a swirl and a nip. She moans for me and my life is complete.

She pulls me back up to her face, and I tell her my intentions. "I was going to…"

"Just be inside me, my love. Complete me." And I do. I slide inside of the love of my life, and we both gasp at the moment. She hooks her legs around my hips, and we stare at each other, locked in the moment. We stare at each other connected beyond words and fears. Then my Hellcat comes out to play and she swivels her hips and I groan at the sensation.

We don't speak as we begin to find a rhythm. I'm gliding in and out of her as she raises her hips and pulls on her own nipples. It's so fucking hot. I increase my speed. Long motions in and out.

"Deeper. Josh. Harder." And I absolutely oblige her. I thrust into her all the way and all the way out. I pull her legs up as I ram back into her and she delights in every move I make. "I'm so close. Make me come." I don't want to. I don't want this moment to end. I never want to be outside of her again. Can we get work done like this? Connected. I moan her name loudly, and it feels like a prayer or a celebration.

"Elle. Elle. My gorgeous Elle. I'm close. You."

"Yes. Come with me. Come with me, Josh." I drive into

her faster and when I'm closer, I reach down, circling her clit, driving her higher. I hear it in her breathing.

"Now." She moans and I put more pressure on it, and the moment I feel her contract around my dick, I'm gone. I continue trying to thrust, but I freeze and fill her.

"Elle. Fuck." She spasms around me, her thighs trembling as I lower myself to cover her. We kiss her deeply. She opens her mouth to mine, and we speak without saying a word. I groan as I pull out of the one place I never want to leave. I head to the bathroom and get her a towel.

She sits up as I clean her up. I see her face looking quizzically. "Forever?"

"Do you have a problem with that?" I ask.

"I guess not."

I kiss her forehead and then laugh at her. "Now, let's find something to eat."

She winks at me, "I can think of something right here that you could eat."

"You're insatiable. Come on, Hellcat." I throw my t-shirt to her.

"You know my clothes are right there. And in the room next door."

"I know. But I want to see you in this. And only this and those epic panties." A mad and wild grin flashes on her face. I head downstairs and hear her scamper after me. She jumps on my back halfway down the stairs, and I carry her piggyback to the kitchen. I deposit her onto the kitchen island and yank open the fridge. Looks like we're having toast for dinner.

"There was chicken. Mrs. Dotson must have grabbed it. I can run to Poppy's."

"Nope. Nobody leaves this property until we've all had at least three more orgasms."

She jumps off the counter and opens the back door. The

dogs rush in. I crouch down to greet them. My face gets a solid licking. I look up, and she's still standing at the back door.

"Babe. What are you doing?" She grabs my keys off the table by the door and calls for Juniper. That puppy trots over to her. Smart dog. I would do the same thing if she called for me.

"Just stay here and see if you can scrounge up a glass of wine."

I wink at her. I have no idea what she's doing. No one is here. I'm glad she's taking a dog to go outside. "Be careful. And don't let anyone see your ass. That's mine now. I decide who sees it. I'm going to need bikini approval from here on out you realize."

"Bikinis? Got rid of them after Bali, and I'm not sure I even own a bathing suit anymore."

"Then I'll get you many, many bikinis. Let's just say they've figured prominently in my fantasies."

She shifts her weight, and I realize she's got my Adidas on. She looks like a kid playing dress up in my shirt and shoes. Her hair is wild and her make up smeared. And with her lips half-cocked, she stares back at me. "What?"

"Take your phone. And you've never been more beautiful." She blushes instantly, and it fills me with such joy that I'm able to do that to her whenever I want.

## 34

---

## ELLE

THERE'S A GIANT BARN OWL THAT I HEAR IN THE DISTANCE. I almost always hear him. I find him comforting. I call him Hal. Hal the Owl. I've never seen him. I make my way through the gravel parking lot down to the tasting room. Juniper runs ahead and then behind like she's circling me to protect me.

I look up to the insane hooting. "It's okay, Hal. It's just me." Then I look down at Juniper. "Come on, girl. Let's go steal some food."

---

I BURST BACK through the door, and he's sitting reading his iPad on the big comfy flowery chair just off the kitchen. My arms are full of crackers, chocolate, cheese, salami, olives, dried apricots, almonds, and baguettes. And ice cream. I'll replace Will's stash. He's sipping something red, and I'll bet it's Malbec. I throw the stuff onto the counter and crawl onto his lap. He accepts me greedily and holds me close. I curl into him with my knees all the way like I'm trying to make myself a ball. He's so tall and strong. I feel stronger in his arms, but I'm also aware that I'm short and tiny. He rests his chin on my head, and we sit like that for some time.

"Did you pay for those items, Ms. Parker?" I look up at his sparkling blue eyes, and he lowers his lips to mine gently.

"Yes, but I forgot to give myself the employee discount since I was recently fired." His lips are hovering just a whisper above mine, and I'm tingling all over again. He sees the evidence in the form of goosebumps all over my arms.

He teases my lips and says, "Good thing. Since you weren't an employee but a contractor."

"Good point. We won't have to disclose our relationship to HR."

"You mean Mrs. Dotson?'

"Exactly." He leans forward ever so slightly and kisses me full on. His tongue is inviting my lips to open. After a deeply satisfying kiss, I head back over to the island to arrange our feast.

He follows behind me. He puts the ice cream in the freezer then grabs all of the food and throws it into the fridge. He turns to me and pulls his shirt over my head. Now I'm naked in the kitchen in my cheekies. "What?" His finger presses to my lips silencing me. He crooks an eyebrow, and I can't resist him. But I'm not going to stand here in the kitchen naked by myself.

I lift his shirt off him as well, my hands savoring each ripple of his stomach. Each sandy-colored delicate hair that covers his pecs. I trace the trail down through his V and he stops me before I invade his shorts. He turns me around and then back towards him as he hooks his thumbs into my panties and slides them down my legs. I crook an eyebrow to him.

"Shh."

He lifts me onto the island then goes into the cabinets for

a large pile of dish towels. He pushes me down onto the island slowly. Half of the pile is placed under my head the other half under my ass. Like he's propping me up for display or better access.

He pulls up my foot to his face, licking my ankle. I gasp again as his tongue moves up my thigh. I'm shaking because of the cold island and the anticipation.

His thumb finds my clit in an instant, and the heat spreads rapidly through me. I arch my back and swivel my hips in response. Then his tongue is all over me. Tasting and savoring the way only he can. I anticipate the swirl that will send me over the edge, and he's teasing me. Lapping up all of my slicknesses and spreading into all the places. He's gripping my thighs, my legs on his shoulders, and he holds me in place as his tongue goes wild on my clit. I groan, gasp, and move in rhythm with him. My orgasm already building. The coil tightening within me, waiting to be unleashed.

He pulls his head up and kisses my stomach while his fingers plunge, searching for the perfect spot. First one slowly moving inside of me then a second in rapid succession, in and out. I scream and thrash my head as he fucks me with his fingers. The pressure is almost too high. He's driven me to this frenzied place so quickly it's maddening. He needs to release me now.

"Josh. Josh. I have to." I beg.

He removes his fingers and leans down to my face. He lightly brushes my peaking nipples. His grin is more insidious than it's ever been, more predatory. His hand kneading one and my other inside his mouth. I'm thrashing a bit while he lightly bites and sucks my nipples. He rolls and pinches the other. He takes as much of my tit into his mouth as he can then slowly draws out his mouth, sucking every bit of pleasure he can get out of me. My body twists tighter and tighter.

"Please. Please. Josh. I'm begging for you."

"Hell no. I'll die with a hard dick before I let you come right now."

"Why? I need it."

"I'm not going to let you come until I hear it. And I'm going to punish you for making me wait so long for it."

He stands and crosses his arms. His dick, the rootstock, is straining against his shorts. I know what he wants.

My hands go to my own nipple and clit to try and finish. He grabs my wrists and pins them behind my head. I move my pelvis into his, greedily searching for friction. He leans deeper into me, and I let go with what he wants. The most deep-seated, loudest moan I can summon.

"Josh."

In an instant, his shorts are off. He tugs me up to sitting, and I wrap my legs around him. Then he picks me up and places me directly onto his dick. His arms are so sculpted and strong.

"OH. God."

"Punishment later. I need to fucking fill you with my cock."

He pushes in, and it's rough and ragged. I'm entirely being controlled by him. My arms are around his neck. My body is pressed to his, sweaty and wanton. I grind up and down.

"Fuck me harder."

And he does. I take all of him and feel his balls slapping my ass. I've never been this full or turned on in my entire life. I feel as if I'm stretched to the limits and I love it. I scream and moan loudly. I'm so tight around him. He grunts and gasps. Then I shake and quiver as I try to hold on to him. I'm possessed by this insanely, deep rippling orgasm that rends me in half. I collapse a bit, but then with one arm, he supports me. Keeping his rhythm going but now his other arm goes to my upper back so I can continue this ride. As I try and regulate my breathing, I'm pulsing and taking his cock deeper than I thought possible.

I regain my wits, grabbing back on to this mountain of a man who loves me.

He pulls me off his cock and sets me down. I'm stunned. He nudges the kitchen step stool with his foot until it's at the island. He places me on the little bench. Then he flashes those deep blue eyes and gently turns me around, his mouth on where my shoulder meets my neck and his hands cupping and rubbing my breasts from behind. I throw my head back into his chest, and he snarls. Then he slowly bends me down until my nipples touch the cold marble island. I moan loudly at the sensation. I feel his tip at my opening again, and he launches inside of me. I groan and arch my back. He holds my hips keeping us at a steady pace. I'm dancing on the edge again and desperate to come. I push past the exhaustion, pain and soreness. I'm desperate for pleasure to crack me open again. The angle that he's hitting is new and spectacular.

"I need to pump into you. I need to fill you with me. I need to mark you from the inside."

"Please. Do it. Do it."

It's only right now that I realize we're not using a condom. That all of this is bare and intense. I only hope the shot does its job. And I'm cresting again as I ride the wave of his thrust.

"Fuck. Fuck, Elle. You feel so fucking perfect. You're tight and perfect. Oh fuck. I'm coming. I have to come in you. I own you. You're mine. Noelle. Elle. Elle. FUCK."

The guttural snap of my name from his gorgeous mouth makes me come again just at the top of his orgasm. I come crashing down on his cock as he almost loses his grip on me. He braces his legs and leans back as I feel a hot blast fill me. I want to hold on to all of it. I own him too. He covers my back with his sweaty and firm body. He whispers in my ear, "I love you, all of you. I love you, Cosmo. I love you, Hellcat. I love you, Elle. I love you, Brittany Noelle Parker Doyle. I love you so fucking much." And as he falls out of me, I feel as if a piece of me has gone missing. He needs to just stay inside of me always.

## 35

---

## JOSH

She turns around in my arms to face me, her stunning face flushed the perfect shade of pink from pleasure. I grab a tea towel for her as well as myself. I remember the last time we fucked without a condom, but that's the first time I've finished inside someone in close to a decade. I'm not going back. Let's shoot her up to protect us from things we're not ready for, but shit that was good.

"I love you so much, Joshua Lucien LaChappelle Whittier."

"It's just Josh. And my Hellcat, feeling all of you for the first time since that first night is everything."

"I'm so tired I can't eat." She pushes her pouty lip at me. I pick up my t-shirt and return it to her body.

I scoop up this gorgeous, sexy, and spent woman. She weakly holds on to me as I climb the old winding creaky stairs. I'm careful to dip her head under the beam on the landing before turning towards my bedroom. I lay her down on my bed and stare at the most breathtaking human that's ever been. The one, I'm convinced, was put on this earth for me. She smiles up at me as if she thinks the same thing about me.

I curl around her as I pull up the old quilt with a map of France embroidered on it by my grandmother. She's purring like my Hellcat should be. She gave me as much as she could. And now she should sleep. I took it all from her. And it's still not enough. This fucking woman is all encompassing. I can never be away from her again. I fall asleep in the sound of her ragged, satisfied breathing.

---

I'M NOT sure what's happening, but in my dream, my cock is hard and wet. Then I hear my goddess moan. My eyes pop open, and her mouth is full of me rising up to the occasion. I have no idea what time it is, but I'm the luckiest fucking man in the world. This woman couldn't even get a good night's sleep without having to suck my dick. She's so good at this. Her hands rubbing my shaft up and down while the tip is getting flicked and licked. I pull my hips back and forth, and she sees that I'm awake. Her gorgeous eyes narrow as she pulls my dick further into her mouth. The tip hitting the back of her throat. No gagging, she just swallows me down. Glorious sucking. In and out and fuck. I push my pelvis in and out in rhythm with her.

"Jesus fucking Christ, Hellcat. So good. Suck me off." I put my hand into her hair.

She lifts her head while she continues to stroke at an accelerated pace. She never loses grip of my dick while she comes up and kisses me.

"You're not in control here. Don't tell me what to do. If I choose to suck you off, then it's my choice, not your command. Who knows what will happen? Only me." I kiss her deeply, my tongue licking into her mouth. Then she says the hottest thing. "But you're in luck, I couldn't wait until morning to taste you."

"Fuck. You're hot. You're fucking perfect. You know exactly what I need, and it's to spill down your throat."

She moans in response to me. Then her hot little mouth continues sucking, and I begin thrusting. I tangle my hands into her hair and feel her head bob. My balls are hard and heavy. They're tight to my body while she sucks those too. Her hand begins massaging them, and she takes me all the way in her mouth. I will not last long. She's got me so deep. And in long strokes pulls me out. Then licks around just the tip while stroking the shaft quickly.

"I'm coming. Sweet god. Elle. Elle. Elle." She deep throats me one last time, and I arch my back growling louder than I ever have in my fucking life. I spill down her throat. She keeps stroking to get it all and then licks up the rest. I can barely speak.

"You took it all."

She licks her lips and rubs her fingers over them, "Almost every drop."

"Why almost?"

She climbs on top of me and shoves her finger in my mouth, "I saved one drop for you. You should know how good your cum tastes too."

There is no one hotter than this woman. She's perfect. Utterly perfect. Dirty in all the right places, smart and stunning. "Now, you." I flip her over swiftly, licking my lips.

"Nope. This interlude was just for you." She swallows a giant glass of water then kisses me again.

I leave the bed to clean up, and when I get back with another glass of water for her, she's already asleep, purring. Like I dreamed it all.

# 36

## JOSH

HER GOLDEN BLONDE HAIR IS SPAYED ALL OVER HER PILLOW and tickles my nose. We've not moved in hours. My arms encircling something that's become treasured overnight. Her scent in my nose is making me hard. I lean into her back, hopefully signaling that I want to explore more of her, but she just snuffles, sleep is still holding onto her tightly. I get up, and my dick is aching for her. I hope it settles for a quick jerk in the shower and a cup of coffee.

I take my full and painfully erect shaft in my hand and close my eyes, imaging her painted hot pink lips wrapped around it. Not only was last night the best blow job of my life, but it was also one of the best sexual experiences I've ever had.

My Hellcat had me from the moment her flowery scent made my dick twitch at Steiner's seven months ago. I'm pumping away at myself, desperately praying she wakes up and joins me. My cock is fat with desire. I'm slapping and tugging it until it's almost raw.

I release with a groan, and it's a pale comparison to what

happened last night, but it will have to do. I scrub and soap myself up several times. I still have grease and dirt on my arms from my attempts to fix the sprayer three days ago. Three days ago, I had thoughts of heading back to Santa Barbara. When I showed back up in Sonoma, I actually had a girlfriend who was supposed to visit today. And then her. That woman who turned my life upside down. I don't know where we go from here, but I know it's together.

I could move to New York, open a branch of my firm there or start a new one. Maybe something else. The thrill of the deal is a bit gone.

Once the sale goes through, maybe she'll join me in Santa Barbara. I do know that she doesn't have the choice of being without me anymore. There is nothing I've ever been more certain about than her. All those walls and barriers that were in place to keep my life exactly the way I wanted came crumbling down the moment she began to dismantle her fortress of solitude.

As the coffee brews, I see her phone on the table. I root around in her open purse for the charger. Once plugged in, her phone comes to life with text alerts. It says she has six from "Asher." My blood boils that he lives in her phone, let alone in any part of her romantic past. I only see part of his message, and it's all emojis. He's a fucking forty-six-year-old man using the kissy face emoji.

My neck stiffens, and my hands ball into fists. What the fuck? Like four months ago, the weasel was parading around with my fucking ex-fiancé. Look, if we're going to do this screwed up swap, at least make it a clean break. He can have all the Serenas I've ever had as long as I keep her. I'll give him Claudia's number as well. But as for Noelle Parker, she's off the market. I want him off her phone and out of our lives. My gut doesn't trust him.

Good god, I'm in deep. I don't know her phone code, or I'd read the rest of the messages myself. How often do they correspond? What's gone on between them while I was in Santa Barbara.

I put the phone down on the counter and consider having it monitored. I pick it back up and try to think like Elle and figure out her code. I punch a few numbers.

"It's 1-3-4-3-6."

I look up as if I've been caught committing a crime. She's standing at the bottom of the stairs in tiny sleep shorts and one of my shirts. Her legs look creamy and delicious. They're long in appearance despite her stature. She's five-foot-five, but from her ball-busting personality and the length of her stems, you'd think she was six foot. Her arms are crossed.

"What's that?" I ask, knowing the answer already.

"My code. It's the address of my building in Manhattan, 134 E 36th Street. I have nothing to hide from you anymore. If you want to see whatever is on there, go right ahead but ask."

"Well, now if you run from me, I'll be able to find you. I have your address."

"My address is public."

"Is that really a good code then? Honestly, Elle, I was just charging it for you, and a text came in and made me—"

She interrupts me, "Asher?"

She crosses the room to me, placing her scarlet nails on my bare chest and looks up at me. My running shorts are not hiding my excitement from her touch. She goes up on her tiptoes, which is the cutest fucking thing, and kisses me. I pick her up and put her on the island again. Her hands never leave my chest as I place mine on either side of hips as I step between her legs.

"He's nothing. But he brought the buyers, so he's kind of

hanging around until the sale. Then he'll be gone. But he's the reason I'm here. I'll always owe him a little bit for bringing me into your world and across your path, my love."

"I do adore hearing you call me that. But you know I would have found you anyway. You were meant for me. You wouldn't have been able to hide away in your ivory tower forever."

I kiss her, and she pulls away and sighs. Then says, "We need to disinfect this island before anyone eats here." I laugh at her.

Her stomach grumbles, and I realize neither of us has really eaten in like a day and a half. All the food she foraged last night is still shoved in the fridge. After I screwed Elle on the kitchen island, we both fell asleep upstairs. Well, she got a quick shot of protein in the night but other than that, she's got to be starving. I pour her a cup of coffee and add a little milk and a pinch of sugar and hand it to her.

"How did you know that? Even that ginger bastard who fixes my coffee three times a week at Peet's doesn't know that." She sips.

"Observation. I heard you tell my dad your coffee order one time." I turn back to fix myself a cup.

Her voice goes to a sing-song tone. "Whatcha doing?"

"Why?"

"I'm just looking at your ass and..." I round on her and take her into my arms, careful not spill the coffee.

"You're insatiable."

"I'm not the one who jerked off in the shower."

I tighten my lips and get in her face. "I see. You were awake? Did you like listening, dirty girl?"

"I did. And it's hard to stay asleep when there's a tree trunk stuck in your back." She giggles, and I shake my head at her.

"And you let me suffer?"

She pushes out her lower lip. "I was super, super tired."

"Seems like someone deserves some punishment for that." Her eyes flash at me, and a little smile breaks across her face. "Hellcat, is that what you were angling for?"

When my lips meet hers they're parted just enough for me to slowly enter her mouth. The tips of our tongues mingle. Her stomach rumbles again, and I pull back.

"More." She moans with her mouth still open and her eyes closed.

"After food, I'll take care of that puddle you've got building underneath you."

I stir some eggs in a bowl for omelets. She jumps off the island and beings scrubbing all surfaces. Then she pulls some plates and silverware out and refills my coffee. She goes outside and rounds up the dogs to feed them. This might be the happiest I've been in my adult life. She pops out for another moment, returning with a citronella candle, setting it in the middle of the table. I put the plates down with some grilled baguette bread and fresh jam.

"What's with the candle? Are you expecting mosquitos?"

"It's our first date. Our first meal together, just us. Other than Juanita Juanita and that wasn't fun at all."

"Mary's Pizza Shack."

"That was take-out, and we never got around to eating. A habit we have. We have sex and forget to eat. The Mary's leftovers were my odd breakfast before officially meeting you that day. I want this morning to be romantic."

I'm dumbfounded. I've never taken her anywhere, and she's in love with me. I've spent hundreds of thousands of dollars wooing women, and she just wants a bug candle.

I bought her an elaborate client dinner and some dresses, but that was an apology, not a present. I do have a replacement pair of Fendi shoes stashed in the closet up at the Lookout for her as well. But nothing really. I'm going to do something for her. I want to show her I can be much more romantic than a stolen salami and Vella Dry Jack cheese omelet.

# 37

## ELLE

As much as I want to stay in bed all day, I'm sore, and we actually have a harvest to run while Sarah and Will are at the hospital. I sneak out of the house while he takes another shower. I may have spilled cold coffee down the front of him as I attacked him while he was doing dishes. Who knew domestic could be so fucking sexy? We've had sex four times since he told me he loved me. He loves me. I still can't believe it.

I stroll into the tank room floating on air. Sammy is straddling Sam and grinding into him as he feels her up. I'm sure they're about to get busy. Sammy has shared that they have an insane amount of sex. She's also hinted that it might be a bit kinkier than I want to hear about.

I did not expect this show. He's supposed to be cleaning the tanks for all the Zin that's coming in today. The sprayers kept them from becoming dried out raisins, but they need to be picked today. I don't know if Sam knows we're back. Jims took over Sam's duties at Langerford as he took over for us after Sarah fell. Alena has managed so much lately, I'm glad Sam could step in and help her. We need her being the winemaker not the vineyard manager, harvest captain, and tasting room associate. Just the winemaker.

"Is that the secret to Langerford Zinfandel?"

Sam glances over at me without his lips leaving Sammy. "Yes. It's been known to give it a certain spice."

"Just keep it in your pants," I bellow.

"No. You leave, and it gets to come out of my pants." Sam commands as Sammy laughs hard. He attacks her lips again. "Your harvest is fucking with my schedule of fucking. You leave."

I roll my eyes and walk through the tank room to the tasting room. I need to grab a few folders I left there. Mrs. Dotson was not pleased that I did the paperwork in the tasting room again. The harvest celebration thank-you event is still on track, but I need to figure out in the wake of Sarah if we're still going to do it. It's scheduled the same day that they sign the papers for the sale.

I also need to tell Evan I'm not coming back for a while. Not until at least the end of November. I walk back through the tank room just to annoy them. They break apart as I walk by.

Sammy follows me as Sam yells out, "Hey! Elle." I turn around. "Why are you walking funny?"

I didn't realize I was, but I guess there's no hiding the stubble burn from his ever-present slight beard and my duck walk from taking that root inside me over and over.

I smile "Because I'm in love, duh."

A large yelp and a woo-hoo erupt from them. "Is he up there?"

"Yes. He'll be pissed I went to work. I think he'd like to keep me chained up in the Farmhouse. But a girl needs to work. And an Epsom salt bath and some rest."

"Sounds about right. I could loan him some things to keep you in place if you need." Sam winks at me.

He jogs out to find his best friend. And I sit with Sammy, going over event details. I also catch her up on what went down between Josh and I. She's particularly interested in the step stool sex. She wants more lascivious information, but I only provide a few details. Sam's got her a bit oversexed.

This party is more about the winery than getting everyone plastered. It's a moment for the employees, both past and present, to say goodbye. The sale happens on the day of the party.

"What's the final offer?"

"Seventy-five million. They owe the bank nothing so after taxes are paid, they'll be set for life. Hell, Josh's grandchildren will be set for life."

Sammy purses her lips at me. "You mean, yours."

"I'm a little lightheaded by that thought. Shut up."

The money is great but his kids, whomever their mother is, won't have this place. I need to make sure Josh is still okay with the sale. He's kept out of it. The contracts are at the lawyer's right now, and I have a copy sitting in my email. I don't think Will and Sarah are up to it with all that's been going on. The final offer came in while we were in the hospital. I don't want to put one more thing on Josh's plate, but I do need him to look them over. I think he'll understand the language better than I can. I may be a marketing genius, but I'm aware that I tune out over the legal stuff. That's always been an Evan thing. My creative genius is also the one who can pick apart the minutia. The yin and yang of Evan.

# 38

## JOSH

"Hey, man! Put on some clothes, I'm coming into the house."

"Shut the fuck up. What do you think I'm Hugh Hefner walking around in a robe and my cock out just waiting to get sucked?"

Sam crosses the room, and we embrace. "Sarah's okay, right?"

"She is. There's a shit-ton of stitches but the real issue, I've just found out, is she has Parkinson's. She's been transferred to a place that has doctors who specialize in it."

"How did you not know that?" Sam shrugs at me.

I punch his arm hard. "You fucking knew that?! Why the hell didn't you tell me?"

"Will asked me not to. Said they wanted to do it. I thought you just didn't want to talk about it." Sam crosses his arms and tucks his hands into his armpits. He used to do the same thing when he was six, but he'd make fart noises. Now he does it to protect himself when he's uncomfortable.

I inquire, "When did you know?"

"Like six months ago. But pretty sure my mom's known since the diagnosis."

"Does everyone know but me?"

He circles the island and I can't help but remember what we've done on this island over the last fourteen hours. And now I just want to find Elle and bury myself in her again.

I snap back to reality at Sam's voice. "Apparently. Did Elle know?"

"Yes, and I ranted at her then reamed her a new asshole. Then fired her. Told her to pack her shit and get the hell out of Sonoma. Told her she had no place in our lives. That I never wanted to see her again for lying to me."

"Then why is she walking funny?"

"Because she didn't leave. Threw my words back at me after the cave. Wherever you go, I go from now on."

"You told her to fuck off and leave, and she showed up to be by your side while you learned your mother has a disease?"

"Yes."

Sam raises his arms in the air. "Tell me you rewarded this goddess for putting up with your shit."

"I told her I loved her and fucked her raw."

"Good man." He nods.

"Dude, then I got a wake-up call in the middle of the night."

Sam slaps his hand on the counter. "That's the dream."

"It is. She is."

"I have never seen you like this."

"In love?"

"Holy crap, you're not even Josh. He doesn't do love."

I walk away. I'm not him. I'm better. I'm Josh with Elle. I was so full of shit before. Sam never even blinked an eye when I went all Joshua. He just stayed by my side and had my back. He knew who I was and just let me get it out of my system, whatever I was doing. Now granted, I've made more money than I need in a lifetime in the past ten years, but as for being a solid human, well, only Sam believed I still was. Elle should thank him for holding onto Josh while I abandoned him for a while.

"Why are you here?" I can tell that something is on Sam's mind. He's been fidgeting since he walked into Farmhouse.

"Have you seen the deal?"

"Elle has it. I'm going to look it over this week before the signing. Why?"

"I'm just a bit uneasy."

"Why? You're not selling outright. You and the other wineries maintain management and your wineries and they will be giving you a wider audience, for a piece of everything. Right? It will finance the next thing you and the guys want to do. Did Becca look at it?"

Rebecca is David Gelbert's older sister and a lawyer in Napa. Baxter swears by her for all of his environmental lobbying crap. She's whip-smart and always had better grades than all of us. We weren't that close, but I trust her with everything. That's the nature of The Five: we inherently trust each other, just like our parents and their parents did.

"All the contracts are with her right now. I just want to make sure you didn't think this was a mistake. Gelberts and Aganos are on board, but Schroeders and my folks are a bit on edge about it. Can you look it over?"

"Of course, man. When do you sign?"

"All the wineries sign at the same time at their different lawyer's offices. But I'm not sure when Will and Sarah's appointment is scheduled."

"They moved it to early afternoon because Mom has a follow up."

"Cool. Cool. I have to get home before Jims fucks up all of our Syrah. Tabi said she could be on call for the next couple of days if you need her. They're just juicing. Call her to help out Alena if you need."

"Perfect. I'll text her," I say dismissively.

"But not today. Tabi's at the aquarium," Sam says as he heads out of the house.

I roll my eyes. "Please tell me she's not fucking a dolphin."

Sam shakes his head, "I don't ask. I mean, she's Tabi, for god's sake. We've known her since kindergarten. I can't go there. I hope this scenario is better than the construction worker or that Montana rancher."

"Is she trying to fuck all the Village People? Man, can you imagine hooking up with her?"

"You did, dude."

I correct him. "I had baby Tabi. High School. She's on her own path now. And if I met her in the wild, she'd scare the crap out of me."

"Don't get me wrong, I don't want to fuck her, but I do applaud her for going after whatever kink she wants."

"Yeah but shouldn't there be limits?"

"Joshie, you don't know what you're missing if you put limits on kink. As long as you know your hard limit, the rest is up for grabs." He crooks an eyebrow and disappears.

I'm uneasy when Sam's uneasy. I need to look at the contract. Nothing rattles that guy. I need to go see how the picking of the Zinfandel is progressing, check some brix, and then get some Sal paperwork pushed through. Another piece of the rackets goes legit today in a Texas Country Club. I'm desperately trying not to go to Santa Barbara. I'll have to go soon. There's a ton of in-person shit I need to do. But not today. Today is about Zinfandel. And Elle.

# 39

---

# ELLE

AFTER A WEEK OF BEING IN LOVE, MY RIGOROUS SCHEDULE OF sex and harvest are kicking my ass. But my legs and arms have never been more toned. The Zin was touch and go, but it's all juiced now. There's only the cab and bit of the Syrah left. The Cabernet is going to be a bear so we gave as many people time off as we could while the Syrah mellows on its skins in the tanks. The remaining blocks can be done tomorrow morning, and then it's just monitoring the heat and the brix with the Cab. It might be a couple of days or a week.

I opened the tasting room this morning with Mrs. Dotson, so the staff didn't have to come in. Sammy will be here in an hour, and we gave Randy the day off. Harvest has been non-stop people flowing through here, and we've sold a ton of wine.

I need to respond to a ton of marketing emails, and Asher's been calling. A bit more insistent that I call him than his standard emoji texts. Not sure what he needs, but he's been helpful with the sale, so maybe it's a congratulation. My back, neck, and legs are sore from pouring and paperwork. I need to go for a walk to at least to loosen everything up.

"Be back in five."

As I round my way up to the storage barn to grab some carrier boxes. Before I can get there, I see Josh standing in the parking lot. He's in a suit. Granted he's hot as hell in a navy suit and a melon colored tie with turquoise stripes. The hair product is back, making it Joshua perfect. I approach slowly. I can't remember the last time I stepped into my Jimmy Choo's, and he's in real shoes. Not boots or sneakers but polished Gucci loafers. He's pressed and perfect. But he's not my Josh. He sees me and instantly speaks loudly and even keel like he's trying to calm down a mental patient.

"I'll be back as soon as I can." With his arms out wide, he continues to try and calm me down.

"Where are you going?"

"Santa Barbara." My breath catches. I stop the tears from flowing by sheer force of will. I freaking hate that place, and I've never even been there.

I nod, and I turn around back to the tasting room. "I have to go."

He walks quickly and closes the distance, catching my wrist. He spins me around to face him. "No. No. Wait. Elle." He places his hands on my shoulders, and I look at him. "When I come back, we're going on a real first date."

"It's fine." I shake my head at him and try to be convincing.

"Stop it. I love you. I'm coming back."

"We'll see." I weasel free, but then he traps me in an embrace. I'm just numb as he pulls me closer to him. I can't believe this is happening again. He's leaving again, and I went all in. Fuck. I'll have nothing left of myself if he abandons me again. At least he told me this time.

"You either trust me right fucking now Noelle Parker, or we don't have a prayer."

"Are you off to meet an exotic leggy raven-haired Santa Barbara Insta beauty? This is just more secrets. Or are there more threats to protect me from?"

"Stop being glib and look at me. I have to resolve some tight issues on three different deals. And there's a face-to-face meeting I've put off for too long. I don't have a choice. It's how I finish this chapter."

"Sal?" He nods. "No fucking way. You're not going to meet a mobster. Will your FBI friend be there?"

"I could lie and tell you yes. At the heart of it all, Sal's a businessman. We'll be in a public place. It's bad business for him to hurt me, he's too smart for that. And Mark still has him under surveillance. But we need to have it out. I need to look him in the eye in order to know that none of this shit will happen again. We meet on an even playing field this time. I'll be safe in my house. My house has ridiculous security. I even have gates."

"You have gates?" I step back from him. I've googled his house, but I didn't see the gates.

"My place is kinda snatched. But you have nothing to worry about. Trust me. I'm coming back."

I yell at him, so he gets the point, "You need to stop telling me to trust you and start showing me you can be trusted. You knew you were going. You applied hair product. You have to tell me before you apply the product. YOU NEED TO TELL ME THINGS. BEFORE they happen." I scream in exasperation as I wiggle free and head back to the tasting room.

He screams, "Dammit, Elle. Just do as you're told for once. Don't worry."

I raise my middle finger and disappear around the corner to the courtyard and scale the little hill that they all call

Lucien's. Josh's grandfather used to stand and lord over his workers. He wasn't the most well-liked of men, but apparently deeply respected. It's a beautiful view of the vineyard, and I need a freaking breath. I can't deal with this. I want to know how long he's known that he had to go to Santa Barbara. It doesn't just sneak up. Even if he knew yesterday, he had to make plans. He knew when he put that stupid suit on.

I'm so hurt and pissed. I bend over to regulate my breathing. Calmer, I tromp back to the tasting room. I am mustering the parts of me that aren't devastated that once again he's leaving. And I wasn't a thought in the process.

He parks the Porsche in front of the tasting room doors like a jackass and yells, "You're right. I should have told you. I didn't know how to talk about it without you blowing up like this. You're not easy."

I come down the hill to him. He's not wrong. I'm not easy. I answer him resolutely, "It's fine. Go. You need to go, and I won't guilt you over your business. You'd let me go if I had business. But, oh, that's right, I fixed my shit, so I don't have to leave. I'm fine." I'm not. I'm dying inside as I say these words to him. He comes around the car and opens the passenger seat door.

"Get in."

"No."

"For once, do as I say. Elle. Get in the car. We're going to be late."

"For what?"

"My afternoon meetings."

Adrenaline shoots through me. "HOLD UP. You want me to come with you? Be with you?"

"Always." All of a sudden, my whole body flushes as he gives me that one lip lifted smile smirk thing that drives me wild. And I launch into his arms. I kiss him quickly.

"Why?"

"I'm showing you. You were right."

My face is in a full-body smile. "I have to pack."

"Taken care of." He pulls a slim duffle and my laptop bag out of the back of the car.

"That's just the cheeky pearl panties, and those sage green yoga pants you like my ass in isn't it?"

"And a toothbrush." He winks and gets in the car. "We can shop. Let me buy you things. Expensive things. Lots of pretty things. Come on, get in the car. Let's see how much money I can spend on you. Consider it a challenge. And you don't back down from those." Then he outstretches his hand. "Do you trust me, Cosmo?" I find it funny the roles are reversed right now, him in his fancy Porsche Spyder, me in my farm gear. Although it's a skirt today, I still have boots and a grubby t-shirt paired with it.

"There's a ton of work and calls. We have to get coverage. And…"

"Get the hell in the car and shut up, beautiful."

———

IN THE TWENTY minutes it took us to drive to the Napa airport, I haven't stopped smiling or holding his hand. He's showing me. He's trusting me with all of him. I get to see his house, and I get lots of pretty things. More importantly, I get to see another part of him. I already know what he sleeps in, but what does his bed look like? I'm excited to see what random beverages or moisturizers he has laying around. I want to know if his house looks like I pictured it. Will it reconcile with who I know him to be and who he was pretending to be?

"Holy shit. Are we flying in that?"

"Why drive when you can fly private?"

"My hair's a wreck. I'm still in my pajama shirt, and I don't have any underwear on. I can't fly in a private plane like this." Damn, I have changed. I used to be regularly dressed in a designer outfit. My pajamas were Dior, and my lounge pants were Miu Miu. Now, they're local swag. I grab a pen from the glove compartment and twist it up into my hair, it's the best I can do. It almost looks like I'm in an urchin exchange program. Like he's giving a homeless person a glimpse of the high life.

"You're stunning."

"I can't believe this. I don't know what to do on a private plane." He leans over, slowly moving his hand up my legs and under my navy-blue midi knit stretchy skirt. A quick swipe of my bush and I'm instantly wet.

"I know exactly what we're going to do for the next hour. I like the skirt." I bite my lip and look at the impressive plane. He takes my hand and guides me up the tiny stairs. A strange man whisks his car away, and another grabs our bags. He looks as comfortable here as he does among the vines. The two halves of his world and mind make more sense to me as he starts to show me the rest of him.

He nestles me in a seat across the aisle from him. A very nice woman brings us a glass of bubbles. She takes Josh's suit jacket and hangs it up. He removes his tie while staring at me and hands it to her as well. Josh neatly rolls up the sleeves of his shirt and even that is sexy.

I whisper to him, "How exactly do you purpose to have me, with her here? I don't share well." He smirks and nods to the door at the back of the plane. "Bathroom?! No, thank you." He laughs and nods again.

"Go look."

I unbuckle and head back to the door. I peek in, and it's a freaking bedroom. I whip my head back to him, "Holy hell. Just how rich are you?"

He curls his finger for me to come to him, and then he pulls me onto his lap. We spill our glasses just a little as he tangles his fingers into my hair, yanking my head back and the pen out of it. He lures my lips to his. It's a dirty and forceful kiss. I want to just be in that bedroom already. I pull back from him and trace his lips with my hand as I ask again. I really want to know.

"Seriously. How much money do you have?" He nips at my finger on his lips, and a wicked little grin appears.

"How much money do you have Ms. Parker?" He asks.

I shake my head at him. "I do okay. I mean, I planned for the future. And I'm a frugal farmer father's daughter. But I do like pretty things. I didn't save as much as I could have. But if I sold my building, I'd be set. Maybe not Manhattan set. But Hudson River Valley set or I could roll fat in Omaha. I'm okay. I mean I don't have private plane scrilla. And I certainly do not have bedroom private plane bank."

He kisses me deeply, and I feel the connection that I constantly crave from him. Then he dips his head, his eyes locking with mine, and winks.

"You do now."

# 40

## JOSH

As much as I want to fuck her on this plane, sadly, we really only have about twenty minutes in the air where we don't need seatbelts. I need to answer some emails. Hope she's okay with that.

I kiss her deeply and stand up, lifting her with me and placing her in her own seat. She pouts, and I want to rip her clothes off.

"I have to work a bit."

"You're telling me that I have to drink bubbles and not have sex on a private plane?"

"Hellcat, we're not in the air long enough for that type of activity. I got ahead of myself."

"Well, I'm never flying private again. What kind of bullshit is that? No orgasm. Whatever."

"Another time, my love. I promise I'll fuck you senseless in a private plane at some point." I kiss her hand and return to my iPad.

The plane begins to slowly taxi, and she clutches my hand pulling my attention to her. I lean towards her, and I see the fear in her eyes. The curtain has been drawn, so the flight attendant isn't really paying attention to us.

"Elle, look at me." She is super pale and sweating. This is not my fearless woman.

"I'm just kind of noticing that this is a tiny plane. I mean *tiny*."

"Are you afraid of flying?"

"Not usually. But this is really tiny."

I cup her chin to look at my face. "You're okay. Listen to my voice." She's sitting in the aisle seat of two seats across from my single seat. She leans into the aisle, looking terrified. She's ashen, and her hands are clammy. I quickly unbuckle and sit down next to her. But I don't let her react to me sitting there as we take off. It's a windy day, and this isn't going to be the smoothest ride. I shift sideways to face her in my seat and run my hand up her inner thigh, gladly remembering that she has no panties on.

"You're not as wet as you should be for me."

"I'm fucking terrified. Who's wet when they're panicked?"

"There are some who enjoy it."

"Well, we found my line. I'm not into panic death kink."

I laugh at her. "Open your legs for me. Let me in. Close your eyes and only listen to my voice." My lips are at her ears. Her hands are clutching the armrests. I reach further up her skirt and run my finger down her seam.

"This isn't going to work."

I put my finger in her mouth. "Suck." She does. "Good girl. Now close your eyes."

I spread her legs wider for better access. "Stop talking. Do you feel my finger? It's just moving up and down, just casually caressing your cunt. Actually, it's my cunt. And I get to do whatever I want to it right now." At the c-word, she sucks in a sharp breath. The dirty talk should distract her. "This pussy needs to know how badly I want to finger fuck it. My fingers want to explore all the parts of you. Curling slowly inside you. Stretching and exploring. I won't stop until you're writhing in that seat. Let go."

"Oh, god." Her chest flushes, and that's a good sign. I dip one finger in and grab the gathering wetness and take it to her clit. I slowly circle it as it becomes swollen. She pushes her hips into me and loosens her grip on the chair just as we get above the clouds. I circle more vigorously, now with several fingers. I'm rubbing her with a bit of pressure. I slip my middle finger deep inside her. She sits up suddenly as the plane lurches. I push her back down. I lean into her and nip at her neck.

"Let go, Elle. Let me give you this. I want you to clamp down on my fingers as they search for that spot. Is it here?" She sits up moaning. "Is that it?"

"Fuck. Fuck. Oh. How can you make me come this quickly?"

"Oh, you want it slower?" I pull out of her, and she moans at my exit. My thumb still firmly in place on her clit. "I'm going to make you come so hard. I'm going to start by doing this." I thrust three fingers into her quickly and then out of her, and she stretches to accommodate me. My thumb remains pressing on her clit, gently massaging it. And she's clutching the armrests for a different reason.

She's whispering to me. "Fuck. Josh. Fuck. Fuck. I need to come. Let me come, Josh."

I turn my body, leaning over her and replace my fingers inside of her, slowly pumping in and out. My mouth on her neck, sucking and nipping. My pinky drifts just below and grazes a different area of her that I've never dared go near. It's enough to detonate her.

A deep guttural noise erupts. "Oh, fuck." She sits straight up and then squeaks at a high pitch, and she crashes into me.

Breathing heavily as I continue to milk every last chill from her. I remove my hand and clean it up with a cocktail napkin.

She turns her head to me and kisses me intensely. "What the hell was that?"

"A distraction. You're now at cruising altitude." I unbuckle, bend over, and kiss her and return to my original seat, pulling out my iPad as she looks at me stunned.

"No. That thing. That little surprise."

"Oh, that. Just something I've been thinking about."

"No."

I turn my head to her. "Really? Your body says different-ly." It was magnificent, and I just grazed her in the moment. It wasn't a thought-out thing, but I wouldn't hate if we explored all of her body.

"Don't you have some work to do?" I look forward smiling.

She's still looking at me slack-jawed. "I guess."

"Your legs are still trembling, aren't they?'

She says indignantly, "Maybe."

I give her a wolfish grin. "Good."

# 41

# ELLE

I DON'T KNOW WHAT THE HELL WENT ON, ON THAT PLANE. I'VE never come that hard without someone inside of me. Damn. We land, and of course, he's got a fancy car waiting.

"How is this here?"

"The Tesla? John dropped it off for me. They have the keys at the front desk."

"How many cars do you own?'

"Three. No, four. Jeep, Porsche, Tesla, and kick-ass truck."

"A truck?"

"It's not like I can haul or move anything in the others."

"I do not know what to say. I don't get it, having never owned a car before."

We get into the Tesla, and it's really lovely. He goes to start the engine and then stops and looks at me.

"You've never owned a car?'

"I drove tractors and such. But I never really got my license until college. And then I just bummed rides. Then Bali, and then Manhattan. Car not really part of the program."

"Is that why you're a terrible driver?"

"I am not."

"Your short term lease car is dinged all to hell. Maybe if you owned it, you'd take better care of it."

"Well, probably not." I roll my eyes at him, but who cares? It's a rental. I probably should buy a car at some point. I'm staring out the window. It's gorgeous here. Different from up north, more rolling hills and cliffs. You can tell it's a coastal town by the way the sun plays off the trees. It has a boosted reflection from the water. There's bougainvillea exploding everywhere in bright, cheerful patches. I'm lost in their colors when Josh speaks again.

"Do you like your car?"

"The Mercedes? I do. I like it a lot. I might buy it after my lease thing."

"The dinged-up car? The one that needs a good vacuuming and new shocks?"

"I don't eat in the car that much."

"All the scones that ginger-bitch-barista provides you. And don't get me started on the sticky mess from the Basque's morning buns in your car."

"Fine. You can vacuum it when we get back, and I'll eat out of the window from now on."

He takes a sharp left turn and then looks at something on his phone at the next light. Then he programs his GPS. When we arrive at our destination, my jaw once again drops.

"What are you doing?"

"Buying you a present," he says with a sly grin as he exits the car.

"No, you are not. Buy me flowers. Or lipstick. I like lipstick. I like it a lot. This is too much."

A man with his hair slicked back approaches us in an off-the-rack suit. I know this because it gaps a bit. He extends his hand to Josh, and I stand there in my pajama shirt, messy bun, no makeup, and stretchy skirt, looking once again like a charity case or a hostage.

"How are you folks doing today? See anything you like?"

"Take this card. She can have anything she wants, but she drives it off the lot today. If you…" He hands a black credit card to the man.

"I am not a kept woman! I can buy my own car." Now I totally look like a sex slave.

He turns to me, and I'm furious that he's treating me like this. "Look, I would have done this differently, but I have to go. We're short on time. Do this for me. If you hate it, we can sell it and give the money to puppies, orphans, and innovative health research."

"Fine. I will do this if you donate the cost of the car to those things too."

"Done." He pecks my lips, sealing the deal.

"Someday you're going to have to tell me how much money you have."

"We have."

"Stop it. We are not married. I am simply in love with you."

"There's nothing simple about it."

He turns back to the dumbstruck car salesman, pulling up to his impressive six-foot-four height and puffing his chest. The man cowers just a little as my belly gets warn as my man flexes his intimidation techniques. "We both have impeccable credit, but I don't want to finance. Put the full price, minus the full price cash discount you're going to give us, on my card. Don't dick around. No extra costs and you get an impressive commission for the day. If she pays over one penny of the sticker, if you screw her around in any way, I will be back. Call whoever you need to call and get this done within the hour. She has places to be."

"I do?" I am baffled.

"Check your phone. John sent you some information. Including directions on how to get into my house. I have to get to my meetings and calls. We're going to dinner tonight, so buy some clothes with the same card I just handed this man. John was picking out some boutiques for you to explore as well." He leans into my ear. "You have a spa and salon appointment as well. I know you haven't had your hair cut in a while."

I kiss his cheek. "Thank you. This is all too much." It is. I'm not used to being handled in this manner. I can do all of these things myself.

"It will never be enough. You don't have to shoulder everything by yourself anymore. Let me do this. Let go, Cosmo. And buy some lipstick as well."

"Well, in that case, if we're short on time, can you wrap up a cherry red C 300 Cabriolet Mercedes right now?"

The man nods. "Just meet me in the office to sign the paperwork. Whose name do I put this into?"

"Mine, I'm pretty sure she doesn't have insurance."

I shrug. I'd been using insurance through the lease. "I should probably get on that."

He dashes off a text with his arm snaked around me. "John is sending that info to you as well. I have to run. I love you."

He kisses me softly but decently. He pulls off the lot, and I turn towards the dealership about to have quite the 'Pretty Woman' day.

---

I SLIP into my new M.M. Lafleur black cigarette pants, and orange textured Sadie sleeveless top after my blow out. I showered after my massage and bought a ton of makeup. My lips are covered with shiny, Guerlain light warm beige named *Beige Lingerie*. I thought it fit since I did buy quite a lot of that today too. Dinner is in an hour and a half, and it feels strange to go to his house without him. After googling Magnus' address, I set off for my new destination.

I'm greeted by a proper looking brunette who appears to have very little time for me. I'm carrying a gift for Josh. It's a wine glasses with our names etched in a heart. I thought it was cheesy and funny. I mean seriously, what the fuck am I going to buy the guy who just bought me a car? I also bought John some chocolates and a tie. I have no idea what he looks like, but I figure a shiny steel grey goes with everything.

"There are no appointments available today."

"Hi. I'm Elle Parker, and I'm here to see Josh Whittier."

"Mr. Whittier is completely booked. Can I set up something for a future date? Please note that Mr. Whittier isn't currently taking on any new clients." This makes me so happy to hear. He is actually getting out.

"Is John around?"

"Ma'am, there's no way around me."

My voice drips honey as I try to circumnavigate this woman. "It's only for a moment." I do not know how to explain myself. I pull out my phone and text John, which I have never done other than to say thank you for the information today.

"I'm sorry." I nod at her and take a seat, much to her chagrin.

*ELLE: John. Sorry to bother you. Are you busy?*

*JOHN: For my liege's queen? No. I could be having surgery, and I'd still take your call. He'd kill me if I let you flounder. What do you need, most magnificent one?*

*ELLE: I'm in the lobby, and the nice lady won't let me come find you.*

*JOHN: OOOH! On my way.*

Within a minute, John is rounding the corner. He's flamboyantly dressed in a gorgeous cobalt blue suit. My grey tie was a mistake. But I did include the receipt. He bows deeply in front of me, and I giggle.

"Stop."

"You are the most unexpected."

"Why? Because I'm not an exotic leggy brunette with a flat ass." He holds my arms out to the side.

"YES! You're delicious. Sassy. Stunning. Curvy. Vivacious. You are a vision. He most certainly does not deserve you." John envelops me in a hug. "Let's be best friends. He'll hate that. Come with me. He's on a conference call and quite prickly today. I do not know what to make of it." He hisses at the scowling receptionist.

He takes me back through this foreboding glass-and-steel building accented with rich mahogany wooden beams. We round the corner to a suite and push through a frosted glass door. His desk is in the front room, and I assume, Josh's office is behind his. There's a small conference room off to the right. It's like his own mini office building.

"I got these for you."

"What are you talking about? Prezzies!!!" He opens the tie.

"I didn't know you would have loved something with a bit more flair, so I went conservative. You can take it back."

"No. Not. Nada. Never. It will pair perfectly with my boyfriend's wrists." I giggle and hand him the chocolates. "You are too kind. And you really love him?"

"Shit. He told you that?"

"No, he's just never let anyone come to the office before. Or asked me to do anything specifically for a woman. We've been together for eight years. I know him."

"To be fair, he doesn't know I'm here."

"My darling. As sure as your panties are in his top left desk drawer, he knows you're here."

"My what?!"

"They're the reason I knew you were different. He wouldn't let me mail them back, even through the Claudia blip. And you have a curvy ass. No former concubine of my master's could have filled out those panties."

"I'm going to die. Can I go in? There's something I want to give him."

"He's on a call. There's not much you can give him while…" I raise my eyebrows to my new co-conspirator.

"Holy, little minx. Go on in."

## 42

---

## JOSH

She walks in, and my heart flips. As much as I want her here with me, I'm in the middle of negotiations. I shake my head at her, and she walks towards me. I'm behind my desk. She looks sexy as hell in her little Audrey Hepburn black pants and flats. She pulls open my desk drawer like she knows what she's looking for. I try to stop her, but she pulls out the padded envelope, extracting her undies. She glares at me and wags her finger in my face like she's scolding me. She puts them in her purse and places a gift bag on the desk. I will confiscate them back from her later. I finish making a point then put the phone on mute.

"What are you doing?" I crook an eyebrow at her.

"I missed you." She flashes a grin that makes my dick jump.

"That's nice to hear."

"What are you doing with these? These are mine."

"They're not. I told you I was keeping them when I took them off your body." I grab her wrist and drag her to me to kiss her. Then pull back and unmute. "That's unacceptable. When I said six-and-a-half percent, I fucking meant it." I mute and pull her to me with more force this time. She licks into my mouth, and I want this call to end. I talk again. "I was there. The value isn't there, and my client isn't going to give you that. The deal is for twice of what you're asking, and you give him the percentage on the return that you already fucking agreed to." She raises her eyebrows as she witnesses business Joshua for the first time. "I'll have your balls. I'll spread the word far and wide that you tried to deep dick me up the ass on this. You'll never fucking close another thing as long as you think you're in business." I lean forward, and she backs away. I'm looking for a piece of paper with the figures on it, and I don't see what she's doing.

Before I can protest, she's got my belt off. I push her head away from my crotch. That doesn't deter her. "That's better, just keep it fair. That's all I'm asking for and what you're going to do." I barely get the phone on mute before she's gone all in. I groan loudly.

She lifts her head, and I come out of her mouth with a pop. "Baby, just keep doing your business. I just wanted a little snack before dinner."

"Christ, woman. You're going to be the end of my career."

"That's fine with me." She takes all of me in and begins pumping her hands at the base of my shaft. I place a hand on her head and try to guide her.

She sits back, "Do you want me to stop? Keep that up, and there will be no release for you. I don't care how much money you're going to make on this deal."

I talk into the phone but also to her. "That's it. That's the way to get this deal fucking done." I mute and look down at her groaning my commission. "Eight hundred thousand dollars. Oh, god. Fuck." She stops.

"Are you fucking kidding me?"

"No. Hold on." I go back to the phone. I can barely breathe, "Okay, let's get this to bed. I have a pressing matter to take care of in my office right now. Send it to John by tonight." I look down at her and give her my full attention. "Now, where were you?"

"I'm not blowing you for your money or the car, you know that, right?"

"Why *are* you blowing me in my office?"

"Because the idea of making you lose control is intoxicating, and I haven't seen this perfect cock in like six hours. And that's the longest I've gone without it since I said I love you."

"I know you're not doing it for money. You didn't spend my money. I checked the card. I'll punish you later for that." I throw my head back.

She moans and takes me back down her throat, and I thrust into her. She working me and I can't hold on. Her lips are glistening and inviting. This might be my favorite color of lipstick ever. Fuck. It's like moments. This woman. I groan loudly, "Fuck. Elle." I spill down her throat, and she continues to suck me, swallowing it all. I collapse backward as she sits back on her heels and wipes her mouth. Then she licks her lips.

"Delicious."

I tuck myself back in and take her arms, guiding her onto my lap and kissing the hell out of her.

"You are perfect. Sexy, smart, and the perfect amount of dirty." She's twisting my hair between her fingers.

"Did you really just make eight hundred grand?"

"Not until the papers are signed, but yes."

"And this was a Sal deal?" She looks worried. She doesn't need to be.

"Yes. He's one of the investors. I meet with him tomorrow to tell him all about it. It's one of his bigger investments."

"Are you meeting here at the office?"

"No. Restaurant. I don't want him near the building. He gets that."

"I don't like it."

"Then I'll just have to keep you so blissed out you won't even have time to think or worry about it." I kiss her as she nods. "Let's skip dinner and head back to my house so I can have my dessert." I squeeze her ass hard, and she squeals.

"Open your present first."

"Didn't I just get your gift?"

I look in her gift bag and remove two red wine balloon glasses etched with our names in a heart and a unicorn flying around.

"It's perfect. I didn't have anything like this." We both laugh at the ridiculously tacky glasses.

"Now, let's go. I'll drive. I don't know if you heard, I got a new car today."

## ELLE

WE'RE LYING IN HIS BED, MY BACK TO HIS FRONT. WE'VE HAD sex five times since we left his office. He's running his fingers up and down my arm. He's lulling me to sleep. We never made it to dinner. We made ham sandwiches a couple of hours ago.

"What did you buy today?" His voice is gravelly and sexy.

"Lots of pretty things."

"You know I wanted to do that for you. Why didn't you use my card?"

"The answer to that question and all the ones like it in the future will be because you bought me a seventy-five-thou-sand-dollar car." He squeezes me closer. I'm beginning to understand the volume of his wealth, but it makes me uncomfortable. And he was right when he told me that his parents certainly didn't need to sell the winery. He could have provided anything they needed.

"Know that I'm not trying to woo you anymore. I just want to do nice things for you. You have impeccable taste. You spend lots of money on yourself, let me do it for you every once in a while."

"Mercedes. I let you buy me a Mercedes."

"Okay, baby. But as soon as I figure out how you smell this good all the time, I'm going to buy all this perfume in the world, so no one else can smell like you."

"I'm not wearing any." I don't know what he means. I switch my shampoo all the time. I don't have a signature scent.

"Interesting, that's just you then. Let's get some sleep so I can bliss you out in the morning before I go. My meeting is early, and I'll be home as soon as possible. I'll let you know when I'm done, so you don't worry."

"That will do it. I won't worry now." I flip over and kiss his soft and swollen lips, his scruff lightly pressing on my cheeks. Then I sink back into his spoon and fall away.

HE HEADS OFF TO WORK AFTER EATING ME OUT, TWICE. I PEEK in the closet, and again the man leaves me speechless. There are rows of clothing I didn't buy. It's all so gorgeous.

*ELLE: YOU! Did you do this? WHEN?*

*JOHN: Did you try on the Prada yet? GORGE. And now that I know your coloring, it's perf for you. It's all so Gucci. And there's Gucci! When he texted yesterday morning telling me you were coming, he sent me shopping. Squeal!*

*ELLE: Thank you.*

*JOHN: Hell, no bish. You do not thank me for this one. That man let me spend a fortune on clothes. So fun. Anything you don't like, let me know. And know that I didn't buy that one pair of shoes. They were already in the closet.*

*ELLE: What shoes?*

*JOHN: You'll know. I made him explain those gorgeous little kittens to me.*

*ELLE: Tell me he pays you well.*

*JOHN: I'm the only assistant in my tax bracket. Ta, girl. Gotta make sure the mobster's paperwork is in order.*

*ELLE: Is he scary?*

*JOHN: I'll spill the tea for you, but do not furrow that perfect brow of yours. Salvatore is actually a puppy dog. He needs a rolled-up newspaper to the nose every once in a while. He won't hurt Josh. Ta.*

*ELLE: Ta*

That makes me feel a little bit better. I walk through the closet, handling all the fabrics. I love them all and can hardly believe all of this is for me. I simply fell in love with a jackass grape farmer, and now I've got a fantasy closet in a massive beach house in Santa Barbara. I will admit that it felt so good to slip into silk and bias-cut anything yesterday. I own four new pairs of shoes and whatever John picked out.

I glance around, and my eyes fall on the center island in his closet. There's a shoebox that looks as if it's got a spotlight on it. I know what they are before I even open them. He replaced my Fendi kitten heels that I ruined in the mud to spite him. He remembered. I look at the fuchsia Prada dress, and John left the tag on it. He bought me a six-thousand-dollar Prada silk dress. There's a post-it note on the tag.

*E,*

*Your legs will look killer in this.*

*Wear it tonight.*

*I love you,*

*J*

My legs can look killer in a Target dress too, but this is beyond comprehension.

I have fabulous clothes in New York, but these are insane. My mom was fashionable for Kansas. She was always impeccably dressed, even collecting eggs or mucking out stalls.

We used to obsessively read B&B, Buttons and Bows, magazine and scout the latest trends. We'd shop our mall and add strategic pieces to our existing wardrobes, but designer clothes were way off our radar. Every fall, there was a big fashion issue and we'd clip the section on purses and take it with us to the mall. We'd scout, hunt, and search every corner to find a knockoff that was close to the high-end pieces that we coveted in the magazine.

I wish I could have bought her a Chanel suit. She would have liked that. She used to accessorize all the farm wives for the big church dance in the summer. She'd piece together scarves or make jewelry that mirrored what they were wearing on those glossy pages. I still subscribe to B&B magazine; it's the only fashion magazine I've ever really read. I do it now mostly for nostalgia sake since the internet can provide real-time images of fashion week. But when I hold it, it connects me to her. I wish she could see this closet. I sigh and scan the rest of the beautiful things he's given me. I should tell him about why I love fashion. I glance at the entire closet, trying to take it all in.

And then I lose my breath. There, among the purses, shoes, and scarves, sits a bag that costs about as much as my new car. He needs to donate more to charity if he's going to casually buy me a hot pink shiny crocodile vintage Birkin bag. It's so pretty I can't even touch it. I just stare at it, standing here pants-less in his Stanford t-shirt. I can't touch it if I'm half-naked. That would be offensive to the bag. I pull on a pair of his boxers and fold the waistband down. I delicately touch it with one finger, to make sure it's not an apparition. Electricity surges through me. It's so beautiful.

*ELLE: You?*

I snap a picture.

*JOHN: HOLY MUTHAFUCKING GRAIL. Is that what I think it is? That's all him, honey. Can I have it?*

*ELLE: No. It's never leaving my side.*

*JOHN: You must give good head.*

*ELLE: The best.*

He went to work early today, or he would absolutely have

gotten anything he wanted this morning. I pick up my purse and bring it to the bed with me. I'm not kidding. It's never leaving my side.

We, my Birkin bag and I, lounge around the bedroom and in these insanely comfortable sheets. I set up a command center and get a ton of work done from this decadent bed all morning. I carefully place the bag on the nightstand when I grab more coffee and a bagel. She doesn't need cream cheese anywhere near her. I've decided to call her Daphne. I don't know how to tell Josh I like her more than the car, who has yet to be named.

The room is light, a yummy warm beige. All the walls, bedding, lights, and blinds are all shades of this taupe. His personality comes through in the textures in the decorating. The super high headboard is a luxurious velvet, the walls are covered with grasscloth, there are leather chairs in the corner, and the rug is sisal. But there's a soft, cozy throw at the end of the bed. Competing textures that feel like him. But the main feature is the entire wall of windows and the French doors that lead to the ocean view. He overlooks cliffs. There are series of terraced patios down towards the water. His infinity pool looks likes it lives right on the edge of the world. He assures me an earthquake won't topple the pool or the house, but this heartland girl is skeptical.

Now I'm showering in a space larger than my Manhattan kitchen. Daphne is tucked away on a shelf with a towel underneath her. There's a chest-height wall that separates the shower room, complete with a bench that came in handy last night. The rest of the room has an overgrown concrete looking bathtub surrounded by floor to ceiling windows. The two sinks opposite the tub match the concrete. The deep sinks blend into the countertops. His towels are this bright turquoise. A bright aqua like the color of the shirt he wore when I met him officially at the vineyard. They're fluffy and absorbent and most likely cost more than Daphne. Looking around the house, I only see Josh in the outdoor areas. The interior and decor are all Joshua. It's gorgeous but a little cold.

I've laid out the Johnny Was scarf-print skirt for the day. It's navy with large scale lilies and peonies on it in pinks, creams, and periwinkle. I grab my favorite black tank from my duffle. It's not a billion-dollar one, just one from the GAP. And I pair it with the most gorgeous leather dusty rose angular slides the world has ever seen from Mercedes Castillo. I adore the angles and square shapes of them. I don't need to wear shoes in the house, but they were calling to me, begging me to put them on.

I'm going to pad around his house today in this skirt until I need to put on the Prada. I've missed dresses, but this is undoubtedly not daytime winery attire. The soft rayon floats all around me as I walk. I feel a bit like a decadent kept woman. I walk down his light gray hallways on the marble tile towards the kitchen. I pass the other two bedrooms that are equally monochromatic, in blue and the other in gray. I run my fingers on the walls as I pass by, taking in his absence from the space. Without him, he only exists in pockets here. There are no family photos, except a couple in his office, buried on the bookshelves. The most personal thing in his space is in the living room. I turn a corner and see it, and it makes me smile.

There's a five-by-seven-foot photograph of an extreme close up of a ripe vine and a grape cluster. I guessed correctly, and he attacked me with kisses. It's a ripe Pinot Meunier, Emma LaChappelle's, his four-times great grandma, the 4G, favorite varietal. It's the reason she got on a boat and came to California. The reason she defied all odds to achieve her dream of creating her own wines.

It's the base of the *Emma* sparkling that Will is secretly

working on. No one but Alena and myself know that he's been cultivating the original root to become a sparkling for Sarah. It's his winery swan song and three harvests ago he finally got some juice. Alena and I picked this year's crop personally and secretly crushed it. That's how I know what it looks like versus a Pinot Noir. Differences are subtle on the vine, but both grapes combined with Chardonnay will produce the perfect sparkling. Alena has a double fermentation rack being built for the back of the caves for her office, as most people call it. It's her secret lair and lab. She does her experimental blending there and it's where Will does his crazy blends. The original proportions for the *Emma* sparkling were found in a handwritten log on the shelves of the Farmhouse.

The photograph tells me that he's always been connected to the land and his family despite all his efforts to be someone else. He'll always be Josh LaChappelle Whittier.

Daphne and I head to the kitchen. I place her down on a dry tea towel off to the side so I can grab some iced tea. I have a special delivery coming for Josh. John told me he's a sucker for macarons. I ordered a bunch to be delivered today. I met the baker yesterday, and he said he'd send someone over.

The double door glass fridge is its own room. You can literally walk into it. We could never eat everything John stocked. There's plenty of cheese, bread, and some milk for cereal. Another interesting thing I picked up about my beloved. His pantry is stocked with like ten different kinds of cereal. He must eat it all the time. I knew he liked it. I didn't realize it was a staple in his diet.

The house is overflowing with lush fruit as well. I'm snacking on an apple staring at the ocean through the living room window when the gate buzzes. I check on Daphne, and she's fine, so I push the button and open the gate for my French pastry delivery.

Josh met with Sal this morning. I was instructed not to leave the house and don't let anyone in, but I got a text an hour ago that it all went well and that he's gone. I'm happy to have this behind us. Now he can eat macarons off me later.

## 45

---

## ELLE

WHEN I OPEN THE DOOR FOR MY DELIVERY, I GASP. MY HEART is immediately in my throat, and I throw my only weapon at him. Salvatore Pietro gets hit smack in the nose with my apple core and puts his arms up like it's a gun.

I shriek. "What the fuck, man? Why the hell are you here? He's at the office."

"I'm not here to hurt you. I swear it on my familia. Noelle Parker, I'm here to see you. I bring a peace offering." He's carrying flowers, a pastry box, and a bottle of wine.

"You think you're coming in here? Holy shit. You! You fucking followed me. You kept him from me."

"I am alone. I swear, Ms. Parker, I come in peace. I have amends to make."

"Damn fucking straight you do."

"What a mouth on you." He shifts his weight and his large frame fills the doorway.

"Cocksucker, you want to fucking play with me? You don't get to judge what language I use considering your profession. Shit. Ass. Hell. Cunt. Muthafucker."

He puts a hand in the air as if he gets my point. "Fair enough. My apologies."

My adrenaline is popping off the charts, and I'm scanning the area for my phone or a weapon.

"I swear on my family and yours, I mean you no harm. I simply want to share a glass and talk a little."

"I don't trust you."

"You have every right not to trust me. I've done wrong by you, and I want to make it right. Josh will not accept anything from me but an apology. But I have a feeling I'm going to need to work a bit harder with you to get you to accept my apology."

It wouldn't hurt to listen to him. "And Josh is alive?"

His gruff laugh fills the house. "Of course, Noelle. Of course. I left him a bit ago. He is fine and shook my hand in friendship. I will never threaten him or any of you again. It was a dire situation, and I reverted to my worst instincts. Mea culpa, Blondie."

"Can we get one thing clear?"

"Whatever you need."

I steel myself and my voice so he understands exactly what I'm saying. "Just this one thing. You owe us nothing. And we owe you nothing. I don't want debts, favors, or vendettas between us. Do you understand me?"

"That's not the way my world works, but it will be with you. In my world, there's always a ledger and long memories."

"Not with me. Do you hear me? These flowers you're holding, I'm taking them because they're beautiful not because you need to make things right. Do not make things right, simply talk to me and promise me none of this shit happens to us again. And not with Josh. I do not want favors."

"I promise. What about the wine?" His lips curl upward into a broad smile.

"Well, we should drink that because we're both thirsty." I shrug at him.

I take the gorgeous bouquet of hydrangeas from him and walk away. As I turn towards the kitchen, I say, "You may come in but don't come within ten feet of me. I am going to carry a giant carving knife around. And I'm wicked good at cooking, so I'm super good with the knife. You cool with that?"

"Works for me."

"And leave your weapon in the car."

"That I can't do, doll. Josh may have forgiven me, but many never will."

"Then you can't come in." I turn after placing the flowers on the counter and take a superhero stance with him. "Seriously, get the fuck out if a gun comes in here."

He nods and leans down to his leg and removes it from its holster. I suck in a gasp. I could die right now. The man has a gun in Josh's house, and my phone is in the bedroom. I'm nauseated. I will not die today. I have way too much to do. He disappears out the door. I exhale and bend over to try to catch my breath. He's much better looking than I imagined. He has gorgeous olive skin. His short, cropped coal dark hair and dark soulful eyes make him seem less menacing than I anticipated. He's built like an inverted triangle. The dark scruff on his chiseled jaw softens him a bit. The broadest shoulders and insanely jacked arms and his body tapers down to long, muscular legs. I hear him come back inside and I stand back up in my faux attack stance. He returns without his black suit jacket. He rolls up the sleeves of his white button-down as he nods to me.

"You win. No weapons. Hey, nice bag."

"That's Daphne. Don't touch her."

"I promise to keep my hands to myself. Nice to meet you, Daphne." I grin as he greets my Birkin bag without calling me crazy.

"Now pop that cork, Blondie. I've got much to say."

"If it's not about stealing Josh from me for months and that we're safe for the rest of our lives from you and anyone who follows in your footsteps, I got no time for it."

"You're a hell of a ballbuster."

"You have no fucking idea."

"Hellcat, you here? My day sucked. I need to bury myself in you. Let's stay in."

"She's out here." My body goes numb at the sound of Sal's voice. I did not know he was still in town. I have shit security. I drop the groceries and our dinner. A bottle of wine shatters on the ground as I bolt to my back patio.

She greets me at the sliding glass door. "Hi, cutie." She wraps her arms around me, and I don't take my eyes off Sal. I scan the area. There are no bodyguards. It's just Sal with his tie undone and eating some Humboldt Fog cheese. It's Elle's favorite. What the hell is going on? I exhale and drag her as close to me as possible.

She kisses me. "Can you open another bottle? Sally and I already went through the red he brought."

Tucking her close to me, I whisper in her ear, "Are you okay?"

She looks at me and puts her hands on my shoulders then goes up on her tiptoes. "I'm fine. We're fine. I'm safe, and we're going to stay that way."

"Not only is your girlie a looker but Blondie is one hell of a fucking ballbuster." I grin, knowing that Elle has indeed handled things. I shouldn't be surprised, but sometimes I have to remember, she's not fragile. She's stronger than all of us.

"That she is." I kiss her head.

"What's for dinner? I'm starved," Sal asks.

"Originally, we were going out, but I decided last minute to grab my favorite take out. It was Coq au Vin from Stella Mare. I dropped it when I thought Sal had either killed you or had you tied up. And now it's covered in broken glass."

Elle's face gets ashen as she exclaims, "Is Daphne alright?"

"Holy shit, who's Daphne?" I panic that there's someone else in my house.

Sal chortles. "It's the purse."

"IT!" She scolds Sal.

"Many pardons to Daphne. She. She's the purse." I chuckle and look at my love's face.

"Daphne Birkin," Elle tells me pointedly. She found my surprise.

"She's fine. Do you like Daphne?" She goes back up onto her tiptoes, and I lower my ear to her lips.

She whispers, "There will never be enough sexual things I can do to you or you can do to me to ever explain to you how much I love her. Thank you." I brush my lips to hers. I'm filled with lightness. Finally, she accepts a present without fuss.

We all laugh as Sal says, "I got too much respect for you, Joshie. I'd never off her in your beautiful home. It would be off property. And let's face it. It wouldn't be me, Joshie. You'd never see it coming."

Barefoot in a long black skirt covered with flowers and her black tank top clinging to places I dream of, she exhales. My Hellcat has an underworld boss wrapped around her finger.

She turns to him. "Don't you even *think* about killing me. I will fucking haunt your ass. I'll get your dearly departed mother to haunt your ass. Capiche?"

"See. Ballbuster. Most people who work for me don't have the balls to talk to me like that."

I say, "Trust me, I know all about her mouth and attitude."

She turns to me. "Well, then, what should we order?"

"Bullshit. Order. What is with that? What's in the house?" Sal stands up from his deck chair. Josh looks at me, and I look at him, and we shrug. "It's the honeymoon phase. You idiots forget to eat. Come, we'll cook and then we'll have a nice chat."

"I don't really, um, cook," Elle says sheepishly. I shrug again, Sal rolls his eyes.

"You lied with that knife threat?" He gives her some side-eye, and my fight or flight kicks in.

"I did." She turns to him.

"Don't do it again. That's not who we are to each other now."

"I won't." He nods at her, and I have no idea what they're talking about. "Come, it's time you had a lesson. Your mama will be so proud when you bring home this gravy."

Elle and I freeze, but Sal interrupts us before we can speak. "Calm it down. I love research as much as this one. I meant Mama Whittier. I know yours is with the angels, like mine." He pulls a medallion from his neck, kisses it, and does the sign of the cross. Elle crosses the patio and goes up on her tiptoes and kisses him on the cheek. Then she heads inside to apparently learn to cook. I shouldn't be surprised, but I'm dumbfounded that she's charmed a mob boss into teaching her how to make dinner.

AFTER HE FOUND some tomato paste and had a specific canned San Marzano tomatoes delivered, Sal made what he called a quick Sunday gravy. I thought he was going to cook brown pot roast gravy, not tomato sauce. Elle made the salad, and he instructed her on how to correctly cut veggies. I, miraculously, made some kind of chicken thing. We pounded and breaded chicken. He kept calling them cutlets. It was all delicious. By the time we opened the fourth bottle of wine for the day, I realize that my darling girl had been drinking for close to seven hours.

She has a soft contented look on her face. She glides through my house as if she's always been here. The ease with which she finds silverware or a platter is heartwarming. She dives into a large pastry box of macarons, my weakness, arranges them on a fancy platter that I didn't even know I owned. I pop a raspberry one in my mouth, and she kisses the meringue crumbs off my lips.

"The two of you. How the hell did you get here so fast? I mean this one was just with that dystopian-looking slender thing. No meat there, no interest. And you Blondie, you were with that useless tool, right?"

She quickly interrupts me before I can answer him. "He who shall not be named in this household. Yes. It was very brief and very wrong. But it did bring me to him."

"I guess you never know when you're going to get bit." He raises a glass to us, "Salut."

We all toast, and I've filled her glass with water. She keeps sipping unconsciously. I'm not letting her passing out.

She blurts out. "You like Poppy Gelbert, don't you?"

"What makes you say that?"

Elle tucks her knees under her on the chair and leans way across the table to Sal. I have no idea what's she's driving at. They met once for a moment.

"Because you lit up when you asked about her earlier. And I've seen her expression when she asked about you."

"Gingersnap asked about me?" He leans back and puts his hands behind his head. A satisfied look crosses his face, one I haven't seen before. And I presented him with a high yield deal today. This is different, more profound. "She's a someday kind of woman. In my world there is no guarantee of someday. For now, I can dream of a time where we aren't who we are. But for now. It is what it is." Sal winks at Elle.

Elle grins and leans over the table towards him. "We're paisanos now. I see you. She's too good for you but keep going in this direction and you might just earn my endorsement."

"Ballbuster." I nod as she laughs and Sal continues, "Now that you know my mother's quick gravy, we're family."

"When did your Mama pass?" Elle asks as she sits back down but not before grazing my lips with a quick kiss. She's remarkable. She somehow charmed a crime boss into teaching her how to cook and opening up about his dead mother. And apparently has secured our safety in perpetuity. Our kids will grow up safe. Our kids. Damn. That's a thought. Slow down.

We should probably think about getting engaged in a year or two. Let's just sit with our relationship for a while. I haven't even seen her house yet. Marriage can wait at least two or three years. The candlelight is playing off her hair, and it's glowing. Her barefoot toes are newly painted a deep shiny green and match her eyes. Or maybe I marry this woman tomorrow or get Sal ordained and do it right now. Lock her down and keep her forever.

I'm so in love with her and every delicate movement she's doing right now. Moving her hair behind her ear or lightly touching Sal's arm. I watch her as she strokes the stem of her wine glass. Then as her ankles are crossing and uncrossing, shifting her weight based on enthusiasm for whatever subject comes up. It's our first dinner party, as unconventional as it is. She's my caught off-guard girl. And I'm ready to be off-kilter for the rest of my life. I also need Sal to leave. I'm acutely aware that I haven't been inside this woman in almost seventeen hours.

"Sal," she says bluntly, and we're all intrigued.

"Yes, Blondie?"

"Can I be honest?"

"Depends." He folds his hands in front of him on the table and leans forward toward her.

She reaches across the table and takes one of his hands. "I look forward to seeing you again. To taking you to Poppy's for dinner or coming down to LA with Josh sometime to see you, but I need you to leave." And somehow she read my mind. Holy shit, she just kicked Sally Pipes out of my house. We wait with bated breath, and a laugh from deep in his soul erupts as he stands up.

"Ball-fucking-buster! Lovers. You two. I get it. Okay. I'm gone." He seems so much older than his actual age. As if he was raised in a different time. He's only a couple years older than me, but I often imagine him thinking of me as a kid. He has a paternal thing to him, possibly because he's the head of a very unconventional "family."

Sal hugs me, and I give him a good slap on the back. Then Elle approaches him.

"Remember. No debts. No favors."

Sal shrugs at her. "Then what are we if not indebted?"

"Friends. We do things for each other because it's nice, not because we want something or have to pay someone back."

She's remarkable.

"Not sure I have friends like that."

"You do now. I will never need something from you that you're obligated to do."

"Are you saying you won't make me an offer I can't refuse?"

I laugh genuinely at his joke.

"I am." She hands him the pastry box. "Leave the gun, take the macrons."

He chortles and kisses my woman on her head and leaves my house. And just like that, we're best friends with a crime boss.

# 47

---

## ELLE

That was a lot of wine. My head is swimming with thoughts of swimming naked. Sal was talking about flowers he wants to plant someday, and I couldn't even pretend I wasn't thinking of Josh naked.

Before I know it, Josh is dragging me toward the patio. There's not a hesitation as he takes me in his arms and slants his mouth over mine. I respond feverishly. Being next to him for so long and unable to hold him has been torture. I tangle my fingers into his hair and twist it tightly as he lifts me up, hitching my legs around his waist. One of my favorite places to be. He softly moans, and I arch into him as he cups my ass. My body molds to his. He begins walking toward the water and stops just before we fall in.

He puts me on my feet, and I begin unbuttoning his shirt and kissing his incredible chest. I'm trailing lower when he puts his arms around me. He just holds me to him, and I can feel him ease into forever. I keep my arms around his warm and wonderful skin.

I could always feel a tug of sadness or anger about either lost time because of Lucien, or mistrust over me, but right now I feel as if I'm absorbing all of his doubt. I can take that all away, and in return, he's taking away my solitude and the sadness that surrounds the idea of giving up control. Without feeling "the sad," I can't possibly feel "the happy." At this moment, we are lowering the last of our walls and I've never been more vulnerable or happier in my entire life.

He kisses my forehead, and then I kiss his neck. Then things ramp up. He pulls my skirt off, and I tug my tank top off. In just a green bra and panties that match my new toe polish, I crook a smile at him while I see his eyes rake over every pore of my skin. I take three steps backward without breaking eye contact and slip into the pool.

He watches me as he slowly takes off his shirt, unbuttoning the cuffs. I remove my panties and throw them at him. He puts the wet pair into his pants pockets and whips them off. His cock springing forward, hard and ready, and in an instant, he dives in and comes up to me. I wrap myself around him in the water.

He attacks me, and we're kissing sloppy and enjoyable. I rub myself against him under the water.

"I'm pretty excited for mermaid sex." I say to him as I lay back in the water and let my hair free float all around me. My back is arched and my nipples peaking from the night air. He's staring with hooded lids and a dark expression. I feel his erection. It's so hot. With his hands on my hips, he moves me gently side to side as the water cascades over my breasts and my hair swooshes back and forth. I can hear nothing but the sound of the water. He reaches down to my clit and pushes down, then explores my wetness inside mixed with the fresh water pool water.

I hear him murmur, his voice obscured by the water in my ears, "Fucking perfect."

## 48

### ELLE

SANTA BARBARA IS LIKE A DREAM NOW. WE'VE BEEN BACK FOR a week and working nonstop. I barely see him, both of us being pulled in a million directions. Sarah is healing, but the process has been slow. Harvest will be done today. It's been incredible, but I could definitely do with a break. Every part of me is freaking exhausted. Everyone is kind of milling about in a haze. Everyone is catching naps where they can. There's been fist fights over the old green La-Z-Boy chair in the tank room. The finish line is in sight. We're having a cookout tonight with everyone's families to celebrate the end. The real party to say goodbye to the vineyard with everyone we could rustle up will be tomorrow night after the signing.

I'm hoping to get a nap in. Last night was the first night we didn't have sex since we said we loved each other. We had to be up at four a.m., both of us putting out fires here and in our own businesses all day. Last night we sat up in bed, both with our laptops, and conquered the problems. I passed out before he was done. But I did wake up in his arms.

I feel as if my hands are going to be permanently purple

after juicing and sorting clusters the last couple of days. I have like a four-hour window where I can get some deep ass sleep before I pick up barrels of potato and pasta salad from Broadway Market for the picnic.

I flop onto the bed, in my panties and favorite soft Stanford t-shirt that doesn't belong to me. I haven't even washed my face. I haven't done manual labor like this since I was sixteen years old. And now, twice that age, I feel it a lot more. I won't need Pilates for weeks. And I can't believe we survived. Will and Sarah are coming home today for the cookout. Then they head back to the city for the night. That way they can get to her early doctor's appointment before the signing of the sale papers. Then they'll surprise everyone at the party. They have large bonuses to hand out to their staff. Josh doubled their salaries for harvest and they don't know it. He claims the money is coming from the wages of the workers who abandoned us, but I know he's covering the cost. It's something that Lucien wouldn't have done but Josh didn't even hesitate in rewarding people for going above and beyond. They all pitched in because of their commitment to Will and Sarah. Josh really wanted to reward their loyalty and caring. He's the Josh I always knew he could be.

Today was also hard because we worked separately. It's like Josh and this town figured out a way for me to be both parts of myself. The New York and Kansas meld here in Wine Country. I understand the soil and the foie gras. Cutoffs and Chanel lipstick. My head is swamped with thoughts that scare me and excite me. Is this my life? Are we really not leaving California? Are we going to go to Santa Barbara or New York? Or should we just buy a beach shack somewhere remote and have sex for the rest of our lives? Did I take enough Advil to make sure my back doesn't give out tomorrow? Lots of questions as I begin drifting off.

After being independent for so long, it excites me to have

someone to make those decisions with me. I can share my burden. My mom was the last person I was able to honestly do that with.

Since my parents and aside from Evan, everyone I've shared anything with has hurt me terribly. Whether it was in business or personally. My heart's been off the market for so long. But he sees me and takes away that control part. I really do need a break from everything being perfect and planned out. I didn't fall apart when I didn't plan every aspect of this picnic tonight or the party tomorrow. Although I did order flowers and cigars for the wives, husbands, and mothers who became harvest widows or widowers. I didn't tell Josh that I tweaked a few things. I did buy the meat from a specific butcher. But I don't know the color of the tablecloths or if there are tablecloths. I may have ordered some to-go boxes and extra goodies for the kids coming. And there's furniture coming tomorrow that Sarah didn't exactly approve. But that's it. And my world hasn't shattered yet. And even though I'm still on guard, there are pockets of bliss in the unknown. I stretch out and curl the comforter under my chin. But I may need to check on the tablecloth situation.

Usually, my thighs glisten at the thought of him, but sleepiness has dried me up for the first time. After a lifetime of men demanding things of me and me rebelling against it, his demands are always about giving pleasure or securing his world around him. I submit to him and struggle with hating myself for it, but in the end, I like it. He has my body. He has my heart. Can I give him my soul as well? I'm so tired that all these thoughts are flowing into each other. Someday it will fly out of my mouth, and I won't be able to stop it. What I truly want. Children, family, forever. Probably on the heels of him fucking me silly. Even as sleepy as I am, he's always on my mind.

"WHAT IF I could make you come without moving?" Josh's newly showered warm body presses to mine. He's in my ear, pulling me out of my dreamy state that I swear I just entered.

"Are you going to talk my orgasm out of me. Because I'm so tired, I can't do anything."

"Not kidding, I won't move, and you try not to. I read something I want to try."

I can't even smile. I'm so tired and my research man looked up how to give me more orgasms.

I murmur, "I'm going to stay over here as the little spoon and if you feel the need to explore some kind of voodoo, go right ahead. Enjoy. I'm bone tired. I've never been this tired. I can't participate, but use me as you like. Don't be offended if I snore."

"You won't."

"No devices."

"No devices. Just let me hold you."

"That would be nice." He wraps his arms around me, and I snuggle back, my ass brushing up against him. He's thankfully not hard. The idea of squirming and thrusting is beyond me right now. His hand moves into my cheeky panties and I feel his dick twitch.

"Thought you weren't going to move?"

"I have to get in position first."

"You're are nuts. Goodnight."

"You're the sexiest thing on the planet. This sleepy, it only makes me want you more. And now I want to control you." A smile tugs at my mouth, but my eyes are still closed. His hand goes deeper, and he adjusts himself closer. Slowly he opens my right leg and drapes it over his.

"I thought I didn't have to do anything." I angry-whisper at him.

"That's it. I only needed a bit of access."

"That's the only help I'm giving you," I mumble.

"If I do it right, you'll buck, thrash, and scream my name. You'll beg me to stop, but I won't. I won't until your entire body comes alive and forces me to stop."

"Grand plans for a very sleepy, dry, and limp girl." His hand separates me and positions two fingers lightly on my clit a little to the left but covered slightly by the hood. It's instantly erotic and pleasant. I can't help but juice up for him, but I'm still settling into sleep. He taps lightly for like thirty seconds. It's a strange but not terrible feeling. It's like he's gently pressing the remote on-and-off switch. Then he just pushes on. Not harsh pressure just a gentle constant presence.

"I own you. You're mine, and I can turn you on and off as I like." He's forcefully whispering in my ear, and the strangest sensation begins. As the pressure remains steady, I begin to slowly pulse from my core and my breathing deepens. My brain clues into what's happening. I keep waiting for him to stop or move his fingers. I expect him to circle my clit, to claw at my nipples, lick me anywhere, but all he does is coo in my ear. Well, his dick digs into my back. As I pant, he gets harder. I imagine all those other things are happening to me, but it's only the tension not letting up with constant pushing on my clit. It's like my clit is the epicenter of this coming earthquake. It's pulsing in light whirls with my breath. With each exhale, the waves spread out further. I feel the upsurge in my upper thighs now. It's getting more intense each time it happens. A chill flows through me at regulated intervals, and then a flash of heat begins to build again.

"Let it happen. I own you. You're mine." He growls in my ear.

My eyes now fully open, and my breathing is rhythmic. I moan lightly on the exhale. The sensation is relentless, unyielding, and dominant. My pleasure pulse gets deeper and fans out like I genuinely have a core that's radiating. Josh doesn't move. He doesn't let up. The constant force of his fingers on my clit and the tide gets stronger and returns faster and faster. The throbbing speeds up. He doesn't adjust or increase the pressure. I can't fathom that he's forcing me to come. That I'm being compelled, and I have no 'out' except to orgasm. I'm bound to this pleasure to escape this moment. And that's so fucking hot I can't contain myself. Now I'm moving my hips into his fingers, trying to get more force and pressure on it. Then I retract. I circle my hips, and yet he does nothing. It's building so rapidly now.

He whispers in my ear, his lips never making contact. It's delicate and sexual. "Tell me. Tell me what I want to hear."

I'm tossing my head back and forth and clutching my nipples that are so hard and now ultra-super sensitive as well. He's only keeping two fingers firmly on me. Inflexible constant pressure. It's insistent, and I feel it in my toes, every part of me awake and tingling, a slave to the surge. I need to come. Harder than I've ever needed to before. I need to be released.

I lick my lips and say, "Fuck. You have me. Josh. I'm yours. Josh, let me come."

"Like Dorothy, you have the power to go home all on your own. Use me. Push against me, I won't move, I promise. Do it for yourself. Let me watch you, hear you, and feel you come." I groan and gasp. I moan like he wants me to. "My favorite fucking sound in the world."

"What are you doing to me? Oh. Jesus. You. I can't. You must stop. I can't take this. The pressure is too intense. It's rippling through me faster and faster with my breath." And all he's doing is two constant fingers of pressure. How the fuck is this working? I'm ready to explode. If he'd just swirl, I could detonate. Or ram himself into me. Something. But instead, he just presses.

"Please. I. Can. Barely. Speak. Josh."

"I told you, you'd beg. Beg me to come or beg me to stop? I may own you, but you're in control. Come or stop?"

"Oh my god." And the power of the pulse is now radiated to my nipples and toes. Fuck me, this is good. I love research. I breathe quickly, almost panting in rhythm with the pulse that now touches me everywhere. The wave comes again and again, and still, his fingers stay. Not into me, not moving, just straight onto my clit. The next time I arch my back and push into him. He simply pushes back, and it's enough. I scream as a shock of pleasure overtakes me, and it's almost like a love seizure. Every part of me shakes as the surges keep coming. It's powerful and different. An intense series of chills hold my body for a second and are instantly replaced with flaming red all over my face and body. I'm sitting in my own wet spot when I finally open my eyes.

I'm sitting straight up, and I don't remember doing that. I'm fully clothed, and somehow this man made me come so hard without penetrating me. He's leaned back on the headboard with his arms behind his head, smug expression on his face. I turn to him, pulling the quilt up around us. His rootstock is straight up in the air.

"What the hell?"

"I know, right? I did not think it would work like that. That was awesome. It may be my single favorite thing I've ever seen or done." I move on top of him and feel that he's not so sleepy.

"That was so odd and wonderful. Holy shit."

He kisses me quickly. "You did it. I was just your catalyst."

I continue, "But now I'm awake. Like every part of me is awake and tingling."

"And I'm bone-tired, so goodnight." And he tries to push

me off him, but I won't budge. I cover his mouth with mine. He sits up, and I wrap my legs behind him.

"How tired?"

"Somebody's Hellcat woke up?"

"I just want more, that's all. I want you inside me. Is that so wrong?" He crushes his mouth to mine, and our hands begin moving all over each other. I'm not sure how either of us has any energy, but I am sure I will get what I want. He's so hard as I rock back and forth against his dick, my hyper-sensitive clit still pulsing as I rub against him begging for more. He pushes me down and rolls me over, removing my soaked underwear. After a quick smack of my ass, he flips me over and mounts me.

"Oh, Mr. Whittier. I didn't know it was going to be like this at nap time."

"That I'd get so fucking turned on by watching and feeling you come that my dick needs to be buried deep within you. You did see that coming, right?"

"Please. I want nothing more." He teases me with the tip. I reach down to place him inside of me, and he smacks my hand away. I'm dying. I need him to plunge into me so deep I never stop screaming.

"Tell me."

"I'm yours. Please make me yours."

"I need to hear from you." I moan loudly. I moan his name as loudly as I can, and then I beg.

"I need your cock inside of me. Please fuck me."

## 49

## JOSH

MY DICK HAS NEVER BEEN THIS HARD AND ONLY ACHES MORE when she begs for it. It feels larger and harder than it's ever been. Watching her release herself onto me was epic. Unlike anything I've ever seen or felt. She's a study in smut, class, and beauty. She's all things. I love that the world has no idea how dirty she can get. It's all for me.

This in control, gorgeous woman begging for me to satisfy her is everything. I slide a finger into her and rubbing from the inside and then I pull it back out. She arches her back, and my sound erupts from her mouth. I can't tease her for long because I need to tear into her.

She reaches up and pulls me to her, digging her nails into my shoulders. I remove my finger once again but replace it in one swift motion with my rock-hard cock. Since we've dispensed with condoms, there's been an intimacy I didn't expect.

When I'm inside her, it's as if she's not her and I'm not me. The lack of separation truly makes us *us*. Sex is more. As is everything with her.

I growl at her. "Don't you come yet. Don't you dare. It's

my turn." I pump away, and she bucks and twists under me. I know she wants to angle on top, but for right now I need to be in control. We speed up, and both of us know we can't keep up the pace and then like fucking rumbling thunder it bears down on me, and I fill her up. I come hard and yell.

"Now. Do it. Come for me. Now."

And on cue, she twitches and screams and writhes. I watch her beautiful face ride another orgasm. Her face is flushed pink, and her eyes fixated on mine. I fall on top of her and out of her at the same time. As I exit, she moans loudly and enduringly one last time.

"I have no words." She's trying to catch her breath.

"No words needed." I kiss her nose and fall on the bed next to her. After a few moments, she rolls over on top of me. Staring at her adoring face and rosy cheeks, I drag a dust-filled strand of golden hair from her face. She grins, and her eyes fill with tears. I caress her cheek. She's leaking happiness again.

"I love you, Joshua Lucien LaChappelle Whittier, and I always will. I want everything with and for you. All the things." It's the loveliest thing I've ever heard from her mouth.

I kiss her softly. "And I thought your moaning was the greatest sound I could hear."

"Blame the orgasms that are still running through my body."

After we clean up, we settle in for a well-deserved nap, my arms around her and her curled into me. "Goodnight, my one perfect thing." I hear her breath catch, but this time her shoulders don't tense when I say it. Could be the exhaustion, could be the orgasms, or it could be that she realizes she is mine for real.

"Night, love." I grin from ear to ear at her words as I drift into a bottomless sleep.

## 50

---

## JOSH

I SNEAK BACK INTO BED WITH A CUP OF COFFEE AND CURL around her. She's laying in my arms balled up like a cat, so soft and warm, I love her. Of course, last night she was a sex kitten, my Hellcat. Now just a sweet and tame purring kitty. The picnic the previous night was exhausting, and after another round of rigorous sex, we finally got a full night's sleep. I stroke her hair, knowing she's awake. We need to find somewhere else to be when my parents finally return to the Farmhouse. We're way too noisy.

"I've decided that after today, we ban Asher from our lives. The sale will be completed, and I need to put all of the sale and him behind us. Can you do that for me?"

She doesn't move but speaks plainly. "He's moving to Europe or something. Asked me to join him, kind of. Says it's time to buy the big house. I'm not sure if he wants me there anyway since I stopped sleeping with him long ago."

I laugh heartily. "When did you stop?"

I move to sit up against the headboard and pull her to my chest. I stroke her hair with my free hand. "The moment you kissed me at Steiner's. Well, like an hour before." She grazes her fingers up my arm in a hypnotic pattern. "That's when I knew I'd never kiss him again. Not totally because of you but because even if I never saw you again, I wanted to have that kind of passion and connection. I wanted that kind of expertise and sex in my life. I wanted chemistry and heat and possibilities. He wasn't it. But I haven't slept with anyone but you since that night."

I kiss her head as my guilt creeps up. "How I wish I could say the same, my love."

She sits up next to me, the blanket barely covering her breasts. I see her peek to the top of my manhood and enjoy the V. Then she refocuses.

I answer her unasked question, "Four different women and then Claudia."

"How? When?"

"LA and Santa Barbara. I got game outside the confines of the Valley. I wasn't sure I'd ever get to speak to you again, and I was desperate to get over you."

"Those poor women never had a chance."

I tickle her. "No. They really didn't. But they didn't know they were messing with cosmic forces that were beyond our comprehension. That I'd already been taken off the market the moment you sipped bourbon in front of me."

She laughs at me and settles back against the headboard. She takes my coffee from me and sips. Flashes of my fantasy from our first night at Steiner's, sipping coffee and being domestic with her in my bed play through my mind. Maybe I manifested this. Her delicate pink lips wrap around the mug that my mother made, and it's perfection.

"Claudia was the only one I asked out more than once. And it was because she was simple, uncomplicated, and compliant."

"I mean she's basically my clone. I feel like you're describing me perfectly."

"They were all pale comparisons to you. After each one got dressed and left. Then I'd once again be flooded with thoughts of you. What about Asher?"

"I've learned that he's a guy who watches his own back pretty well. I'm sure I was just something he needed to get something. I don't know what he wanted, but I do know that I'm probably a chess piece in whatever game he's playing. He doesn't do anything out of the goodness of his heart. There's always an angle or annoying compliments. He's the king of hollow flattery. He's a suck-up."

"I told you."

She smacks my face lightly. "Yes, you did. We get it. You're smarter than the rest of us. He's smarmy."

"Exactly."

She shifts to face me again. "Even looking back when Asher invited me places, I was either eye candy or a ringer who knew marketing angles. Including dinner with your parents."

"What was this angle?"

"No clue, but I miraculously sat next to two people who needed a marketing firm. Maybe it was just to draw me to the West Coast?"

"My parents, your sudden appearance here, and his helping with the buyers it doesn't quite add up. What does he get out of it? I'm rather grateful my parents did hire you, though."

"No idea? But as long as I was getting things I wanted out of it all, I never worried. Now with the deal done, your parents stand to sell the vineyard for a tidy sum. And they had a team of accountants and lawyers working on this deal. But after today I won't ever have to see him again."

I pause for a moment while this gorgeous creature stares at me, her green globe eyes round with anticipation of my next words and thoughts. She could get me to do anything right now, anything. I feel that it's destiny to be here with her, something neither of us could stop from happening. Our hands are intertwined while I think.

She's mine, and I begin to wonder how she came into my life. I don't doubt my feelings for her, but what if this temptress was positioned here on purpose. This spitfire of a blonde fuck demon who has bewitched my cock and my heart just appeared in my life. She's grabbing a towel and heading to the shower, and although I'm enjoying the view, I need some answers. I pull on a pair of jeans and a t-shirt. I want to get some more coffee.

She arrives downstairs with a laptop in hand, and I set up next to her to re-review the contracts my parents are signing today. I didn't see anything out of order, but maybe I missed something. But Sam still feels strange. I need to see them again.

We work side by side, and it's comforting. I know she has a shit ton to do, and with harvest done, we will all have to take our next steps. Mom enters her first round of clinical trials next week, and then they want to go to Denmark. For all these years that they've spent living off Denmark Street, they've never been to the country.

The contract seems straightforward. I know their lawyers and our lawyer friend, Rebecca 'Becca' Gelbert, have gone over it back and forth. As I'm reviewing all the names of the signatures required, there's one I don't recognize. It's the only red flag I can find.

I ask her. "Hey. What if it was me?"

"If *what* was you?" She stands up stretching as she asks the question.

"What if Asher knew I'd hate the idea of the sale but be charmed by you? So eventually I'd allow it. Has he ever seen you around clients? Charm a room?"

"It's how we met. I hired him to host a wine dinner for my top-tier clients."

"Did you do a lot of business at that meeting? I've seen you in the room. You're unstoppable. You can get anyone to do anything."

"Except you."

"No? I mean, I clearly I came around."

I grab her and drag her towards me as she now stands between my legs, and I kiss her. I continue, "But it's like you have the Marketing Exec you and then the you that's here that's with me now. She's the one who made me come around. And come and come."

She looks at me inquisitively while stroking my face with her delicate fingertips.

I continue, "You did a hell of a job marketing my family's vineyard and drove the price up, did you not?"

"Damn straight, I did. But I'm the opposite of what people would have thought was your type."

"True. But maybe he never thought we'd get romantic and you'd just annoy me? What are the final numbers?"

"I got it up to around seventy-five million, baby. It all started at about two."

"I still can't believe you did that. My parents are getting seventy-five million."

"Now I may fuck you for your inheritance."

I smack her ass, and she flops down on the couch opposite the kitchen island by the window. Her face framed by the sunlight and her hair glistening, mocking everything around her. Nothing in the world right now is as stunning as she is.

She looks at me with a quizzical face. "I'm not sure Asher's ever seen Elle. He only knows Noelle. Why? Do I feel like I was a ploy? Like I knew this would happen?"

I cross to the room in a flash and kneel in front of the couch.

"NO. No. Of course not. No one could predict this would all happen. Not at all, but you are a distraction." I kiss her hand. "I'm so happy by whatever means brought you to my bed and my life, but I'm beginning to think it wasn't an accident."

"You're starting to not make sense."

"I'm reading this contract and just wondering how involved Asher is in this sale. What does he gain? Why did he work so hard to bring you buyers? I mean he brought a couple of companies to the table. And then he made sure this particular group got the sale. Why doesn't his name appear on the paperwork? Surely there was at least a finder's fee. I mean, you said it yourself, he doesn't do anything out of the kindness of his heart. Was he in all the meetings and dinners with the Vino Groupies?"

"Yes, he was. All of them. No one ever met with the Groupies without Asher in the room." I stare back down at a signature page and the paragraph that outlines who becomes the steward of our property during the sale transition.

"Was there a man named Darren involved?"

"I don't think so, but I have all the business cards and emails."

"Search for a Darren Marcus."

"Who is that?" she inquires.

"It's a name that's on the contracts. If Asher was hustling, you and the deal that hard, then surely, he'd get a taste. We need to figure out about this other guy. He gets management control over the properties as the custodian for a year. And gets a piece of the profits after that year. It's just worded strangely. Search the board of directors of the Vino Groupies."

"I thought the other wineries maintained management control."

"They do essentially. They run their own operations and maintain quality control and oversight. The custodian position is usually someone from the board of directors. They oversee reports, insurance and read the boring paperwork stuff. It's largely a figurehead position."

She screws up her face like she's thinking super hard, and I'm still worried. Something's not adding up.

# 51

# ELLE

JOSH IS PACING THE FLOOR, FLIPPING THROUGH MY BUSINESS cards as I search my email. I'm starting to think he's on to something.

"I'm proud of you. You did this. But something's up. Where's Asher today?"

"Downtown at some meeting."

"Shit." Josh stands stone still and stares at me.

"You think Asher is at the sale?" I ask.

"I'd bet your sweet ass on it." He slaps my ass for effect.

"But why? He's not listed on the memo for attendance. The only name we don't recognize is the one you mentioned. And I've never met that man. I've known all the players. He must be an angel investor or something."

"There's not much on Google. There's a principal in Ohio and some college kid in Louisiana, but I don't see anything that would be relevant. Why isn't there at least an address or a mention of this guy Darren in California?"

Josh bolts upstairs and comes back down in an instant with a phone I don't recognize. He smashes a text out and then shows it to me.

*JOSH: Need help immediately. Who is Darren Marcus, and why doesn't he show up on Google? I need all the info on him. I need a picture of who this man is and what he does. Like yesterday. Time is of the essence.*

"Who the hell did you text?" And while I'm asking, my own phone pings, and I read the response.

*MEL: Tell Josh that he was supposed to toss that phone. He gets a bill this time now that you're safe and in his bed. Or I'll just take it from his account. Heh Heh. Hold a second.*

I look at Josh incredulously. "Mel? My Melissa?" He nods and reads my phone over my shoulder.

*ELLE: Holy fuck. Mel! Melissa.*

Then he crosses the room scrubbing his jawline.

"She fixed the Sal shit." My jaw goes slack as my phone pings again.

*MEL: Sup, Elle. I know it's Elle now. I like it better. Hi, baby-doll! Glad you guys worked it out. He cares a lot for you. A fuck of a lot. Okay, so this Darren guy scrubbed his own data. He's good. I'm better.*

I stare at the phone in disbelief. My heart beating rapidly as I wait for information.

"You're going to need to tell me all about your dealings with Mel."

"She's a trip. But know this, she saved my ass and yours and I'm eternally grateful." I roll my eyes at my beautiful man. I'm glad I was nice to her when I fired her.

*MEL: The dude changed his name. His dad was in some wine scandal involving Josh's grandfather.*

Holy shit. This can't be what I suspect it to be.

*MEL: Damn, girl. You into something now. Can you tell Josh that Darren is your ex-boyfriend? I don't want to be the one to tell him that. He changed his name to Asher Bernard...*

I drop the phone and shriek a bit. Josh runs to me and

ignores the texts that keep coming in with more information, worried about me.

"What the hell just happened?" Josh looks panicked at my reaction, and he should be. My eyes cannot be wider. My throat is dry, and my jaw is slack. I can't believe this. Fuck. I can't believe this.

"Darren Marcus. MARCUS." I say way too forcefully.

"Yeah?"

I say, "As in Barry Marcus."

I pick up the phone, and Mel has texted us an image of Darren Marcus at his mother's funeral eight years ago. I give it to Josh. It's an article from the *Sacramento Bee* dredging up the entire Marcus thing.

*MEL: I'm out, doll. Call me if you need me. I might keep digging if I get bored.*

*ELLE: Thank you. Thank you.*

*MEL: Be careful.*

I say, "He's Asher. Darren is Asher. He looks different, but Mel says it's him."

Josh is yelling and pacing. "Darren fucking revenge Marcus is Asher Bernard. I have to text my dad. Holy shit. Holy shit."

"OH MY GOD!"

"How the fuck did I not know it was him?" Josh scrubs his jaw in disbelief.

"You were so young. But Will and Sarah? And everyone else? No one recognized him?"

"He looks altered. His face is different. He was young when he left here. He fucking played them like a fiddle. And I wasn't here, so he took advantage. He played us all. Shit."

I step up on the kitchen step stool so we can be eye to eye. He laughs at me but fuck him. I know I'm short.

"This is not your fault."

He puts his hands on either side of my face. "It's not yours either. He played the hell out of you too."

Shit, he did. I'm an idiot. I throw my shoulders back and look into Josh's eyes. "Whatever happens, we can fix it. I know we can. But they can't sign it. None of them can. I can fix anything, and you are the master of the universe. We'll protect them. We'll bury anyone who tries to fuck with our family, any of the families." He looks at me with a new layer of love. I smirk and comment, "You like that I'm a shark?"

"Fuck yeah, I do. Now text the bastard to see where he is and if you can get him to give you some information. I'll try and contact everyone. He doesn't know what we know. Find out his angle. And why does he want that ceremonial management post?"

"He doesn't always answer unless it's dirty."

"Wait. How often have you sexted with him?"

"A couple of times in the beginning, but I use a flirtatious tactic if I need an answer from him. Jealous?"

"More than you could possibly know. Keep it fucking light. If he crosses a line, give me your phone. Dammit. I knew something was fucking off about that guy."

"You did, Suit."

"I can't stand the idea that anyone else in the world has been with you—but *him*, it kills me."

"That's sweet, but neither of us comes clean to this relationship." I'm still up on the stool, so I kiss his cheek move down to my mouth. "How about this? Will this make it better? I'll never be with anyone else again."

# 52

# JOSH

"BETTER."

I sit down on a kitchen chair, and she straddles me. I'm still too spent to get hard, but I can feel my cock struggling to find a way. She throws her arms around my neck.

I say the most vulnerable thing I've ever said, "There will never be a moment when I don't love you. When I don't want you or need you. But we need to get this shit done, Parker." She gently brushes my lips, and I seize her.

"I love you desperately, Whittier."

I knew there was something I hated about Asher. He hates us. What kind of scum would take advantage of a woman with Parkinson's? He's so slimy. Shit, they can't sign the contract.

"Flirt but no sexting. Find out what's going on if you can. I'm going to call one of the losing competitors and figure out who's been brokering. Also, text and call Sam. Then Gelbert and Tommi or Baxter. Call the Aganos family. All of them. What the fuck is Asher up to? They need to know it all."

"Sarah and Will are only showing up at the end of the meeting to sign. They don't want to hear the details of how they're going to break up the vineyards. Lodi and the coast included."

"They're breaking them up?" I ask.

"They'll keep the name, but basically all of our Lodi and coastal grapes will become homogenized and harvested with others into recipes for mass consumption. The contract never says plans for the farm, just that it's up to Vino Groupies discretion after the next harvest. But if they stick to my marketing proposal, all the wineries will be fine. They'll be marketed in a ladder format to wine shops and distribution. I hope. If they destroy even a vine here at Emma farm, I'd be devastated."

I lean in and attack her lips. Her soft juicy mouth is happy to receive me. I grab the back of her head. We're at a point where there's no separation between my lips and hers. I tear my lips away and sigh.

"What was that?" She puts her hands on her hips.

"For loving the winery, the land, and my heritage as much as I do."

"You do? I thought you were done?"

"You should know, sometimes I have to be faced with losing something before I realize how precious it really is."

Her arms stay wrapped around my neck as she tries to ascertain what I'm actually saying. "Really? You want this? Because they can't do it and it's a lot of money."

My whole life flashed in front of me when I realized the winery won't be ours as of today, despite who's buying it. "This land, these people, these vines, they're as much mine as you are. They're a piece of me. I fucked up so much. I have all the money my parents will ever need if they'll take it from me. Game faces, Shark. Let's stop this shitty sale now. I have a winery to inherit."

She flashes me a demon look, and I see her click into full-on corporate mode. "Cosmo, get to typing some flirty things and save our legacy." She tears up instantly as I reference forever. There is no plan B. It's not needed. She's A to Z. And so is LC/W

She winks at me. Her sexy stare has me crazy. A hint of jealousy bubbles up. She's never allowed to see another man's dick again. I will have a hard time even watching Game of Thrones with her. I'm confident that I'm sufficient in that department, but I don't want her shopping around.

I NEED HIM TO KNOW THAT I WOULD RIP OFF ALL MY CLOTHES at any given moment if he asks. I'm still shaking at the thought of that crazy clit thing he did yesterday afternoon. Okay. I must focus. I need information, stop the sale, and then pull off a massive party tonight. I can fucking do this. He thinks he can save his mother and father. I can help him do that. His heart is so large.

"Okay. Dirty text number one. Dirty text..." He's behind me and biting my ear. He wraps his hands around me from behind and unclasps my bra. He's cupping my breasts and playing with my exhausted but hard and sensitive nipples. "Oh, come on. Fuck Josh. You have to stop."

"Never."

"Try." He reaches down and begins to play with my hair.

*ELLE: Asher. Hello. I was just thinking of you.*

"That's like the most boring thing ever," he says. "So formal and cold."

"You have to let me do this. He's not that sexual. If I wanted you to text me back, I wouldn't say hello."

"What would you do?"

"Talk about my aching cunt." She twists her hair up and says that phrase offhandedly. She's in professional mode. This Hellcat. This woman. Jesus, she's perfect.

"I can tell you that you wouldn't finish that text before you were filled."

She smiles at me full of this newfound deeper love and lust. "Go get in touch with Sam and your parents. *Now*. The Langerford, Gelbert, and Aganos meetings are this morning. Schroeder is a little later and then your mom and dad. Go. I got this."

I rehook my bra and get down to business.

*ASHER: Where are you? Can I bring my member to you?*

# 54

## JOSH

Her phone dings, and I look over her shoulder to read. "He most certainly may not bring his cock to you. You're busy."

"Told you to trust me. I said next to nothing, and Asher brings up his cock."

"Member." We both bust out laughing.

*ELLE: Where are you?*

I kiss her neck and position my hands on her hips. While she types this asshole, I might just remind her how good I am at kissing different innocuous parts of her.

*ASHER: In the city. Thought you were in San Fran today too.*

*ELLE: Plans changed. I wanted to wrap everything up here at the vineyard before tomorrow.*

*ASHER: Good. I want you out of that place. Thought you were already out. You need to leave immediately.*

"Oh god. You. Stop. Stop. I have to type." I steal kisses while she attempts to answer him. But why does he want her out of here?

I invade her yoga pants. "Don't mind me. I'm going to make you feel good while he thinks you want him." Her body goes soft against me. She gasps. I can't resist. Her back arches into my chest. And then she suddenly pulls my hand out of her and steps away.

"Dude. I need to focus, and so do you. Call your parents."

I get in her face and tower over her. "I will do this only because the winery is at stake but don't you ever, I mean EVER brush me off to sext with another man again."

She grins widely. "I promise. Now go!" I keep an eye on her text while I call my dad.

*ELLE: Why?*

*ASHER: I need the deal to go through, and you won't be welcome there after it does. Now, I'm in a discreet location. I want to know about your thoughts on my willie?"*

"Um. He just called his dick his willie."

"You are shitting me. He's like an old man."

*ELLE: Why won't I be welcome?*

*ASHER: What do you want to do with my love gun?*

"If you want to stop. Do it. I don't want you to have to be subjected to this."

"I can do this. I'll be vague."

# ELLE

JOSH KISSES ME ON MY FOREHEAD, AND INSTANTLY I FEEL SAFE. The slight tickle of his constant stubble on my flesh is an erotic and comforting sensation. He picks up his phone and heads into the next room. He's trying to get a hold of his dad and their lawyer will. He's trying to get a hold of everyone before they sign. To delay all of this until we can figure it out. Meanwhile, I keep leading asshole Asher on.

*ELLE: What do you want me to do with it?*

*ASHER: Where is this coming from?*

*ELLE: Thinking of you making a big deal is a turn on.*

*ASHER: Then you're going to be Niagara Falls.*

*ELLE: Oooh. Do tell.*

*ASHER: Because of the excellent work you did, and I'm proud of you. I didn't know you were that good.*

*ELLE: I am that good. I'm actually better than you know. I've been slumming it lately.*

*ASHER: What else?*

*ELLE: I want to hear how powerful you are. Tell me about your deal.*

*ASHER: Jesus, baby. I have to sign some papers. I get a finder's* *fee on this deal of 1.5%, and you drove that from 2 mil to 75. And the overall deal with The Five that you sweetened, that's close to 332 million fucking dollars. I get $4.9 million all to myself. And the best revenge for my family.*

I yell out, "He gets one-point-five percentage of the total. Like five mil."

Josh yells back, "That's a shitty finder's fee on a three-hundred-million-dollar deal. He's a fucking idiot. He should have a minimum of ten percent on the gross." I adore my businessman's mind.

*ELLE: That seems like an awful lot of money for a family-run wineries. They must love wine.*

*ASHER: My hands need to feel your breasts.*

I don't know what to text. I'm so creeped out by this whole thing. I have barely said anything sexual. He's done it all.

"Babe. He's getting creepy."

*ELLE: Why so much money?*

*ASHER: OH. It's the land and the grapes they want. They have plans for the property that don't involve wines. they don't give a shit about the wine. Then they'll harvest all the inferior and younger grapes for mass production box wine. Then slap the reputable names on random juice from wherever. They're going to do it with all the wineries.*

"JOSH!!! Shit. Come here! Tell them! Don't sign. Stop them!"

He comes running into the room as I'm running out to find him.

"What?"

"They're not going to keep your staff or the smaller vine-yards. The deal buys their land, not their distribution. They're not going to keep your labels pure. They're going to Inglenook all of them. And then do something else with all the land."

I reference the story from the 1970s when a big conglomerate took over the once prestigious Inglenook label. They began to mass-produce jug wine in Chablis and Burgundy at low cost and virtually destroyed its reputation as a winery and its legacy. It took Francis Ford Coppola over three decades to restore its status as a family-owned and esteemed winery label. And most of that wine still has to be called Coppola to sell.

"I'm going to kill that muthafucker. I'm going beat the shit out of that smug fuck. All of this shit because my grandfather was an asshole and his dad was a shit thief."

I put my hand on his arm.

*ASHER: I'm going to be late for the meeting, but I need to get off. Speak to me of your breasts.*

"Okay. I'll kill him after we stop the signing." He kisses me quickly.

"Cut his balls off."

"Happily," he says to me as he redials his parents. We have to get in touch with someone.

*ELLE: Josh just walked into the office. Have to go. Sorry.*

*ASHER: That fucker always ruins everything. But meet me at my home, and I'll be there as soon as possible. Wear that black thing from Healdsburg.*

I smile and show Josh the text. I bought us a couple of minutes, but we need to get downtown. His mom and dad are a little ahead of us, headed to the bank office, but hopefully, their lawyer has answered. We jump in the Porsche to get to San Francisco as fast as possible. I start calling Sarah and then Tommi, and he calls his dad. No one is picking up. I madly group text anyone in The Five.

Josh gives me side-eye and says, "You know you're going to have to burn that black thing from Healdsburg."

"I do." I take his hand, and his entire body is strained.

I leave a voicemail. "Sarah, Asher's real name is Darren

Marcus. He's Barry Marcus' son. And the sale is to break up the wineries and sell the names. Don't sign."

I call Will as well and leave a more detailed message.

I say with urgency while Josh tries to get Sam on the line,

"WILL. Don't sign the contract. Asher is Barry Marcus' son. It's a bad deal. Asher put the whole deal together behind your backs. Walkout. He gets a finder's fee. But the Vino Groupies don't want Gelbert Family Wineries, Langerford, Aganos, Schroeder, or LaChappelle, they want your high yield vineyards and the names for box wine production. They don't want the wineries. They want the land for something. Don't sign."

"Call Sam and Jims. Call all of them."

I leave a similar voicemail for Sam, Tommi, Jims, Baxter, and David. I call Poppy but she's at the cafe. I tell her to find her mom and uncle and stop them. Josh finally gets a text. I read while he drives.

*SAM: Don't sign. I just got Elle's text. Fuck. What did we miss? It's a bad deal. We got trapped. Call me later. We're already fucked. Everyone is. WE all signed. Will is with his lawyers now at another building. Trying to head there now.*

Shit. I hope we're not too late for everyone. Fuck. The wineries. Oh, god. All these people. Asher. Shit. Darren got us. Oh shit. I answer Sam with Josh's phone as the Spyder madly weaves in and out of traffic.

*JOSH: It's Elle. We can't get a hold of Sarah and Will. We're speeding to the city. Almost there.*

*SAM: The contracts were the same. We've all already signed but your parents.*

*JOSH: Shit. Can you go find Sarah and Will and stop them?*

*SAM: I'm stuck on the bridge, accident. I'll try Bax and Tommi. Why was fucking Asher there?*

*JOSH: He's really Darren Marcus.*

*SAM: And that is...*

*JOSH: Barry Marcus' son.*
*SAM: WTF!*

I say to Josh in an urgent voice, "He convinced your parents to hire me to ratchet up the sale, which I did, but the purpose was selfish. He gets a one-point-five percent finder's fee. And he convinced me that I had to pitch this piece of business. That only I could do it. Fuck. I'm so sorry."

He takes my hand. "You did nothing. Except come into our lives when we needed you. Asher does not get to own any part of our relationship or the winery. He owns no part of you or the reason you're here. He can't. We must stop this. Keep calling Tabi, David, my mom, anybody. Keep trying."

I smile at him. "We have to stop this. "

I take his hand and squeeze it as he weaves in and out of traffic in a frantic pace, trying to get to his parents. "Elle, if I've learned anything in the past eight months, it's that you can't stop destiny. And LaChappelle/Whittier is that for us. We'll find a way or the universe will. I've never been more sure of anything in my life. Keep trying them."

"Destiny." I say back to him. Mine, it turns out, is nowhere close to what I was planning. My carefully laid out plan A and plan B all flew out the window the night I sipped bourbon at Steiner's. The universe had its own master plan. And I couldn't be happier to take a back seat to the universe's schemes. I just want to bask in the love of this future grape farmer and the life we're building. As soon as we stop the sale. If we can stop the sale.

### End of Book Two

Thanks for reading! Josh and Elle's story continues in
### Uncorked
Click it. I'll wait. Got it? Cool. Enjoy. See you on the other side.

Other 5 Families Vineyard Series Books
All book are available on Amazon and Kindle Unlimited!
Each winery's story is interconnected but not dependent on
each other. And can be read as standalone.

**Stafýlia Cellars Duet**
Over A Barrel & Under The Bus

**Gelbert Family Winery**
Meritage: An Unexpected Blend

## STAFÝLIA CELLARS DUET

**Over A Barrel** is a friends to lovers, opposites attract story about the steamy and stormy history between US Senate Candidate Baxter Schroeder, and bold, brash Tabitha Aganos. Best friends who think they can ignore fate.

This friends to lovers story begins with Over A Barrel and concludes in Under The Bus.

## GELBERT FAMILY WINERY

### Meritage: An Unexpected Blend

Natalie Lloyd is the most efficient woman on the planet and she just figured out how to convert bad boy player David Gelbert into a boyfriend.

David's in love for the first time in his life and it happens to be with two women. One doesn't want children and the other is still in diapers.

The Juggle is Real.

He's a DILF way over his head.

Click Here for Meritage: An Unexpected Blend

# HEY KELLY, WHAT ELSE CAN I READ?

**RockStar Romance? I've got you covered.**

A steamy and funny standalone duet.

**<u>Shock Mount & Crossfade</u>**

Always random and off on a tangent, film festival director, Meg Hannah, moves from Sonoma to New York in this duet. It's a reverse age gap-rockstar-love triangle-no cheating-HEA guaranteed extravaganza.

Meghan Hannah tripped into their lives, much as she trips into almost any room. Now each man wants to catch her. Meg's not sure she'll get back up if she falls too far.

## MEG

I have no clue what I'm doing. I mean, I thought I was really good at being married. Turns out that's not true. I thought I was really good at hiding certain parts of my past. Also not true. I even fooled myself into thinking that I am good at relationships. I'm a mess of myself, but at least I have my friends and my memories. I hold them all very close. But now my whole world seems to be flipped by one innocent night that ended with a broken watch. Perhaps I can course correct and get that happily ever after. And maybe all I need is a more lyrical life and good sex.

---

**Side Piece**, a workaholics standalone romance.

**A hot, hilarious, angsty Instant Connection- A story about cheating on their jobs not each other.**

Married to their work, Tess & Alex find that sex is the easy part. But can they actually stop working long enough to find love?

Side Piece is an instant connection sweeping romance where Tess and Alex simply don't have time for romance. Their work schedules dictate their worlds, and they like it that way. But their pull towards each other is undeniable. The relationship feels like a torrid affair cheating on their everyday lives. Perhaps there could be more, if only their schedules overlapped long enough to fall in love.

Join me at www.kellykayromance.com to make sure you're up to date on all the cheeky, daffy nonsense.

Did I thank you for reading? Wait. Yup, I did But it's worth saying again, thank you.

Talk soon,

xo

Kelly K

## ACKNOWLEDGMENTS

My friends, old and new, who have come out of every corner of my life to read and enjoy my words. It means the world to me. Thank you.

Thanks to my sister Allison for eternally being there for me and my words. I'd also like to give a shout out to my SIL Amy Spitznagel, who has always supported me and has this amazing ability to always think that everything is always possible. I'm pretty lucky to get to be around her and her infectious belief that life is good for decades now. Love you both.

There's a gaggle of people in Sonoma that I want to thank for supporting me through the years and with these books: Jill F, Kevin, Anthony, Gary, Sondra, Kevin, Rosemary, Bill, Tiffany, Becky, Vickie and Jane. I hope we get to sit across from each other and sip something delicious someday soon.

Erin Young, my editor, this book and the others wouldn't exist without you. Thank you very much.

Holly Jennings, thank you for catching all the tiny things and calling me out on the larger things. I'm grateful to have found you for copy editing and proofreading.

Tim Hogan, I promise to keep providing the hooch in exchange for dirty pictures. Thank you my friend.

Let's all collectively thank the teachers of the world. I knew they were valuable but since having to open up my own home school in the wake of the quarantine, good night, we don't pay them enough.

Thanks to the medical workers and first responders on the front lines of something unimaginable. And hands up for the stock people at Amazon, postal workers, grocery store workers, the good folks providing the world with hooch, food delivery people and farmers who are still doing their jobs while we try to flatten the curve by watching way too much Netflix.

Eric and Charlie, I know that I could not do any of this without the two of you. I love you. And to my in laws, Lynn & Ron Sutton who let us escape to the woods for a quarantine with a view. Thank you.

# ABOUT KELLY KAY

I used to create "dreams" with my best friend growing up. We'd each pick a boy we liked, then we'd write a meet-cute that always ended with a happily ever after.

Now I get to dream every day, although it's a little steamier these days. And I've discovered I can and will write anywhere I can. I have photographic proof.

I'm a writer, married to a writer, mom of a creative dynamo of a nine-year-old boy and currently a little sleepy. I'm a klutz and goofball and love lipstick as much as my Chuck Taylors.

Random good things in the world: pepperoni pizza, Flair pens*, road trips, coffee, sidesplitting laughing fits, matinees on a weekday, the Chicago Cubs, a fresh new notebook full of possibilities, bourbon on a cold night, Fantasy Football, gaggles of friends, my city, witty men, local zoo in the rain and that moment when a character clicks in and begins to write their own adventure. I'm just the pen.

Oh, and wine. I like wine. (duh)

*purple is my favorite Flair pen

www.kellykayromance.com

Made in the USA
Middletown, DE
05 October 2021

49545584R00194